TWINNED WITH THAILAND

TWINNED WITH THAILAND

Keith Wadsworth

The Book Guild Ltd
Sussex, England

Swindon Borough Council Library Services	
Askews	
	£16.95

First published in Great Britain in 2002 by
The Book Guild Ltd
25 High Street
Lewes, East Sussex
BN7 2LU

Copyright © Keith Wadsworth 2002

The right of Keith Wadsworth to be identified as the author of this work has been asserted by him in accordance with the Copyright, Designs and Patents Act 1988.

All rights reserved. No part of this publication may be reproduced, transmitted, or stored in a retrieval system, in any form, or by any means, without permission in writing from the publishers, nor be otherwise circulated in any form of binding or cover other than that in which it is published and without a similar condition being imposed on the subsequent purchaser.

All characters in this publication are fictitious and any resemblance to real people, alive or dead, is purely coincidental.

Typesetting in Baskerville by
SetSystems Ltd, Saffron Walden, Essex

Printed in Great Britain by
Antony Rowe Ltd, Chippenham, Wiltshire

A catalogue record for this book is
available from the British Library

ISBN 1 85776 665 2

*This novel is dedicated to my
dear daughter, Panida, and especially
my wife, Souwanee, for her help,
advice, and understanding.*

1

Hook a Duck, (Prime Numbers Win the Jackpot)

In the darkness of a drawer, amongst all sorts of household paraphernalia, a gold ring gleams above all else. Chris puts out a hand and with a trembling finger and thumb he plucks the ring from the dark abyss. Chris sidles into the light of a bedroom window. With his arm extended in an upright position like a prop leaning against a washing line on a breezy day, Chris looks up, fixing a steely gaze on his wife's wedding ring. The glorious blue sky cuts a swath through the band of precious metal and the slanting rays of a low sun fall through the double glazing, straight onto Chris's eyes and lashes, tired and sad eyes, with puffy eyelids that now resemble the hinged lobes of two Venus's flytrap leaves. And as if his harboured torment were not enough to wrestle with, those sad eyes form two centres from which the faint but settled wrinkles of despair spread out like silken spokes in two spiders' webs. Combined with the passing of each restless night, those spokes, each a tell-tale sign of mental anguish, appear more defined, clearer, and visible, as though having the misfortune to be covered by a white hoarfrost at dawn. Chris takes one step backwards, out of the bright sunlight and into the shade. From there he scrutinises the wedding ring and its ominous-looking split. Chris gives a slight grunt of disdain. Then quite unexpectedly, he experiences a sudden sense of foreboding, like a hidden inferno, feeding quietly, and consuming all vestiges of his marriage and soul. With haste, Chris returns to the drawer and drops the ring inside.

A small black book catches his eye. The right-hand corner of its stiff cover has been sliced off in such a manner as to destroy its very purpose. Chris is staring at his past, a testimony to his love life. He opens the book. Inside the front cover is an inverted blue stamp bearing the word CANCELLED. A thin cardboard beer coaster falls to the floor. Chris smiles and picks it up. It's from a tropical bar. On the reverse side, written with an insecure hand is a name and address. The black ink has faded now, but Chris doesn't need to read it. The address is indelibly engraved in his memory forever. He turns a few more pages, passing his youthful and amusing photograph. Finally, he stops at immigration stamp 24 NOV 1985, a day he will never forget. His expired passport is awakening memories, memories of another Chris, a man whom he can hardly identify with now, a much younger, naïve Chris, searching for his destiny.

Chris wiped his hands on a moist, warm flannel, and looked about the aircraft with indifference. His fellow passengers, all of them men, filled the entire aircraft. An air hostess with the faint hint of sexual desire flitting under her make-up, handed Chris a crisp immigration card. Chris, plunging his hand into the pockets of a travel bag, pulled out his passport and pen.

'I see ye've been to the Seychelles,' a deep-toned voice said.

Chris turned to face the man sitting beside him. This man, who resembled a member of Spandau Ballet, was staring at Chris's only passport stamp. Chris cast an eye at his fluffy, bouffant hairdo, which wobbled comically as the aeroplane shook. Chris checked an embarrassing smirk.

'Yes,' whispered Chris.

In a flash the stranger seemed to sprout six inches taller.
'Did ye shag any of their lasses?' the stranger asked, leaning towards Chris.

'No, they wuz all devout Catholics.'

'Oh! I won't go there then. Ye won't have that problem in Thailand, I've been here six times,' he replied, eyes rolling mischievously. His raucous voice had caressed the word 'Thailand'.

'When did yer fust cum here?' Chris asked, wondering.

'Three years ago – Whitsun nineteen eighty-two.' Chris detected a sly, confiding half-smile on the stranger's thin lips, as if nursing a pleasant imperishable memory. 'I'm staying in Bangkok,' the stranger resumed, 'what about you?'

Chris, now grating a fingernail across his overnight stubble, replied, 'Nine nights in Pattaya and three nights in Bangkok.'

'Ye'll be okay then,' said the stranger, grinning broadly, 'most of these guys are going there . . .' He paused, shuffled his feet slightly, and then asked, 'Why did ye decide to come to Thailand?'

Chris fell into deep thought.

'I saw it on *Wicker's World*,' he offered vaguely, and then added, 'one day when I wuz in the Seychelles a young English woman saw me at my worst. I wuz having a bad day – yer know, fed up and lonely. So out of the blue she told me to go to Bangkok. Yer see, she'd bin everywhere and said it wuz ideal for me.'

'Reet, but why didn't ye shag her?' the stranger asked sharply, looking quizzically puzzled.

The pilot adjusted the wing flaps, forcing Chris to raise his voice.

'She wuz getting married and her fiancé wuz with her.'

'Oh reet,' the stranger replied, but his thoughts were elsewhere and he turned away.

Presently, the raising of the window blinds made Chris lift his eyes from the form he was filling in. He craned his neck and peered through a window. Outside the dark night sky had erupted into a fledgling sunrise. Much nearer, the actual windows themselves seemed to stand out with an amber pink light of their own distortion, oval and translucent like a row of cod liver oil capsules under the watchful gaze of a pharmaceutical inspector. Chris stood up and his eyes began to glisten. Below, lay the exotic Far East, passing as if unwound endlessly like a long piece of green tartan cloth, its criss-cross weave of paddy fields sending a wet gleam skywards.

The aeroplane approached the city and Thailand's agricultural backbone gave way to a concrete suburbia. Now the view below reminded Chris of an autumnal dawn. Scattered here and there, like mushrooms sprouting through the earth's skin, were the white and pearly grey tower blocks. An obese python, of sorts, appeared through a hazy vista of yesterday's pollution. It was the Chao Phray River throwing back the sun's early rays in a salmon-pink glow. Approaching that lustrous river, its size and importance now became clear. This river was the reason for Bangkok's very existence, in its past the very life and soul of an ancient and small port.

'There's the Grand Palace,' somebody yelled excitedly.

Chris could see it too, rising from its darkened slumber in a profusion of colourful gleams. Then quite suddenly its gilded roof tiles were caught in the sunlight, resplendent and brilliant, dazzling the atmosphere above the sacred precinct with a brief, explosive flash of golden light.

Chris's ears sharpened. The passengers began to chatter excitedly. A copious flow of words filled the aircraft. In the whole gathering of wagging tongues no voice uttered a coherent sentence, only a mumbled jabber of candid jocularity. Chris sensed a mysterious expectancy in the air. He could see a glint of excitement in many a man's eye.

'Bangkok!' somebody thrilled, as if bewitched by the city.

Chris sat rather silent throughout the whole spectacle, bemused, and yearning to understand their sudden outburst of raw emotion. It was difficult to put his finger on it, but there was definitely something going on here, a hidden agenda to say the least.

Presently the aeroplane landed and in the long, dusty shadows of an untidy construction site beyond the runway the saplings of palm could be seen placing an oasis amongst the sand and cement of a rapidly, expanding airport. Palm trees were good, thought Chris, their feathery foliage an indication of warmth and an escape from a disheartening winter. Chris gave a deep sigh of relief. At long last the flight was over. The aeroplane came to a gentle halt and everyone waited for the ground crew to arrive. Suddenly the cabin doors were flung open and the passengers' air-conditioned environment was filled with a ferocious heat, fiery and strength-sapping, with an unremitting persistence like the repeated bark of a neighbour's dog that seemed to weigh heavily on tired bodies.

With the airport behind him, Chris found himself travelling in a minibus with several other tourists towards the beach resort of Pattaya. A silence soon fell. Outside, quaint foreign characteristics immediately caught Chris's eye, such as strange variants of company logos, well-known companies, with their distinct trademarks amusingly altered to cater for Thailand's squiggled alphabet. A screaming motorcycle overtook them with two small children clinging precariously to their mother's torso. Chris's jaw dropped, he was totally aghast. He counted four people on that motorcycle, with their jet-black hair flapping in the wind like galloping horses. Family bonding takes on a different perspective here, he thought.

They passed a large advertising hoarding bearing an artistic impression of a new housing estate. Depicting a plush air-conditioned house, with a beautiful wife and successful husband, their idyllic family life seemed to come straight out of a religious magazine. There the two adults sat, outside, on a patio, watching a well-groomed pedigree dog play ball with two angelic children. From what Chris had glimpsed so far, it was all a lie. Bangkok had more than its fair share of slums and even in the affluent suburbs there was nothing to resemble this advertisement. Perhaps it was the start of a new era, but somehow Chris disbelieved the artist's vision.

Their minibus driver was trying to make up for lost time, as he had wasted over two hours attempting to leave Bangkok's notorious traffic. He overtook a mechanically unsound pick-up truck fully laden with sugar cane. A few anxious farm labourers clung to its tilting, suicidal load, like the crew of a ship hugging a lee rail in a howling storm.

A road sign in Thai and English announced that Pattaya was 125 kilometres away. Two hours later they arrived in Pattaya and their driver began to drop off his passengers at their various hotels. Third stop was an economy-class hotel. Two very young men, perhaps students on a gap year, in torn denim trousers and tee shirts that advertised their favourite rock legends, disembarked with roomy rucksacks.

A fellow passenger turned in his seat, puffed out his cheeks and, leaning forward slightly, whispered to a friend, 'I'm glad we aren't staying there.'

His friend made a grotesque, scornful snigger.

These malicious comments got right up Chris's nose and when the driver finally hollered, 'Nipper Lodge next,' Chris was delighted to see that the two men remained seated, whilst he collected his luggage.

After checking in, Chris decided to explore his surroundings. Having spent 20 minutes or so walking around the hotel grounds, he was pleasantly surprised as to how good it was. The three-star hotel was undoubtedly great value for money. Chris strolled around the swimming pool and through the spacious garden, which after the blinding glare of the water seemed dull in comparison. Guests, mostly men, slept on adjustable sunbeds. Occasionally the dull, heavy tread of a waitress's flip-flops returning to serve a cold beer would open a few lecherous eyes.

A hotel security guard, remaining dignified and aloof from the waiting taxi drivers outside, had caught Chris's eye. His polished badge glinted in the bright sunlight as he paced back and forth in front of a large, wrought-iron gate. Clad in a navy-blue uniform with knife-edged creases that ran down his trousers, the tin badge which seemed part of a child's cowboy outfit informed the guests of his importance. Chris approached the gate. There was a rush of vigorous activity in the street outside. The security guard wrung his hands slightly, saluted Chris and opened the gate. The hinges squeaked, embarrassingly. Chris smiled to himself as he passed through the portal. After all, he thought, it's not every day that someone salutes you.

'Taxi! Taxi! You want taxi sir?' a man hollered and swiftly approached Chris.

'Massage, you want lady sir?' the man asked in a much quieter voice.

'No thank you,' replied Chris.

Several other drivers gathered around.

'Massage!'

'Massage!'

'I take you to lady.'

'You want lady?'

Chris shook his head at all of them.

'You want man?' Chris frowned at the offending driver, flashed him a scornful glare and strode away in defiance. To Chris's annoyance one persistent driver followed him down the street.

'Where you go? It too hot to walk,' the driver insisted.

Chris turned round and shouted crossly, 'Go away!'

Then rather reluctantly, the taxi driver returned to his chums.

The sun was high and to Chris's disappointment he had forgotten his panama hat. A gap appeared in the traffic. Chris crossed the road. Now he was on the grassed promenade where he sought shade under the trees. Chris had walked a few hundred metres, when suddenly he heard the long toot of a car horn. Chris stopped and saw a young Thai woman dart through a narrow gap in the traffic. The sea breeze forced the cheesecloth dress that she wore to press against, and accentuate, the curves of her thighs and mobile breasts. She wore no bra and her swollen, erect nipples pointed towards the hissing surf.

To Chris's surprise she approached him and asked, 'What is time please?'

Chris raised his wrist and looked at his watch. Before he could utter a single word the woman slid her hand inside his elbow and grabbed Chris's arm. It was a well-rehearsed move.

'Hello, where you go?' she asked him.

'I'm going for a walk,' Chris politely replied and jerked his arm away from hers.

'I go with you, I help you enjoy holiday,' she urged.

Chris stopped and stared into her tired, bloodshot eyes.

He shook his head slowly and responded, 'No thank you, I'm going back to my hotel to eat.'

'Where your hotel?'

'I'm going now, goodbye.'

She pursed her lips and in a clear expression of rebuke uttered a loud, 'Tut!'

With haste, Chris turned round and walked towards the safety of his hotel. Glancing back, he could clearly see that the woman had now returned to her preferred observation point. She was not alone. Two other women stood beside her, seemingly engrossed in Chris's movements. Chris's initial enthusiasm had been tempered.

On returning to his room, Chris sat brooding on the pink bedspread. How could he cope with all these marauding prostitutes? Chris shuddered at the thought. He gazed around the room, a pleasant room to say the least. Next to the door was the *en suite* toilet and shower. At the foot of the double bed, pushed against the far wall sat a cushioned, rattan chair. A pinewood table and orange table lamp stood beside it. To his left was the window, where thick velvet curtains hung from ceiling to floor. Next to his bed, on a smaller table, sat a flask of drinking water and a hardback book entitled: *The Teaching of Buddha*. Written in English and Japanese, it had been donated by the Buddhist promoting foundation. Standing opposite the bathroom, against the far wall, was a dark brown wardrobe and matching chest of drawers. More importantly, next to the chest of drawers stood a mini-bar stocked with chilled beers, soft drinks and snacks. Behind it, a huge wall mirror the size of a door framed Chris's every move.

There was a knock at the door. Chris opened it. Outside, buttoned up in a waiter's green jacket, stood a young Thai man with a flowing mane of black hair.

Whilst peering into his room the waiter said, 'Compliments of the hotel sir.'

He held out a tray of sliced whole pineapple, garnished with a pink orchid. Chris beckoned the waiter inside and watched him place the tray onto the table.

'Thank you,' replied Chris and tipped him ten baht.

The waiter walked towards the open door, stopped and turned round. There was an uncomfortable silence in the room. The waiter eyed Chris carefully and then emitted an unobtrusive cough.

'Sir,' the waiter said, 'I see you go for walk. You come back quickly sir, do you have problem with street lady?'

Chris nodded with a wry grin.

The waiter shook his head sadly and grumbled, 'We have too many street lady in Pattaya – they no good for you.' He paused, and his voice perked up, 'Sir, the hotel have guides. You can see Pattaya and you have no problem when you go for walk.'

'Oh!' Chris exclaimed with some relief, 'how much money for a guide?'

'Three hundred Baht for one day sir.'

Chris felt quite chuffed. It was only six quid.

'Okay,' responded Chris eagerly, 'book me a guide for one day please.'

The waiter held one hand towards Chris. Chris handed him the money.

'I go to reception,' explained the waiter, tucking the money inside his pocket and slamming the door shut behind him.

Chris grabbed a bottle of Singha beer from inside the mini-bar and instantly cursed as the bottle opener eluded him. He searched through the tables and drawers, until, to his dismay, he finally saw it mounted high on the wall beside the bathroom door. Most hotels have their little peculiarities, thought Chris. Quite often a bedside light switch can turn on the bathroom light, or the shower can insist on remaining too hot or too cold. This bottle opener was a clear example of ergonomic failure.

15 minutes elapsed and Chris was drinking his second beer. Someone knocked the door again. Chris opened it. The waiter eased himself into the room. A young Thai woman with a smiling heart-shaped face stood behind him in the corridor. She was a woman of striking beauty. Small and lean in stature, her inky hair was parted down its centre and evenly cut on each side. A badge bearing her name, Wanna, was pinned to her smart, sky blue dress, which also

had deep pink flowers that complemented her red-gloss lipstick. The waiter beckoned her inside.

The woman, smiling demurely, entered the room and greeted Chris Thai-style by holding the palms of her hands together, saying softly, '*Sawasdee ka.*'

Chris smiled, 'Hello, my name is Chris Pepperdine.'

'Hello Kiss,' the woman said, 'my name Wanna – I your guide.'

Chris's smile broadened on hearing her mispronunciation, but he let it pass without any comment. Her exotic voice could say his name wrong, anytime. Wanna saw Chris delve into his pocket and tip the waiter 50 baht. The waiter looked impressed. He thanked Chris, and without looking back he proceeded at a rapid pace towards the door, whispering something in Wanna's ear as he passed her. Wanna let his smug comment pass without flinching.

'Kiss,' she asked, 'can I have drink please?'

Chris nodded and watched her pour out a glass of iced water from the chrome flask.

Standing straight backed and sideways on, with her petite breasts glorified against the light of the window, she took several sips and asked, 'You want see Pattaya?'

'I want to go for a walk,' Chris replied, 'but fust I want to eat lunch. Will yer join me?'

Wanna wrinkled her brow. It was clear that Chris would have to speak the Queen's English with no trace of an accent.

'Shall we eat lunch?' Chris asked slowly.

She nodded in agreement and they went to the hotel coffee shop.

'What do you want to eat?' Chris politely enquired. Wanna looked at the menu and replied, '*Kow tom . . .*'

Her voice halted with an abrupt silence. An embarrassed expression flitted momentarily across her face. Chris smiled to reassure her.

'Kiss,' she explained, 'I sorry I speak Thai. I want eat rice soup.'

'That's okay,' Chris said, 'I want a ham sandwich – can you tell the waitress, please?'

Wanna spoke to the waitress in her own language. The worry and anxiety that Chris had harboured regarding the Thai language fell from him, like a flurry of sparks emitted from a chain of Chinese firecrackers.

Presently, their food arrived. Taking exaggerated care to try and string together a voluble conversation, they both succumbed to shyness and found themselves making fitful remarks in between bites. The open-air coffee shop was situated next to the garden and the sound of running water drifted in through the window frame. Outside a gardener watered the grass and flowers with a red hose. Soon, the fresh smell of a quick-drying garden after a summer shower blended with Wanna's aromatic soup.

After lunch Chris paid the bill and they strolled around the garden. It was walled on three sides, allowing unfamiliar ivy to spread along the brickwork. Colourful, tropical flowerbeds flourished beneath several palm trees and the air seemed heavy with a perfumed essence. Chris had not noticed it before. Perhaps Wanna's pleasant company had something to do with it. They decided to retrace Chris's aborted venture along the promenade. They strolled through the gate and Wanna silenced the annoying taxi drivers with several harshly spoken Thai words that brought a broad grin to Chris's face. The street women stayed well away, although Chris did detect a derisive glare as they passed them.

'These lady have no home,' Wanna said vaguely.

Chris peered at a small bar where women sat on high barstools.

'What about these ladies – do they have a home?' Chris asked, pointing a finger.

Wanna nodded and explained, 'They work for bar owner – they stay in her home.'

They continued to walk, passing more bars and more bored looking women. Chris guessed that they were waiting for the sun to set, for it was then when Pattaya would probably come alive. One of the women crossed her legs slowly, as if by chance, providing Chris with an exciting glimpse of her pink underwear and suspenders. The woman blatantly ogled Chris.

Wanna observed her too, and quickly said, 'This lady no good for you.' Chris smiled at Wanna and nodded in agreement. They walked the full length of the beach road and turned round to retrace their footsteps.

The oppressive heat from the afternoon sun intensified.

'Wanna,' Chris said gasping, 'I want to drink a beer please.'

Wanna selected a pleasant open-air bar and they each mounted a vinyl barstool. A plump, middle-aged woman of short stature with a round beaming face welcomed them. There the woman sat, in the centre of the bar, enthroned in a teak rocking chair. Wanna ordered their drinks. Chris peered around. The layout of the bar was circular in construction, similar to an English fairground 'hook a plastic duck' stall. In spite of this, the clientele were not fishing for yellow plastic ducks. A couple of western men sat on the far side drinking beer. Each of the men had a Thai woman snuggled beside him. Several other women garbed in tee shirts and hot pants sat around the bar. Some entertained themselves by playing cards and dominoes, a strange variation on the western game, that used canary yellow dominoes with perhaps as many as 20 black spots on one domino.

Presently the waitress returned with their drinks and she dropped Chris's bill into a small glass tumbler. Wanna muttered something to the waitress who in turn spoke to the plump, middle-aged woman. The woman continued to sway backwards and forwards in her creaking rocking chair. She smiled at Wanna, displaying a row of uneven teeth. The waitress eyed her boss carefully and after a quick nod of approval she removed Chris's bill and placed it under the counter. Chris observed the gesture.

How strange, he thought, and he quickly turned to Wanna, asking, 'What's happening?'

Wanna calmly took a sip from her glass of iced water, paused a few seconds, and said, 'Everything okay – I save you money.'

Chris grinned and drank his free beer, a lot of beer. The beer rose in him and he felt great. Sweat soon formed on Chris's thighs, creating a bond between his flesh and the vinyl seat. Wanna had already lifted her dress over her right knee and was sitting cross-legged, directing what little breeze there was towards her own heavenly thighs. Chris, now in a relaxed frame of mind, rotated about his seat creating an amusing, erotic noise similar to parting Velcro. In the embarrassing silence that followed Wanna stole an amused glance at Chris. For that short moment Chris's eyes widened, inwardly thrilled. The waitress inserted a cassette into a ghetto blaster and the bar owner began to clap and rock to the rhythm of the western pop music. The tempo grew to a crescendo and the women around the bar joined in, laughing and cheering as she rode the chair like a rocking horse.

A few hours later Wanna and Chris returned to the hotel and, rather surprisingly, Wanna fetched his key from the reception.

'Wanna,' Chris asked, 'shall we have another drink in the bar?'

Wanna whispered into his ear, 'Kiss, your mini-bar cheaper.'

She glanced around, to see if any of the hotel staff had

heard her comment. Nobody was in his or her immediate vicinity. She opened Chris's door and they strolled into his room. Wanna kicked off her sandals by the door. Chris stood watching her, overcome with awe as she slid his chilled beer down the side of a tall glass. She handed him the glass. Chris sipped it slowly and lowered himself into the cushioned, rattan chair. It creaked and the sound was embarrassing in the erotic silence. Chris's heart quickened. Wanna re-opened the mini-bar and took out a bottle of coke. Once more she walked towards the bottle opener fixed high on the wall. The air was crackling with sexual awareness. She slid the bottle top inside, yanked it downwards and comically spilt the frothing beverage down the front of her dress. She looked steadily across at Chris, and pointed a finger to her wet dress. The blue and now, almost transparent cotton clung to her body. The outline of her petite white bra could quite easily be seen.

'Excuse me,' she said softly and walked over to Chris's chair, halting when her knees made soft contact with his.

Neither of them moved, their kneecaps almost kissing through her thin stockings.

Then Wanna turned round and calmly said, 'Unzip please.'

Chris stood up and slowly pulled the zip down towards her pink sateen pants. The noise aroused him even further. She stepped out of her dress and unhooked her wet bra, which revealed fresh pinch marks on her smooth, unblemished back. Wanna gave him a coquettish turn of her head and completely turned round to expose her upturned breasts. Chris responded with a libidinous smile and they embraced. Chris inhaled slowly and the fragrant mixture of exotic spices and the perfume that anointed her skin rose to his nostrils. Chris kissed her red, shining lips. She had a unique flavour and scent, as if licking a foreign stamp for the first time. Her seasoned mouth made a dainty titbit. They sat on the bed, still kissing. Then the noise of another zip could be heard. Wanna pulled his shorts down, over his knees. An immense strain was released, as if two geological tectonic plates had jolted apart. Chris glanced down, and saw that his underpants were now nestled comfortably inside his shorts. They kissed again, a slow kiss, and her hand felt the strength of his reproductive spear.

'Excuse me,' Chris said quietly and he stepped out of his shorts and underpants, discarding them on the carpet.

Chris went to the bathroom and opened his new box of condoms. At last, he thought, I can use them before they become out of date.

Chris returned to see Wanna sitting on the edge of the bed, swinging her legs from side to side. She was naked, allowing him to see in all its glory her wonderful fertile patch. Wanna stood up and beckoned him to lie down on his back. Suddenly she straddled him and, without haste, her dexterous hand guided his seed dispenser inside her love corridor. She was warm inside, and Chris also warmed as if he was back home beside a glowing coal fire on a winter's night. Her lean and agile body worked hard, disguising his ignorance of technique. She had a purpose to her lovemaking. Her taught body was drawn like a crossbow. His heartbeat increased rapidly, and their warm body scents rose to overpower the air-conditioner. She swayed her head from side to side and shuddered in an uncontrolled convulsion. Chris's body responded in sympathy by discharging its alkaline fluid that nourished his sperm.

Wanna rose from the bed and turned the air-conditioner to high. Her back glistened with beads of sweat as she calmly walked towards the bathroom. Chris lay on the bed motionless, apart from the occasional palpitation of his penis. He gazed around the room, locking his eyeballs now and again onto the imitation Thai antiquities. He could hear a great stream of water falling from the shower as Wanna cleansed her body. With Wanna still luxuriating inside the shower, jet lag finally overcame Chris and he fell asleep.

2

Deity

Fortified with pride and joy, Chris awoke with an aura of divine status. An aching burden had been lifted from his soul and a metamorphosis had now taken place. Dionysus, the earthly Greek god of wine and pleasure had allowed Chris to worship him, worship him in the form of ecstatic, orgiastic hedonism.

Wanna was sitting in the rattan chair. The orange table lamp illuminating the delicate features of her bare shoulders. She had a white bath towel wrapped tightly round her torso. Chris smiled and looked at his watch. It was 7.15. He sighed and smiled again. He did not really care what the bloody time was. Glancing inside the bedclothes, Chris discovered that what only a few hours earlier had been proud and symmetrical was now distinctly flexible, powdered and lopsided. With great care and thought, Wanna had cleaned, dried and talcum powdered his love hose. He had slept through the whole thing, missing the experience completely. Chris almost regretted not having witnessed such care and attention. He prised himself out of the bedclothes and sat on the edge of the bed, his knoblike spout dangling down in front of him like a tamarind drooping from a branch. Wanna closed her magazine and stood up. In an erotic, yet swift manner she unwrapped her towel allowing it to fall to the floor. Her rounded buttocks were brush-stroked orange as she walked past the table lamp. She approached Chris, held his hand and, like a woodland nymph, led her deity away for ceremonial washing under the shower. Chris was pampered like a sacrificial lamb and, with the care of a nurse, Wanna applied the creamy lather to his skin, massaging, kneading and purifying every pore and orifice.

They left the shower and she dried his body in front of the wall mirror. Chris stood still and admired his naked reflection. Occasionally her wet nipples brushed against his arms, inducing excited gooseflesh along his neck and spine. Chris, now dry and sitting in the rattan chair, watched in awe as she poured a cooled libation and raised the tall glass to his lips. Wanna slowly poured the beer down his dry throat and, without hesitation, replenished his glass.

'Wanna,' Chris asked, 'is there any good restaurants in town?'

Wanna looked disappointed and replied, 'Nice restaurant in my hotel.' She paused awhile and timidly said, 'It good for me – my boss will happy.'

Chris smiled and said mildly, 'Okay, I understand.'

'Me change clothes first,' Wanna suggested.

'Where are your clothes?' asked Chris with growing curiosity.

'In hotel – we have staff rooms,' she explained.

'Can I see your room?'

Wanna shook her head in a forcible manner, saying, 'No, I stay with two waitress.'

'Oh! I see.'

Chris sipped his beer. Wanna dressed and left the room. Chris also got dressed, putting on his smart trousers and a new short-sleeved shirt purchased especially for his holiday.

There was a knock at the door and on opening it Chris saw Wanna standing in the dim corridor. She wore a V-necked black evening dress, with a meshed top that just showed a hint of cleavage. Standing in the orange light thrown from the table lamp, her lips shone like the burning embers of a fire. Chris held her hand, stepped outside, and slammed the door shut behind him. The loud noise echoed down the empty corridor. It was dark now, but what hit Chris first, full in the face, was the intense blast of heat. The setting of the broiling sun had made little difference to the fierce temperature.

They strolled through the scented garden, and above their heads the moon shone brightly with its surface features tilted at a strange and unfamiliar angle.

Wanna pointed a finger skywards, towards the waxing gibbous moon and said, '*Loy Kratong* soon.'

Chris smiled in ignorance and held her hand tightly. The footpath snaked its way towards faint and distant violin music. Lizards, beetles and other nocturnal creatures scurried from their threatening feet and the air was thick with an abundance of frenzied moths attracted to the decorative lamposts.

The violin music grew louder, and now the sound of laughter could be heard. They entered The Captain's Table. Inside the astutely-named restaurant everything resembled a sailing ship deck, with mock rigging, poop deck and mast. Wanna and Chris sat in a small, secluded alcove. A candle flickered in the centre of their table with its yellow flame reflecting in Wanna's brown eyes. In a corner of the room sat a western man in animated conversation with a Thai woman. Two bottles of wine stood on their table, of which one was empty. With no social grace whatsoever the woman cackled like a witch. She talked, chewed and laughed with an open mouth that displayed her food to all and sundry. This woman, thought Chris, was a fine example of the gaiety and exuberance of a drunken woman performing a social gaffe. The western man also appeared to be befuddled with drink. His appearance fitted his offensive manner. He wore a lewd tattoo on his arm, his hair in a ponytail and a large gold earring that a much younger person or a swashbuckling pirate should have worn. The skull and crossbones flying high above their table would have complemented their skulduggery and the restaurant's decor. In spite of this, an elderly, yet competent musician continued to play his violin to the unappreciative couple.

Eating alone at separate tables were three other western men. One by one, they each cast a furtive glimpse at Wanna. A waiter arrived and Chris recognised his flowing mane immediately. Possessing an enormous appetite, Chris eagerly ordered their nourishment and booked Wanna for the next nine days.

Their meals arrived and the soothing music eventually stopped, to leave Wanna and Chris to suffer the high-pitched squeaks of a distinctly dodgy air-conditioning unit. Chris watched as the befuddled man twirled his earring with a finger and thumb and then, rather reluctantly, he tipped the violinist a few baht. The musician found this unexpected baksheesh as little short of miraculous. His bow was now idle. So with a swift rise of his eyebrows Chris beckoned the musician to their table. He approached them and began to play.

'Wanna,' Chris asked, 'how old are you?'

'Twenty,' she replied.

'I'm twenty five – how long have you worked here?'

She thought awhile, almost hesitating, and then answered, 'Nine months.'

Like fine vintage wine, the music aided their digestion. Because Wanna worked at the hotel, the violinist played through most of their dinner. It became slightly embarrassing for Chris, but when the musician finally stopped Chris did tip him a generous 50 baht.

Later, Wanna and Chris decided to walk along the beach road. Under the cover of darkness they discreetly held hands for the first time in public. Pattaya had grown into a hanging garden of neon; neon signs that would have caused an outcry back in the U.K.: 'Caligula Go – Go Bar,' 'V.D. Clinic,' and a huge, phallic ice cream cone topped with a cherry, a cherry that, quite unashamedly, dripped semen-like confection onto bemused pedestrians below. This was no place for puritans, thought Chris.

They stopped outside a small arena. The unmistakable plosive voice of an excited boxing commentator filled the entire street. They watched from the pavement as a kick-boxing bout unfolded before their eyes. Despite the illegal weight difference, a short and fragile-looking Thai man fought with a tall, beer-bellied Australian. Pretty soon the tourist gained the upper hand. The Thai boxer fell to the floor on several occasions, only to miraculously regain his senses just before the tenth count. The Australian was well supported by a group of friends who would cheer him on ecstatically and exchange bets with a disgruntled-looking Thai waiter. In spite of this, the sideways craning of the waiter's neck towards the dazed boxer suggested to Chris that something sinister was afoot. Chris smiled in anticipation. Then, as Chris had expected, the Thai boxer suddenly produced a devastating blurred kick to his opponent's chin. The Australian dropped like a kangaroo caught in the path of a hunter's bullet. There was an expression of intense satisfaction on the Thai boxer's face. Chris grinned. It had all been a confidence trick and now the impoverished Australians looked on, anxious, and as stunned as their prostrate friend.

Wanna and Chris continued their walk, passing discos, bustling bars and night-clubs. Thai women garbed in hot pants and tight tee shirts would openly disregard the Thai social taboo of kissing men in the street. These beguiling women would stop to admire a seductive dress or gold jewellery in a shop window, whilst their inviting eyes suggested a world of sexual fulfilment for their partner. The happy tourist would then feel obliged to purchase the item selected. Chris peered at Wanna and smiled at his good fortune. He could do no wrong. Dionysus had shown him the way and he proudly showed her off to all the men. Dionysus had gifted Chris a power, the power to judge human frailties. These men, not unlike himself, had each in their own way sought romance, but sitting on the sideline so to speak, with no rancour whatsoever, succumbing to the allure of a prostitute seemed an extraordinary choice of behaviour.

Suddenly Wanna jerked Chris's arm and they both came to a halt. She pointed a finger towards a busy bar where men sat and drank with glamorous Thai ladies, ladies wearing expensive evening gowns.

'Lady man,' Wanna said vaguely.

Chris gazed at her with a puzzled brow.

'Lady man,' she repeated and discreetly pointed to her own petite breasts.

Chris stared at the women. They were statuesque for oriental women, with large breasts creating an almost westernised figure and now, as he looked more closely, their facial features made him shudder with unease. It was quite conceivable that they were transvestites.

'Wanna,' Chris enquired, 'are they men?'

She nodded, confirming his suspicion. Chris sighed with relief as a horrible vision materialised in his brain. Thank goodness he had returned to his hotel room first thing that lunchtime. Chris felt safe with Wanna and she was certainly turning out to be a good guide, pointing out all the horrors that lay beneath the gloss.

Wanting to observe more of the liquid action unfolding around him, Chris suggested that they stop at the bar where he had drunk free beer earlier that afternoon. Wanna smiled and showed him the way.

'Wanna,' Chris asked as they both sat down, 'will my beer be free again?'

She shook her head sadly and said, 'No you must pay.'

'Okay, what would you like to drink?'

The hefty bar owner began to rock gently in the wooden rocking chair, her eyes glaring at Wanna as she waited for her reply.

'Singapore sling please,' Wanna replied cheerfully.

'Great,' Chris said quickly, 'I'm pleased you want a proper drink.'

Their drinks arrived. Staring at his tall beer, ruminating, Chris watched the condensation slowly form on the outside of his glass. In a rather childish act, he used his finger as a pen and wrote Wanna's name just below the rim. Small rivulets, of sorts, trickled down the glass to soak into the cardboard beer coaster. Wanna watched his playful activity and smiled. Chris placed her hand onto his thigh, and he gulped his beer.

'Wanna,' he said, 'I have a good nickname for this bar.'

'What is name?' she asked him.

'I want to call it the hook a duck bar.'

Chris sniggered at his own joke. Wanna just continued to smile. Chris knew she did not understand.

The evening grew older and Wanna began to chat freely with the women sitting round the bar. They all spoke Thai, and Chris just sat listening to their tonal and mesmerising language. All the other men enjoyed their drinks, and the occasional subtle, erotic touch of a female hand. A small boy aged no more than nine with brown, cow eyes, walked round the bar selling red roses. Chris brought one for Wanna and she pinned it to her dress. Chris leaned forward and sniffed its sweet aroma, his chin resting against Wanna's breast. Then suddenly the voice of Don McLean singing 'American Pie' was heard above all else. Another bar had turned their music up in an attempt to drown out all of its competitors. Chris watched keenly as his bar owner instantly leapt to her feet, leaving her rocking chair swaying violently back and forth. Her face was enraged as she yelled and stabbed the offending bar with a podgy finger. The music was quickly turned down.

'What's happening?' Chris asked Wanna.

'That bar no good,' she replied vaguely, pointing a finger.

From what Chris could see, the bar had no customers whatsoever and all of its women sat alone looking fairly disgruntled.

'Oh, they are jealous,' Chris observed, and laughed in a farcical voice hoping to show his contempt for their actions. Somehow he had taken sides, treating the hook a duck bar as if it was his local pub.

His bar owner soon calmed down, and Chris allowed his eyes to wander. Flickering annoyingly above an office doorway was a blue neon sign. It read: 'passport, visa, and marriage certificate translation.' Chris wondered how many Thai women actually ended up marrying a tourist. The very existence of the sign proved that the customers were out there.

Chris drank some more. Faint laughter could be heard far away, growing in intensity as it came nearer and nearer like a fast-approaching *tsunami*, cheeky, girlish laughter, moving from bar to bar like falling dominoes. Everybody stood up and craned their necks to see more clearly. The bar next to them joined in the *mêlée*. Then the hook a duck bar burst into loud, impromptu laughter. Looking wonderfully proud, sauntering along the beach road were two red-headed men wearing kilts.

'Why they wear dress?' Wanna shrieked in dismay.

Chris grinned, shook his head, and explained, 'They come from Scotland – it's called a kilt.'

For several minutes after the women continued to laugh and giggle with each other. In one satirical gesture, a woman pushed her own breasts together enhancing their contours. This suggested that the Scottish men only lacked breasts if they too wanted to become women.

Suddenly and unexpectedly, Wanna clapped her hands drawing everybody's attention. She held them closed and placed them out of sight on her knees. The bar owner watched Wanna with a steely gaze. Wanna shuffled her feet slightly and then the moment was forgotten. A few minutes later Wanna opened her hands and displayed a crushed mosquito to Chris. He understood her message. Mosquitoes were on the prowl. Casually they finished their drinks and went back to the hotel.

As they walked along the shadowy corridor, Wanna twirled Chris's door key, rather girlishly. They passed a man staying at the hotel and the embarrassing jingle of the key brought a wry grin to the stranger's face. Wanna opened the door and with a long, libidinous smile she walked inside. In an instant Chris felt the cold air rush past his face. He followed her inside and quickly slammed the door shut. They were in their cooled environment now, like two Inuit immured in an igloo. Chris sat on the pink bedspread drinking another beer, listening to the subtle, sensual sounds of Wanna taking a shower. Pretty soon she emerged from the bathroom wearing a bath towel wrapped loosely round her body. She placed her clothes on the rattan chair.

'Wanna,' Chris urged, 'put them in the wardrobe – they are nice clothes. You don't want to crease them.'

She smiled back at him and replied, 'Okay sir.'

As she returned from the wardrobe the towel was much looser now, almost billowing open to reveal her flourishing oasis. Wanna saw his excited eyes and allowed the towel to fall to the floor. She sat beside Chris and kissed his mouth. Acting lovingly, Chris could feel her tongue rubbing and cleaning his teeth. Chris unzipped his trousers and pulled them down. He broke away from their kiss and stood up, dropping the rest of his clothes to the floor. She lay on her back and raised her knees, swaying them in an inviting gesture. Chris pried her legs open and he began to taste her coral shell, its conch-like overlapping whorl teasing and delicious. Her sensual smile gave way to a short intake of breath as his lance entered her. This time Chris took control of their lovemaking. Zeus, father of Dionysus watched from Mount Olympus and above the headboard a small green lizard scampered along the wall, glancing with indifference at the events below. Chris placed his right hand onto her left thigh, stroking its curved contours and shape. The gooseflesh texture of her skin vibrated with every contact of his fingertips. Wanna held Chris's shoulder blades tightly and moved her hands up the back of his neck, pushing her long fingers through his short hair and running them along his scalp. There was more thrusting, slightly quicker than before. Sweat glands opened and excreted their cooling liquid. Chris could feel her heart hammering away behind her ribs as a synchronised rhythm was established. They both worked hard, moving feverishly until they accomplished their goal. Chris rolled over, gasping like a cod out of water and he could hear Zeus applaud from Mount Olympus. The lizard was on the ceiling now, motionless, directly above their naked bodies. Wanna grabbed the silver flask and poured out a glass of iced water, swallowing it with large gulps. She handed Chris his glass of beer and he finished it off. Chris turned the light off and, holding each other tightly, they curled up into a tight ball. Soon, they fell asleep.

Chris awoke the following morning with Wanna still beside him. His watch read ten o'clock and she appeared to have been awake for quite sometime.

'Good morning Kiss,' she chirped.

Chris nodded to her. A single beam of yellow sunlight cut a path through a small gap in the curtains. Fine particles of dust floated in and out as it projected across the room. Wanna lifted the sheet up and stared at Chris's triumphant reveille. She smiled at him and her head went inside the bedclothes. Soon she was holding and squeezing his bugle. He could see the outline of her scalp move the sheet up and down in a constant rhythm. In an act of devoted worship to Dionysus, Wanna was now performing fellatio. The yellow inclining beam of sunlight illuminated the sheet each time she reached her uppermost point and, as if in a cinema, the beam of light thickened and intensified as the room filled with more dust particles. Chris opened his mouth in disbelief and then bit his tongue softly. He closed his eyes, enjoying the experience to its full potential. Bubbling with an uncontrollable excitement, he soon ejected his life-giving fluid. Wanna's head reappeared from under the bedclothes and she opened her mouth to show it was empty. Chris felt like a dentist, bemused, not knowing what to say.

'Kiss,' she explained, 'I eat your water.'

Shocked, Chris lifted the sheet up and saw that his pleasure fountain was dry. Totally dumfounded, his eyes followed Wanna as she walked to the bathroom, the beam of sunlight gently kissing her shoulders and naked body as she passed through the ray of light.

She showered and, after cleaning her teeth returned to say, 'I get clean clothes now.'

Chris nodded and watched her dress. She left his room, slamming the door shut behind her. A wisp of stale breath whistled through Chris's lips. He too got up and quickly cleaned his teeth.

A short time later, Chris and Wanna both ate breakfast in the coffee shop. Quite soon Chris came to the palpable conclusion that the bars had had a busy night. Several male guests sat and ate with young Thai women. The women ate indigenous food, whilst their partners tucked into bacon and eggs, or continental breakfasts. An unpleasant thought entered Chris's head. Perhaps some of these men would think Wanna to be a prostitute. She was his guide, but how could he tell them? Chris began to talk aloud, asking Wanna questions about her job and hotel. This seemed to cause her some discomfort, but he continued until he was sure their conversation had been heard.

Wanna and Chris spent the rest of the morning beside the clear glimmer of the hotel swimming pool, never wandering too far from the wonderful erotic atmosphere of their little igloo. Chris's bed was on standby, waiting for any lustful urge, and after lunch their frenzied lovemaking spoiled the maid's effort to clean his room. Soon they both fell asleep, exhausted.

That evening, Wanna woke up first, and in a rather worried voice she said, 'Kiss, we go see *Loy Kratong* now.'

She quickly got dressed and urged Chris to do the same. His watch now read 7.00 and they both took to their heels, scurrying across the moonlit beach like two startled crabs. In the distance Chris could see a crowd of people huddled around a crackling fire like a coven of witches, their playful shadows undulating across the rippled sand like mischievous demons summoned from hell.

'Wanna,' Chris asked, 'what is *Loy Kratong*?'

She pointed a finger towards the sea and replied rather mysteriously, 'We have fire on water.'

Chris frowned, as he did not understand. The silver disc of a full moon stood reflected, upside down on the wrinkled sea, and around the vast darkness shone the lonely lights of fishing vessels. Much nearer the shore, strange and unfamiliar lights bobbed back and forth beyond the gentle waves. They approached the crackling fire and Chris soon realised that candles were being lit and placed into banana-leaf boats. He browsed at their selection and chose two waxen banana leaves that he considered the most seaworthy. Illuminated by the moonlight and flickering flames, Chris struggled to read a short leaflet explaining *Loy Kratong*. The fire licked Wanna and Chris's candles and they shuffled along the sand shielding the flames with their hands. They approached the bubbling surf and launched their offering to the goddess of water: *Mae Khong Kha*. Suddenly the gulf of Thailand threw a terrific wave over their fragile boats. The candles went out immediately and the boats sank without a trace. Wanna stood still, looking fairly disappointed. So Chris decided to surprise her. Whilst she was watching the other guests, Chris returned with two more boats.

'Kiss – no!' Wanna yelled in horror, 'we do one time or it bad luck.'

Chris laughed haughtily and said, 'It's all right, I'm not Buddhist.'

Wanna frowned and rather reluctantly helped to launch their boats once more. Almost at once, and now fairly ominously, both boats sank and were swept away to Davy Jones's locker.

3

Girlfriend

For Chris, the next couple of days became a blurred memory. One morning he woke up bleary-eyed and wheezing like an old man. In spite of this, the hedonistic haze of the past few days instantly cleared when he sniffed the air. Chris sat up startled. An irritating, heady smell pervaded the whole bedroom. Its odour, quite odious in the sweet aromas of Wanna's creams and perfume, was familiar, but Chris could not place its source. Wanna sat at the foot of the bed, her arched back facing Chris. She was naked, with her chin resting delicately on her right knee. Chris crept out of the bedclothes and crawled forward, peering over her shoulder. Wanna applied a little more cherry-red nail varnish to her toenails and then glanced up at Chris. A delicious smile spread across her face. Slowly his whole body melted into hers and his large hands came round to cover her silken breasts. Chris gazed around the room. Most of his clothes lay loosely across the table. But on this morning, with his head clear as a bell, he remembered it all. During a passionate moment Wanna had suggested she move into his room. Chris had agreed and now the bedroom and bathroom lay cluttered with feminine items that were alien to him. One item in particular, labelled a 'lady douche', had caused him considerable concern the previous evening. While cleaning his teeth in front of the bathroom mirror, to glimpse that grotesque item lying at the bottom of the shower looking every bit like a one-horned sea creature, really gave Chris quite a turn. However, as he now hugged Wanna on the bed, Chris smiled with contentment.

After breakfast they decided to visit the small coral island of Koh Lam, which was about one hour away by boat. Wanna settled comfortably into a shaded wooden bench, while Chris stood on the deck with his back to the wind, gazing ahead eagerly. Once again it was a hot, clear day, windy enough for Chris's tee shirt to flutter incessantly around his trunk. Chris watched the white hotels of Pattaya grow smaller as their boat made its way towards the still landmass, peeping out, proudly, above the flat horizon. Pretty soon, as the engine stuttered on discordantly, Chris joined Wanna and allowed the soft, rhythmic flow of water peeling away from each bow to soothe and relax him. Suddenly a clanging bell sounded from the bridge. Chris craned his neck, searching the sea. His eyes fell on a small archaic fishing boat and, as they approached it, its wrinkled hoary fishermen smiled and waved their rough work-hardened hands. These dedicated fishermen, Chris mused, seemed trapped in a time capsule, relics of Pattaya's past and a rosy future was far from guaranteed. Wanna and Chris's boat held its unswerving course and the fishermen's craft rocked helplessly as they passed alongside. The angry fishermen put out their clenched fists and cursed. Chris looked up at the bridge and carefully observed the captain. The young captain, unmoved and expressionless, continued to stare ahead. Chris shook his head sadly.

Presently their boat neared the shoreline of Koh Lam. Chris looked up at the sky. A blizzard of white seabirds filled the air, their screams howling like a menacing squall. Soon their boat moored alongside a jetty built on a short stretch of beach and Wanna and Chris stepped ashore with the other tourists. Suddenly hoards of waif-like children carrying small cards, white with unconvincing glass bead encrustations that ranged in colour from sea-green to pastel pink, surrounded them.

'Ruby, emerald, sapphire for lady sir,' urged a rib-skinny boy aged no more than ten. Chris shook his head and followed the tourists into a beach restaurant, which was now rapidly filling up. Through the maze of bodies, Chris noticed two vacant chairs beside the portly figures of a middle-aged western couple.

'Can we sit here please?' Chris asked them.

The man nodded and Wanna sat next to the woman. In a show of contempt and disgust, the woman pursed her lips and moved her chair away from Wanna as if there had been something between them. Her salient body language had made it quite clear that she thought Wanna to be a prostitute. Chris sat down and Wanna ordered their lunch. Chris tried his best to ignore the rude woman by shifting his gaze and rubbing his shoes in the sand. Wanna glanced under the table. Chris followed her gaze. In a perfect procession, workaholic ants heaved their provisions towards a hidden nest. A grain of rice, a shred of seaweed, no item was missed. In an act of mercy he pulled his feet out of harm's way. Wanna smiled.

Their Thai lunch arrived. Throughout all of this, the rude woman remained silent, while periodically flashing a fierce look of repugnance in Wanna's direction. This resentment towards Wanna, this hostility had gone far enough, thought Chris.

'Are you two married?' Chris asked her in a derisive tone.

The repugnant woman looked startled and nodded. She didn't know what had hit her and turned towards her husband, who gave her no support whatsoever.

'This is Wanna, my Thai girlfriend,' Chris snapped again. The woman leaned towards Chris, seemingly embarrassed, and quickly said, 'She's lovely.'

There was an expression of intense satisfaction stamped

on Chris's face. He had shown beyond doubt that some of the Thai women with tourists were not prostitutes. But then Chris paused a moment, in deep thought. Chris realised that he too had fallen into the same trap as this narrow-minded woman. Who was he to judge who were prostitutes or not when walking the streets of Pattaya? Most important of all, it was none of his business anyway. Chris now felt ashamed and took a large gulp of beer.

After lunch, to Chris's disappontment, he realised his camera had run out of film, So leaving their footprints on the beach, like dinosaurs roaming a Jurassic earth, seemed the only way to prove Wanna and Chris had ever been there.

During the last few days Chris had experienced new emotions and feelings that were alien to him. This day was to be no exception. The return trip turned into a nightmare. The sea and a strong headwind threw their vessel up and down like a fairground Ferris wheel. Chris, his head spinning for the first time in his life, cast a pleading gaze towards the captain. The captain, now grinning unpleasantly, kept his venomous eyes riveted on the horizon. Chris, shielding his mouth with a hand and hardly daring to look at Wanna, groped his way to the stern and cowered out of sight. If all else failed, he thought, he could of course blame the Thai food, but he was sure Wanna would see through that lie. Wanna's keen eyes observed Chris with sympathy and pretty soon her soft slim fingers held his hand reassuringly.

Eventually they reached Pattaya and, to Chris's shame and embarrassment, his lunch was now feeding the gulf of Thailand's marine life. Wanna took his arm and led him back to the hotel. That evening sex was out of the question. He could still feel the waves rocking inside his head long into the evening. Wanna ate from the room service menu, while Chris lay with his head buried deep in his pillow. She offered him the last slice of succulent pineapple. Chris refused, with several heaving noises that nearly uprooted his intestines.

By next daybreak Chris felt much better. While lying on the bed reading his Thai guidebook, Chris noticed that the bathroom door was slightly open. His girlfriend was in the shower and a small amount of steam crept into the bedroom and rose to the ceiling like dry ice. Chris peered surreptitiously into the bathroom. The shower curtain was open and water had formed a small pool on the white tiled floor. Chris's girlfriend stood under the shower, sideways on, looking like a nymph. With her head tilted backwards, hands akimbo and face directly under the shower rose, he had a clear view of her glorious breasts. After so many years, finally experiencing this erotic fantasy of his caused Chris to dwell for quite some time. Wanna's eyes were closed as she enjoyed the warm water streaming over her face. His gaze fell once more on the small pool of water. It's okay, he thought, he could easily wipe it up later. Wanna straightened her neck and opened her eyes. Facing the blue-tiled wall for a few seconds, she happened to turn her head towards the door and her eyes met his. A flicker of guilt swept over Chris's face and he lowered his eyes once more.

'Kiss,' Wanna said in an upbeat tone, 'we shower together.'

Chris hesitated, uncertain whether he should enter. Finally he pushed the door wide open, allowing more steam to rush into the cooler bedroom and coat the wall mirror with a thin layer of condensation. Chris quickly closed the door behind him and undressed. Then, rather gingerly, he stepped into the shower and stood in front of Wanna, pulling the curtain shut behind him. His girlfriend turned to face the chrome shower taps and bent forwards, allowing the water to pound her shoulders and run down her arched spine. Wanna pushed her hips backward in an inviting gesture. Her crescent-shaped back formed an escarpment, which allowed the water to run over her rounded buttocks like a cascading waterfall. Wanna held the cold shower tap in one hand, taking control like the helmsman of a ship, while her other hand made a delicate detour, searching blindly for evidence of his unspoken desire. Chris's vertical mast, however, spoke in the international language of love, like a steamer communicating with three flags on her foremast. A moment later her roving hand held that love mast tightly and, with a slow spiral motion, she carefully steered Chris towards her deep whirlpool of pleasure. Chris thrust his hips forward and the cascading waterfall immediately shut off, allowing a small pool to form against his groin and her buttocks. Chris had created a dam and with every thrust he could open and close it at will. Chris looked at his girlfriend's honeyed hands. She now held both taps tightly, bracing herself, as if operating the dam sluicegates with the vitality and enthusiasm of a skilled craftsman.

Wanna, still bending low, faced the tiled floor. Chris began to caress her back, dancing his fingertips across her taught honey-coloured skin like hammers thrown against the strings of a piano. Chris found that he could master the various aspects of irrigation, by directing the flow of water left or right of her spine. He continued to invigorate and tantalise her back, while allowing nature's water to soothe the rest of her body. Small rivulets ran down her legs and along her feet, bringing sensual pleasure to her manicured toes. Wanna began to sway her hips from left to right excitedly. The shower curtain clung to Wanna's hip, forcing her to calm down and decrease the movement to a gentle but effective wiggle. Chris stared at the chrome shower taps. Their reflective characteristics mirrored it all, the resplendent water running over Wanna's naked flesh, and the grimace of sheer pleasure contorting his lustful face. Chris made his final thrust and held the dam in place for several seconds. His eyes refocused, and he looked down at the pool of water trapped against his groin. Slowly he withdrew and the water level dropped. Wanna squared her shoulders and turned round to face him. She smiled happily and looked him square in the eye, saying with conviction, 'Kiss, I love you.'

Chris's jaw dropped, and he stared into her almond eyes, perplexed.

'Kiss,' she added, 'I love you, I want you be boyfriend for long time. I want you see my mother.'

'Wanna,' Chris urged, 'let's get dressed.'

He walked over to the towel rack, grabbed two towels and handed her one. Chris wiped the bathroom mirror and peered at his unshaven, lantern-jawed chin. He was grinning like a large reptile.

'Does your mother live in Pattaya?' Chris asked wondering.

'No, Nakhon Sawan,' Wanna replied excitedly.

'Where is that?' Chris enquired, observing her attentively.

'I show you in book,' she answered and promptly walked over to the bed. 'Here,' she said, placing a finger on the map.

Her fingertip lay near the centre of Thailand.

'How far is it?' Chris grumbled.

'Three hundred and fifty kilometres,' Wanna responded in an upbeat tone.

'That's a long way,' Chris moaned, putting up a possible barrier.

'We can go in one day,' she insisted, kicking his barrier aside.

After breakfast, Wanna and Chris strolled through an outdoor market awash with vivid colours, and heady smells. With goods displayed in a rather haphazard fashion, the market still met the townspeople's demands for fresh fish, vegetables, textiles and live animals. Here, like an unexplained emotion, a secret fear, or deep mistrust passed down through generations, customers would be required to haggle. Confronting the market trader with a smile, and hoping to persuade him or her that their goods would perish before the day was through, had now become second nature to all Thais. Wanna agreed a price and held up a fresh ocean fish, a red snapper.

'We eat tonight,' she declared.

'How will we cook it?' Chris asked with a wry grin.

'I take to hotel kitchen – they cook for us,' she explained and smiled, adding, 'I save you money.'

'Okay,' Chris replied, still unconvinced with her idea.

Wanna examined a whole pineapple and purchased it.

They walked through the town and a sign caught Chris's eye. It read: 'Passport, Visa, Air ticket, Air-conditioned bus ticket.'

'Wanna,' Chris suggested, 'let's buy a bus ticket to Nakhon Sawan – we can go tomorrow to see your mother.'

His girlfriend's face lit up and, in a clear breach of social convention, she kissed him in public.

Back at their hotel, Wanna left Chris in the lobby and took the fish into the kitchen. A few moments later she returned with a glinting kitchen knife.

'What's that for?' Chris asked her.

'To cut pineapple in room.'

'Oh!' He replied.

Later that afternoon Wanna and Chris took a dip in the cool swimming pool. While drinking cocktails under the shade of a palm tree, in a textbook example of paradise, Chris wondered what the men back in the drawing office would think of him if they could see him now. Lucky bastard, probably. Chris took another gulp and crunched ice. His glass was empty. He turned to Wanna and her dilated pupils suggested another agenda. In a mutual understanding they stepped out of the pool, straight onto several brightly-lit tiles scorched by a short strip of sunlight. With Wanna at his heels, Chris's footsore feet set the pace towards his bedroom. Their swimming costumes dripping water down the inside of their thighs, leaving a trail of guilt along the corridor floor, a trail towards uncontrollable passion. They were ready to indulge in the sweetness of an erotic moment, inside that curtained room, with the unclouded glare of orange light illuminating Wanna's glistening body. There Chris stood, face to face with Wanna, with an almost farcical poise of the head, his knees held together by taught elastic and water dripping slowly from his naked genitals. Wanna tugged at his swimming trunks and pulled them off his knees.

'We have to dry ourselves, or the bed will get wet,' Chris told Wanna flatly.

She laughed, pivoted on her heels and reached for their abandoned towels. As if preparing for a picnic, she laid a damp square of white towelling carefully on the pink bedspread. Armed with his last condom and a self-gratified grin, Chris returned to his girlfriend.

She lay on the bed, with her knees raised and legs apart.

'Kiss,' she insisted, 'make sex to me.'

It was a request he could not refuse. Like an asteroid blending darkly with a feeding black hole, what was once two now joined to become one. Chris cradled her head in his hand like a nest of fragile eggs, while slowly stroking his fingers across her damp scalp. Moving slowly, back and forth, in and out, crutch to crutch, they gently made love. Both focused on the pleasure of giving and receiving each other's touch. It was mutual, relaxing and exciting. Excitement that grew with the stirring sensation of nerves pulsating with life. Chris's knees rubbed hard against the towelling material. Their bodies warmed, evaporating all traces of the chlorinated water. Wanna held her lips together, and like a cow giving birth she let out a long nasal moo. She had climaxed and Chris wanted to join her, he continued thrusting, quicker and quicker, and like a slow release of pressurised steam he let out a long hiss between his teeth. To Chris's surprise Wanna mooed again. This was different. Her body had reacted in an unfamiliar way.

A short time later Wanna sat up and smiled at Chris.

'Kiss,' she explained, 'I finish two times.' She grinned, and looked him square in the eyes, saying joyfully, 'Kiss, I want your baby.' With an enigmatic half-smile, exulting like an emperor, and utterly delighted at hearing such sentiment Chris sprang to his feet.

'Kiss, I love you – I want your baby,' she added softly, her eyes slowly panning up and down his naked body.

She was admiring him.

Suddenly, Wanna yelled in horror, 'Kiss, look!'

Chris stepped back in fear, searching the floor for a lizard or perhaps a snake.

'What is it?' he cried.

'Look!'

She pointed towards his legs. Chris peered down and on seeing what had startled her he laughed aloud. His knees now shone like red peppers, the result of friction burns from the towels. They kissed and embraced. Slowly tears pooled in Wanna's eyes and trickled down her face.

'What's the matter now?' Chris asked softly.

'I think you forget me when you go home.'

'I won't forget you, stop crying,' he insisted, trying to reassure her.

They kissed again.

Later that evening, whilst sitting inside The Captain's Table Wanna ordered their red snapper. Striding resolutely, with haste, the waiter returned, averting his worried glances from Chris's disconcerting eyes. In an apologetic tone of voice he spoke to Wanna in her own language. Chris cast an eye at her. Wanna could not conceal her anger and her face shone a scornful glare towards the poor waiter.

'Wanna,' Chris offered, 'what's the matter?'

She paused and pursed her lips, openly expressing her disappointment.

'The manager see fish in kitchen,' she whined, 'he say no cook for me – we must eat from menu.'

Chris felt sorry for her, but he was not surprised at the manager's response. They complied with the manager's wishes and ordered from the menu.

'Wanna,' Chris said smiling warmly, 'it's okay, I understand.'

He was full of sympathy, offering to take her to the disco to help cheer her up. She agreed.

Inside the disco, a dizzy whirl of multicoloured lights ran across the wooden floor. Revellers gyrated through billows of dry ice, dry ice that remained detached, free to wander and creep above that solid medium known as the dance floor. The whole room flexed with the beat of the music, which pounded with a limpid resonance. Above the revellers' brows spun a ball of mirrors, from which beams of light briefly touched a cheekbone or a hand. Whilst waiting for Wanna's return from the toilet, Chris peered around the room. This was a popular place, a place for happiness, thought Chris.

A red light briefly illuminated a darkened corner. Chris's pulse quickened as he caught sight of his girlfriend's crimson face. Wanna stood quite still and, like a chameleon, her flesh changed with each splash of colour. She was smiling and talking to a short, willowy woman. Chris recognised the woman immediately. She worked at the hook a duck bar. He continued to watch Wanna's body language. It intrigued him. Wanna placed a fingertip onto her own eyelid and ran it down her cheekbone. She was miming her crying performance. A shudder ran down Chris's spine and his skin bristled with gooseflesh. He had caught a moment of complacency. There was something insulting in Wanna's actions, the debasing taint of concealment. Dionysus had punished him for having the audacity to dare to join him as a deity. He had brought about madness with a naïve theory of romance. Chris's libido ran down the plughole in an inevitable spiral motion. He craned his neck to see more clearly. The two women now held each other's elbows girlishly, as if celebrating a major achievement. With a bewildered look on his sweat-streaked face Chris sat down, flicking his nails anxiously. He allowed his brain to assemble the pieces of a vast jigsaw puzzle. Chris asked himself what had happened over the last few days.

One – the free beer at the hook a duck bar and then later, after he had had sex with Wanna, he was required to pay.

Two – Wanna laughing and talking freely with the women prostitutes at the bar, and now, as he sat here, she was miming her phoney tears to one of them.

Three – collecting his room key every time from the reception, with no questions asked.

Four – her clothes, toothbrush and make-up were now all inside his room.

Five – 'I want you see my mother.'

Six – 'I love you, Kiss.'

Seven – 'I want your baby.'

The evidence was overwhelming. He had been blind and needed a fucking white stick. She was a hotel prostitute. A short time later Wanna returned smiling affably. Chris smiled back at her.

'Let's go back to the hotel,' Chris calmly suggested.

'Yes sir,' Wanna replied with enthusiasm.

As usual, Wanna opened the door to his room and kicked off her shoes. Chris followed her inside and decided to confront her.

Chris planted his shaking arms akimbo and yelled, 'Wot's going on?'

Wanna's blank face stared back at his petulant expression. Chris was angry and dropped his pretence at speaking the Queen's English.

'Do yer think I'm stupid?' he hollered.

'What the matter Kiss?' Wanna asked mildly, with the slight quiver of her lips.

'I wuz watching yer talk to yer friend in the disco, yer showed her how yer pretended to cry to me earlier.'

She shook her head and insisted, 'Kiss, I do not understand what you say.'

'Wanna – you are a hotel prostitute, aren't you?'

'Oh! Kiss, Oh! Kiss . . .' Wanna wailed.

She pulled her silken hair and covered her sobbing face, squinting at Chris through the gaps between her fingers. Chris stood quite still, not really knowing what to do.

'I love you Kiss,' she muttered, her mouth quivering uncontrollably.

'Kiss, I want you be my boyfriend. I love you – I want your baby.'

'You really are crying now – aren't you?' Chris said spitefully, adding, 'and by the way my name is Chris not Kiss.'

Wanna threw herself onto the bed and rolled over, weeping and burying her head in the pillow. Chris sighed, as he now regretted being so spiteful to her. He walked over to the mini-bar. The muffled sobbing stopped. Chris placed the bottle of beer into the wall-mounted bottle opener, the very one which only a few days earlier had aided Wanna to disrobe. Suddenly a flash of orange light in the crude outline of a knife ran up the wall. Goose pimples erupted silently on the back of his neck. Chris turned round. Wanna had grabbed the kitchen knife and was holding the shaking blade against her wrist.

'Wot the fuck are yer doing?' Chris shouted.
More sobbing and 'I want kill myself,' she declared with trembling lips.
Chris opened the door and ran down the corridor. Green lizards scampered up the walls as if running from a raging fire. With his self-esteem savagely eroded by Wanna's actions, Chris approached the security guard in a state of apprehension.
'Quick! I have problem with Wanna,' Chris cried.
The security guard looked perplexed and asked him, 'You want change lady?'
'No, come quickly,' raved Chris, trying to hold his composure.
Suddenly the security guard looked mortified. He now realised that Chris was in fact pleading for help. They both strode towards the room, stiff-legged and hugging the shadows. Pessimism filled Chris's brain. He wondered what the other guests would think if a Thai woman lay dead in his room. More importantly, what would the Thai police do? They would certainly be involved. What penalties would he incur if he were found guilty of driving one of their very own to suicide? Then there would be a scandal back home. It would devastate his parents, especially his mother.
In the distance Chris could see a narrow strip of orange light running across the corridor floor and then, as if refracted through a glass prism it bent skywards, up the opposite wall. Chris's door was still open. Then to Chris's horror, the latch of another bedroom door sounded to his rear. The slamming of the door and the smacking of flip-flops soon followed. To Chris's immense relief the noise receded. The person had walked the other way. His heart-beat increased like a pounding drum. They approached his room, passing through an invisible wall of cooler air that had seeped into the corridor. Chris strained his ears. He could just hear his air-conditioner rumbling away, inter-

spersed with a faint sobbing sound. Thank goodness Wanna was still alive, Chris thought, but had she cut her wrist? The security guard's pensive face glowed orange from the light that fell through the slim gap between door and doorjamb. He peered tentatively into Chris's room. Chris craned his neck to look over the security guard's shoulder and it took a few seconds before his eyes were attuned to the orange glare. Wanna sat in the rattan chair, still holding the blade to her wrist. She saw the security guard's pitiless face and her sobbing stopped. She was frightened of him. The guard drew in a deep breath and strutted across the room. In an instant, Wanna dropped the blade to the floor. The security guard yelled at Wanna in her own language. He pointed and jerked his head towards Chris, throwing his arms into the air. Chris had no idea what he was saying, but he had a pretty good idea. Wanna exchanged glances with Chris and then placed her head in her hands.

The security guard turned to Chris's anxious face and said mildly, 'Wanna okay now.' He picked up the knife and held it at arm's length, frowning slightly as he examined it. With discretion, he hid it inside his uniform jacket and left the room. Somehow, out of all the commotion Chris had emerged totally unblemished.

Chris opened the bottle of beer and poured it into a glass. He sat down on the bed and asked Wanna, 'what did he say?'

Wanna looked at Chris with scorn and began to cry again.
'He say my job make you happy.'

'Then I was right – you are a hotel prostitute,' Chris said, nodding to himself.

Wanna held back the tears and said, 'I want to be girlfriend – I want your baby.' Chris shook his head slowly. With slumped shoulders she added, 'I know I bad girl, but now I have good job in hotel.'

'You used to work in the hook a duck bar, didn't you?' Chris insisted.

Wanna nodded, paused awhile, and with a slightly upbeat tone replied, 'Now I work in hotel – I have good job.'

'Yes, but you are still a prostitute,' Chris retorted.

Wanna sobbed again.

'My school no good,' she cried, 'I have no work at home.'

'Why do you want to love me – when I have paid for you?' Chris asked her.

'You talk like boyfriend – I think you love me one day,' she explained.

'I spoke to you like a boyfriend – because I thought you was my girlfriend,' Chris admitted. He gulped his beer and added, 'But I realise now that it was my mistake. I knew nothing before I met you. I'm sorry you think you love me, but I cannot love you.'

Wanna stood up, grabbed a few belongings from a drawer and walked into the bathroom. There was the sound of running water, and then there was an uncomfortable silence. It seemed an eternity, and Chris began to worry. Perhaps she had taken an overdose of his paracetamol tablets. Finally he knocked the door. The door clicked open and Wanna's shapely frame stood encased in the doorway. Chris stood in front of her, with a cold, distraught expression on his face. A fleeting moment of triumph twinkled in Wanna's eyes. Her triumphant eyes had told Chris that the grimace on his own face was her greatest revenge. Wanna's appearance had shocked him. While in the bathroom she had inflicted upon herself the most degrading thing possible. She now looked every bit a street prostitute, by wearing thick, heavy make-up, stockings, and pink suspenders. Chris could hardly recognise her.

Wanna gave him a scornful glare and said, 'I do my job now – I make you happy. I am bad girl.'

'Don't talk that way,' Chris said softly, feeling fairly guilty.

Wanna slipped inside the bedclothes and said sharply, 'Come to bed, Kiss – you pay for my sex.'

Chris shook his head and responded, 'We can still go to Nakhon Sawan, but I don't want to see your mother.'

Wanna stared at him in silence. Chris drank many beers and watched her fall asleep. In his mind he thought deeply about how his own naïvety had fooled everybody, even himself.

The idea sounded preposterous, but the next day Chris did go to Wanna's hometown for one night. Chris felt guilty. He blamed himself for what had happened. In spite of this, he declined to meet Wanna's mother in her home, or in the ice shop where she worked. Wanna was distraught throughout the short trip. But she insisted on staying with Chris for the rest of his stay in Pattaya. Apparently her boss would have given her trouble if she had not. Chris brought her a gold bracelet and expensive clothes before he left for Bangkok. Chris knew that he was following in the very footsteps of the men he had foolishly ridiculed a few days earlier. As Chris sat on the mini-bus waiting to depart for Bangkok, he felt Wanna's eyes burning into his skull. Chris turned round and saw Wanna staring at him from the hotel doorway. She looked as though the whole world had abandoned her. Chris knew she was a prostitute, but it was now that he felt obliged to confront the recurring agitation of mind. Would Wanna have to work that night? The answer troubled him deeply.

4

House Party

That evening, while strolling around the lobby of his new hotel, Chris felt encased inside an egotistic, protective blister. Chris glanced past the reception desk, which looked oddly deserted. In front of the large glass doors that led to the street stood the diligent figure of a doorman. Chris approached the doors. Suddenly the doorman put out a regal hand, holding it above the brass doorknob like a wasp irresistibly drawn to a jar of golden syrup. Chris halted, teasing the doorman a little by making a pretence of carefully checking his watch. Finally he put him out of his misery and continued on his way. The doors were flung open. The doorman's identity badge caught Chris's eye. Chris bit his lip, suppressing a smile. His photograph bore little resemblance to the ancient age he now occupied. The picture was at least ten years out of date, and showed him wearing a white suit with flared trousers. The image evoked was that of the actor John Travolta in *Saturday Night Fever*. Chris glanced once more at the doorman's attire. He was still garbed in the very same suit. Perhaps this doorman, Chris mused, would work at this hotel until he died, forever trapped in a period costume, of sorts, like a ghostly apparition.

Chris stepped through the doors, exchanging the plush surroundings of his hotel for the dusty concrete metropolis of Bangkok. Taxi drivers spilled out of their parked cars and began to converge from all directions.

'Taxi, Taxi sir, you want massage sir?'

Chris shook his head and paced towards the main road. He was brimming with confidence and, after his experiences in Pattaya, was ready for anything Bangkok could throw at him. Chris crossed the road via a pedestrian footbridge, thus keeping the ubiquitous taxi drivers out of harm's way. A taxi driver who resorts to hanging around hotels, Chris reflected ruefully, was only interested in the tourist dollar. As far as he was concerned they could wait for months before they laid their hands on his money.

A so-called normal taxi emerged from the cacophonous traffic and pulled up at the kerbside.

'Pat Pong please,' Chris hollered confidently.

The driver quickly studied the traffic, then glanced up at Chris through his lashes.

'Eighty baht,' he replied with guttural sounds.

Chris shook his head and suggested, 'sixty baht.'

The driver hesitated and then rather reluctantly nodded in agreement. Chris smiled and stepped inside the air-conditioned car. Progress was slow, but never boring. Bangkok had far too much to offer with its extraordinary scenes of everyday life. Through the tinted window, Chris caught sight of a street vendor cooking for a well-dressed family. There they all sat, on rusty tin drums big enough for one of their toddlers to stand up in. Suddenly a huge yellow flame mushroomed into the air, and rather dewy-eyed, Chris looked on. The driver saw Chris's bemused expression and asked, 'Your first time in Thailand?'

Chris faltered and quickly replied, 'Yes.'

He had foolishly let his guard down. The driver wasted no time to exploit Chris's lack of knowledge.

'Where you come from?' the driver asked.

'England,' Chris replied.

'Oh! England,' the driver said. His words had embraced the word 'England'. 'What your name?' he resumed.

'Chris.'

'Why you go Pat Pong?' the driver queried in a voice that questioned Chris's sanity.

'I want to have a drink and see the shows,' explained Chris.

'You want lady?'

'No,' replied Chris.

The driver paused awhile, staring intently at Chris out of his rear view mirror.

'You want man?'

Chris laughed his derision at the suggestion, and said, 'I just want to have a drink and watch the dancing ladies.'

The driver shook his head and urged, 'Pat Pong expensive – too many tourists. I can take you where Thai man watch lady – it very cheap.'

Chris thought awhile, his curiosity aroused.

'Okay!' Chris responded in an upbeat tone, 'let me have a look then.'

With his eyes half raised in quizzical amusement, the driver looked around and decided he needed to go in the other direction. Like a scene from *Starsky and Hutch*, he turned the car round and with the aid of a bus lane proceeded to drive against the oncoming traffic. Chris's forehead furrowed. Pretty soon he could see the flashing headlights of a number 13 bus hurtling towards them. To Chris's horror the driver put his foot down and accelerated towards the oncoming vehicle. The mass of the bus rapidly filled the windscreen. It seemed capable of digesting them. Chris was petrified, sitting so stiffly, that a walking stick could have run between the nape of his neck and the newly-purchased snakeskin belt that held up his trousers. Then to his relief, the taxi braked and the driver swerved into a quieter side street filled with parked motorcycles. The driver seemed quite unconcerned. Not a hair on his head was ruffled, or a drop of sweat on his brow. They continued for nearly half an hour, travelling far away from the brightly-lit city. Eventually the taxi turned into a dark and squalid alley, passing a line of parked cars, and pulled up outside a slum building. Chris peered around the alley. It disturbed him. There were no shops, food vendors or pedestrians. Altogether, it was an awfully lonely place.

'Why have we come here?' Chris asked, eyeing the driver with caution.

'It okay,' the driver replied, and pointed towards a roller shutter door, adding, 'Inside is show.'

With the barest flicker of an eyelid, Chris peered at the driver's Bangkok taxi licence displayed for public view. Chris decided it was genuine.

'Okay, let's go inside,' Chris declared.

Chris followed him to the roller shutter door. The driver was small, rather thin and stooping, perhaps the result of spending thousands of hours in Bangkok's stationary traffic. He rattled the roller shutter door with his hand, and on realising it was locked kicked it three times. They waited, and waited, as if part of a signal. Finally the shutters rolled opened and a stout man with a thin moustache stood inside. He spoke to the taxi driver in a muffled tone, as though trying to speak with a new set of false teeth. Thai pop music seeped into the alley. The driver and Chris were ushered into the house, through another door, and into a smoke-filled room overflowing with Thai men. They were inside someone's home. The back room had been converted into what Chris could only describe as a private club. Twenty or so revellers sat on all-weather, plastic garden chairs, the type found in garden centres all around the UK. A photograph of the King of Thailand hung high on a wall, looking darkly handsome, he stared out from a lacklustre gimcrack frame. The stout man approached a table and whispered into a customer's ear. The customer promptly vacated his table. Chris felt like a VIP and he glanced regally around the room. There were no dancing women, so he turned his attention to the crowd of men. They all drank liberal quantities of Mekong Thai Whisky. Chris ordered two beers, one for himself and one for his taxi driver.

The lights in the room dimmed. Three spotlights, each covered with red, green or yellow cellophane illuminated a small stage at the front of the room. The cellophane was torn, creating a weird psychedelic effect similar to a sixties' pop concert. The chortling and chattering slowly receded and all heads turned towards a dusty crimson curtain. The curtain opened and out stepped a nude chubby woman in her early forties. She had a wicked grin and almond-brown eyes that wandered around the room.

'Your drinks, sir,' the stout man said to Chris and he placed two beers on their table.

He folded the bill in half and casually dropped it into an empty glass. Chris peered at his scrawl. It read four hundred baht.

In disgust Chris turned to his taxi driver and moaned, 'Look at this, it is too expensive.'

The driver beckoned the stout man over and spoke into his ear. The stout man's fleshy, indulgent face glared back at Chris with scorn. He pointed towards a darkened corner. Sitting alone, and looking wryly amused was a weasel-faced, slightly balding westerner. The foreigner drank a beer as he watched the woman keenly.

'Look! He pay same you,' the stout man replied in a peremptory way and spread his arms dismissing Chris's complaint.

Chris decided that he had few friends inside the room. The clientele now appeared to take on different personas. A black patch over an eye or a bloody bandage wrapped round a forehead would have fitted in nicely.

'Okay,' Chris said flatly and kept his mouth shut.

The woman on the stage danced and sang a Thai pop

song. It became embarrassingly obvious that she was long past her prime. Having disinherited the taut prettiness of Thai blossom a long time ago, she was now attempting to make a living the only way she knew how. Her voice put Chris's teeth on edge. However, Chris could not understand why these men wanted to watch her. They must have known she was awful. She even had an angry boil on her right buttock.

The Dickensian stout man began to act out a well-rehearsed scene, in which he served an unopened bottle of beer to the weasel-faced westerner. Laughter broke out in the crowd at the stout man apologising with exaggerated gesticulations and amusing facial expressions. Now the grotesquely comical woman waited, dryly amused. She watched from the stage and then walked over to comfort the foreigner, stroking his balding head while stealing his bottle of beer. The foreigner's eyes twinkled. More laughter was heard from the crowd and the weasel-faced foreigner clapped his hands as if he knew what was about to happen. The woman's eyes swivelled in Chris's direction like a crab squinting out of its shell and without warning she winked at him. Chris suddenly became aware of his own vulnerability and he turned to face the weasel-faced westerner. For a moment the westerner's gaze seemed to settle on Chris and he smiled unpleasantly. Chris smiled back, wanly. The woman paraded around the stage flicking the bottle top with her thumb. No bottle opener could be found. So utilising her human body like a Swiss army knife, she skilfully inserted the neck of the bottle into her love tunnel and yanked it to one side. The bottle top dropped to the floor and rolled along the stage. The cheers and clapping of hands reached fever pitch. Chris sat in silence, with his mouth agape. The woman removed the bottle and allowed the beer to overflow like champagne, thus proving the bottle top had not been loose.

'God's teeth! How did she do that?' Chris asked the taxi driver.

The driver smiled and shrugged his shoulders. The woman poured the beer into a tall glass and placed the drinking vessel onto the stage floor. The stout man brought out three ping-pong balls and standing rather rudely, with a wide gait, he handed them to the woman. Now the masses clapped in unison. The woman lubricated the balls with that flexible mass of muscular tissue known as tongue and one by one she sowed her low-lying meadow. Then, like a chubby schoolgirl in the gymnasium, she performed an awkward handstand against the wall.

Chris cringed as her abdomen compressed like bellows and one ball was harvested. It shot high into the air and plopped straight into the glass of beer. The crowd went wild with applause. Her abdomen compressed again. The second ball emerged and, with a sharp ping, hit the rim of the glass, bounced across the stage and dropped onto the floor. A disgruntled man instantly trod on it with the heel of his shoe. This time there was a mixed reaction from the audience, some cheers, and some groans, followed by large drags on unfiltered cigarettes. Money was passed across the tables. It suddenly occurred to Chris that the bastards were betting on how many balls she would get inside the glass. Chris shook his head sadly, now he knew why they had come to see her. Some men at the front stood up to see better, the rest followed and more cigarettes were inhaled. The smoke thickened. There was an ugly atmosphere developing. Chris was sure the woman knew what was at stake. She appeared nervous and realigned herself, edging her feet tentatively along the wall. This caused immense irritation to the gamblers. Cigarettes wagged as they argued. Her final compression proved to be hard work. She needed all of her skill to squeeze the last ball out and, like a hen laying an egg, it finally saw daylight. It flew high into the air, arcing its way through the mass of smoke particles straight into the centre of the glass. Money had been won and lost. Voices cried out, shouting and cheering at each other. Then rather cheekily, the woman handed the glass of beer back to the weasel-faced westerner, complete with two floating balls. She left the stage, a heroine and a villain.

In a quirky sort of way, the second feature bore no resemblance whatsoever to the woman's decadent performance. Two glass containers were brought onto the stage. Each had a lustrous Siamese fighting fish swimming inside, one red and the other blue. The containers were placed side by side. Without hesitation, the fish attempted to attack each other by slamming against the glass wall. More frantic betting took place with depreciating humour. Things were getting out of control. The room was charged with energy. It was only a matter of time before it turned into a *mêlée*. The fish were dropped into a larger, cylindrical container and each took up a side by side, stand-off position. Greed and pride electrified the stale air. There were extraordinary scenes when four men waved handfuls of money into the air like batons, fiercely urging their fish to kill. The Dickensian stout man could only mutter a strangled complaint. The fish obliged by nibbling at each other's fins and tail. Occasionally a fish would break away and take a large gulp of air, and cigarette smoke, from the water's surface. This would invite more shouting until it returned to fight. The stout man became the referee, crouching low and rubbing his moustache whenever a skilful offensive move had taken place. Neither fish appeared to be harmed. Nevertheless, to the annoyance of some of the crowd he declared the blue fish to be the winner. Once again money had been won and lost. More drinks were poured onto chunks of ice.

Chris became agitated. He was a foreigner with money in his pocket. Chris's heartbeat increased and he rubbed his hands in a nervous manner. Disgruntled men squinted across at Chris and prodded each other on the arms. Chris wiped the sweat from his brow, imagining them as desperate criminals who killed and robbed their victims. As if to mock his discomfiture, the stout man returned to see if he wanted another beer. Chris refused and seized the opportunity to expedite an escape.

'I want to go now,' Chris pleaded to his taxi driver.

'It not finish – we watch snake and mongoose fight,' the driver insisted.

'I want to go – I want to go back to my hotel.' The driver shook his head and raised his glass. Chris grabbed his elbow forcibly, and urged, 'I want to go now.'

'Okay,' the driver replied, disgruntled.

Chris paid the bill and followed the driver into the alley. At last Chris could breathe the welcome scents of foul drains and rubbish. Anywhere was better than inside that room, Chris thought. Then, amongst the clumps of mysterious shapes Chris heard a faint rustling noise. The doors of the taxi had yet to be opened. Fearing an assailant, Chris turned round slowly and peered into the darkness. He saw the faint gleam of two eyes returning his glare from the shadows. His heart raced. Chris tried to speak, but his voice faltered. It was a rat. However this was not a normal rat, it was a Bangkok rat, an unnatural mutation, of sorts, and because of its great size it could have been a game substitute for the bloody mongoose. The driver opened the doors and Chris leapt inside. Chris flopped onto his seat, exhilarated. Nothing like this had ever happened to him back in the UK.

The driver continued to remonstrate that they had left far too early. Chris wasn't angry. He was merely bewildered by the turn of events and ignored the driver throughout. In spite of this, Chris's spirits soon rose when he recognised a more affluent neighbourhood gliding past his window. They arrived at Chris's hotel and, in readiness, the doorman opened the huge glass doors.

'You want show tomorrow?' the driver pleaded.

'No thank you,' Chris said flatly.

'Where you go now?'

'I'm staying in the hotel bar,' Chris replied.

The disconsolate driver frowned and drove away.

Still charged with emotion, Chris strode to the hotel bar and ordered a drink, slopping it on the counter as he raised it to his lips.

'Are you all right?' an English voice enquired.

Chris swivelled round in his barstool. Two men in their late twenties drank at the bar. Chris returned to his Black Country accent.

'Yes,' Chris replied, pausing a few seconds to compose himself. 'I've just cum from a weird place – where Thai men gambled on anything under the sun.'

'Wicked!' the nearest stranger exclaimed.

'Some of them lost a load of money,' Chris resumed, 'so I decided to scarper.'

The men stared at Chris and then at each other. There was no tongue-in-cheek elitism, only genuine concern.

Smiling nervously, Chris added, 'I almost expected the actor Christopher Walken to cum in and play Russian roulette. Yer know – just like he did in *The Deer Hunter.*'

The two strangers burst into laughter.

'Where was this piss-pot of a place?' the other stranger asked.

'I don't know,' Chris whined, 'a taxi driver took me there.'

'Pat Pong is the place to go,' the nearest stranger resumed, 'the three of us come here every six months.'

Chris looked at him with a wrinkled brow and asked, 'The three of yer?'

'Yeah – me,' the stranger placed a stubby finger against

his own chest and then pointed to the other man, 'that's John, and our mate Philip.'

'Where's Philip?' Chris asked, wondering.

The two strangers grinned, and then John explained, 'He went inside a massage parlour around the corner. He's still inside there – we ain't seen him for three days.' They all grinned. 'We're going to Pat Pong now, do you want to come?' John asked Chris.

'No, I want to stay here and drink at this bar.' The two men finished their drinks, shook hands with Chris, and then left.

The young woman serving behind the bar counter stared at Chris through her wire-rimmed, John Lennon-style spectacles.

Quite unexpectedly she asked Chris, 'Sir, I listen you talk friends – you not happy in Thailand?'

The woman's lashes blinked more than usual.

Chris shook his head vigorously and said, 'I am happy in Thailand – but I do not understand . . .' his voice trailed away. Chris paused, sipped his beer and added, 'What I mean is – the people here are lovely but, because I am a tourist, so many women and taxi drivers think I have come here for sex.'

The waitress nodded and sat back in her chair, her teeth gleaming through her smiling mouth.

'I was in Pattaya and a girl prostitute' . . . Chris paused and gazed into her sympathetic eyes. She understood all right, thought Chris. He continued with, 'This woman told me she wanted my baby.'

Chris stopped and watched her reaction.

She remained silent, deep in thought, and then said softly, 'I think she love you to say this word. Some man run away if lady say this – I think she love you.'

Chris was surprised at her reply. He gave a long sigh and remained mute, drinking and ruminating the time away.

One and three quarter hours passed swiftly by and Chris happened to turn round. In the distance, through the open doors that led to the lobby, he caught sight of his taxi driver, the very one who had taken him to the show earlier that evening. The small and stooping driver talked animatedly with another, much taller man. The taller man had his back to Chris. Suddenly he turned round and Chris saw his features. He could not believe his eyes. He blinked them, but the picture of the weasel-faced westerner did not go away. These men had come together and they appeared to be looking for someone. This intrigued Chris, which caused his eyes to linger for quite some time. Suddenly the taxi driver caught sight of Chris and nudged the other man. The two men entered the bar. Chris flinched.

'Hello Sir,' the driver said to Chris in a guttural voice, 'this my German friend.' The weasel-faced German held out a long, bony hand. Chris shook it. The men threw themselves onto a barstool and ordered two beers. Chris immediately felt uneasy. This was not a coincidence, he thought. Something sinister was afoot. The German grinned, his glassy eyes now on the same level as Chris looked at him with a steady gaze. Behind those eyes lay a dubious character, sombre and menacing.

'Sir,' the taxi driver asked Chris, 'when you go England?'

'Soon,' Chris said flatly, projecting a torpid state.

'We have friend in England,' the driver said quickly, raising his voice a shade. Chris gave a short grunt as if he had lost his tongue. The German menace sipped his beer and grinned incessantly. His very presence made Chris feel creepy all over. There was an aura of evil emanating from the man. Chris was anxious and offered no intercourse.

He gazed around the room with indifference, until he finally said, 'I'd like you to leave me alone.'

There was an instant pause of profound silence and then, without hesitation, the two men stood up and smiled to each other. Only at the very last moment, as though to justify his very presence, did the German thug speak.

'You are very good,' he said mysteriously, leaving Chris even more puzzled than before.

The two men left the hotel. Chris could only guess what all the shenanigans were about. Drugs probably, but of course he would never know. He looked at his watch. It read 11.35. Chris sighed and wondered what Wanna was doing. He feared the worst.

5

Addictive Bangkok

The following day Chris purchased a ticket for a highly-recommended rice barge tour, which would take him along the *klongs* (canals) of Bangkok. Chris was very interested in this tour, as unlimited free drinks were available on board. He was missing Wanna, so he had decided to get drunk at somebody else's expense.

A silver-haired taxi driver, with a distinctive undertaker-like calm picked Chris up from his hotel. Bangkok's unmerciful stop-start traffic bore him no menace. The driver had seen it all before and calmly drove west towards the Chao Phraya River. Gradually, Chris began to notice that the traffic was moving more freely than before. For no apparent reason all the traffic lights remained green and the faint glimmer of a smile came across the driver's lips. The driver began to mutter to himself and promptly put his foot down. Somehow the driver saw the full meaning of the situation. His hands squeezed the steering wheel and his eyes glared ahead with an enormous, concentrated effort. Gushing drivers exchanged grins through tinted windows and, like huntsmen in red coats or autumn leaves caught in the eddy of a brook, they joined in a chase across the city. It became a trial of wits, of which the essence was to keep up with the vehicles in front.

'What's happening?' Chris asked his driver, excitedly.

'VIP,' the driver replied, half aloud.

Now, on every street corner, policemen stood with walkie-talkies. They had rigged the traffic lights to allow an important person a quick and trouble-free journey. Chris glanced behind and saw that whenever they passed through a set of traffic lights they instantly turned to red. Chris's driver seemed to be faltering. He began to sweat and Chris could hear him breathing heavily as if having sex. With all the excitement, his driver's unruffled calm had now disappeared. Chris's driver was no match for the younger drivers ahead of them. Chris knew that very soon their luck would run out. Nevertheless, he too joined in the excitement. This was an opportunity to beat the system. Chris urged him on with encouragement only reserved for important sporting occasions. They were last now, and to Chris's irritation his driver fumbled a gear change. The lights ahead turned to red and his driver emitted a long sigh of frustration. They stopped. In spite of this, having travelled for ten minutes without halting, they had now covered the same distance that would normally have taken 45 minutes or so.

Eventually they arrived at the river, where a sleek long-tailed motor boat lay moored against a dodgy wharf. Approximately 20 other tourists had already boarded her. Chris climbed aboard and they sped off, crossing the wide expanse of river and turning into a bustling *klong* with its foul, penetrating essence.

Two children on board held their noses and shouted, 'Pooh – it stinks.'

Everyone looked at one another, grinning broadly. They travelled along an intricate network of endless waterways. Here, palm trees and blossom grew beside simple wooden houses built on stilts, each linked to its neighbour's dwelling by a rotting gangplank. And around these homes, all with a gleaming television aerial sitting sublimely dignified above a dull corrugated iron roof, stood the wooden electricity poles sprouting from the calm water like bulrushes in a pond, each linking this out-of-date way of life to the modern world.

A bare-backed man, with his chin and chopsticks buried in a bowl of noodle soup, caught Chris's eye. This man, sitting cross-legged on a raised jetty in front of a house, glanced without interest at the passing boat. Chris was fascinated by his charming uncomplicated existence, which almost made a mockery of the tourists' rushed lifestyles. They passed another house, where a mother washed a dark-skinned toddler's hair. The stark-naked child stood in a red plastic bowl, crying loudly, as his mother worked up a huge lather that clung to his shoulders like epaulettes.

On reaching their destination the boat moored alongside a genial rice barge.

'Please everybody,' their guide hollered, 'follow me – we see snake show.' They disembarked and gathered around a long bamboo table. A stocky, middle-aged man in an egg-yolk yellow shirt stood waiting for them. He stared at his tarnished, imitation Rolex watch, suggesting to their guide that they were late. A lidded basket stood on the table and a large crate of snakeskin belts lay on the dusty floor. Chris thumbed the belts, and curled his lips in distaste. In amongst the tourist kitsch, a pair of long pearly fangs beamed an implausible smile from a viper's skull picked clean by a mass of ants or maggots. Chris's eyes shifted in the direction of the crowd. Now everybody watched the basket. The snake handler whipped the lid off and instantly froze like a statue, his hand hovering precariously above the opening. There was many a raised eyebrow in the crowd. Then the snake handler plunged his arm inside and pulled out a black cobra. Some ladies in flower-sprigged, afternoon frocks were not prepared to be shocked. They yelled out in horror. This caused a teenage boy to quickly retreat behind a much younger brother. Like an agitated cat, the pale, trembling boy grasped his sibling's shoulders and nervously peered over his head.

'Stand back,' their father shouted.

The two boys took two paces backwards. The snake was dropped onto the table and it quickly slithered towards the edge. The whole crowd stepped backwards in unison like synchronised dancers. Without blinking, the snake handler grabbed the reptile and mockingly held it close to his face. The irritated snake spread its hood and lurched forwards, spitting glistening venom onto the snake handler's lips. The man remained motionless, standing idle, while staring into the snake's intimidating bronze eyes. Slowly he sealed his thin mouth shut. Chris watched as the colour drained from his lips. He was lucky, thought Chris. The viscous venom had fallen onto his lower lip. Slowly it trickled down his shaven chin.

'What's that, dad?' the younger boy called out.

'Death!' his father yelled.

Their flustered guide ran into a wooden house and returned with a rag. He approached the snake with trepidation. Slowly he slipped his hand beneath the reptile's head and, while avoiding the cool abstract stare of the snake, he wiped the translucent poison from the man's jaw. Their guide retreated. Then, as if the snake handler had grabbed a red-hot poker, he threw the reptile into the basket and replaced the lid. The snake handler smiled to his audience, foolishly.

'Please,' their guide urged, 'we go to rice barge and have drink.'

'I think we all need one,' Chris scoffed loudly and opened his eyes wide, theatrically.

Several chuckles sounded as they strode off. Peering towards the house, Chris could see the snake handler washing his face in a bucket of water. Chris felt sure the provenance of his next item of tourist kitsch now lay inside that basket.

They all boarded the rice barge, which had been converted into a floating bar and fruit buffet. It was afternoon and their shadows skated across the deck as the boat slewed through the labyrinth of waterways. At the start, their guide had tried to show some interest by patrolling the deck with his hands clasped behind his back. Now he sat alone, with a drink in one hand, gazing wistfully at the passing flotsam and allowing the three waitresses to go about their work. He was a small, moustached man who enjoyed clinking his glass at every opportunity. His lean face appeared worn and tired, with dropped eyelids, leaving Chris with the impression that he was an alcoholic. Chris decided to sit next to him. There was scarcely a moment of hesitation before the guide spoke.

'Do you go with Thai lady?' he asked Chris, smiling affably.

'Yes,' Chris admitted. The guide nodded, as if it were exactly what he had expected.

'Last week – very old man from Australia ask me for Thai lady,' he told Chris. Chris was getting interested, and started to grin. 'He say he want good sex before he dead,' the guide explained.

'Really,' Chris replied.

'I worry very much,' the guide admitted, 'I think if lady too good he will die.'

'So what did you do?' Chris enquired excitedly.

'I take him for massage with old lady,' the guide replied.

Chris laughed, and they raised their glasses of Scotch whisky in a toast.

'Did he enjoy it?' Chris asked, wondering.

'Yes, he enjoy.'

Chris smiled again.

Distant laughter sounded above the drone of the engine,

eddying across the water like pollen caught on the wind. Chris's shadow swooped across the deck once more. He looked ahead, and around the corner the ghostly silhouettes of children came into sight. The children, all wearing black and white school uniforms, appeared to be aligning themselves for the obligatory school photograph. Chris looked impressed, as he could now see their happy faces in profile against the grand building. Each child, some with their heads shaved, held gleaming bells mounted on sticks, triangles, and cymbals, while the younger pupils, many of whom sat cross-legged on the floor, gripped kazoos between their teeth. To everybody's joy they suddenly struck up with a percussion version of *Hawaii 5–0*'s TV theme music. It was perfect, and Chris smiled, imagining he was surfing down the *klong*. These impoverished *klong* families clearly had access to a modern state education, thought Chris, recalling the terrible TV images from other Third World countries. Chris placed his glass onto the deck and rocked back on the bench, hugging his knees. A blissful stillness pervaded their journey, as the animated way of life unfolded before his eyes.

More than one hour had elapsed and Chris was feeling slightly drunk. He wished he could have stayed all day, but the time came when they crossed the river and his excursion came to an end. Chris's taxi driver was fast asleep in his seat. A sharp blow to the window revived him. The driver managed to give a faint, watery smile as Chris peered at his face.

'You enjoy?' the driver asked.

'Yes, it was great,' replied Chris.

They drove away and made good time. Soon Chris began to recognise neighbouring hotels as they drove closer to his. Suddenly, like a prehistoric dragonfly fossilised in amber, they were encased in Bangkok's traffic. They remained stationary for minutes on end, as if the tyres had melted and solidified to the tarmac. Chris's bladder swelled like a weather balloon.

Sitting with a distressed expression on his face, and crossed-legged in an attempt to stem any discharge of urine, Chris whined, 'I want a toilet.'

The taxi driver pointed hopelessly to the cars in front of him.

'It's no good – I have to go now,' Chris said quickly and tipped the driver 20 baht.

Chris left the taxi and wended his way towards his hotel. A cheap-looking jewellery shop caught his eye. A toilet, Chris thought. He entered the shop. Inside everything was neat and orderly and the air was sweet from a vase of flowers that stood next to an electric fan. Chris was the only customer and a young salesgirl with a cascade of luxuriant raven hair sat behind the showcase. Despite the fan, the shop was hot and the top three buttons of her white shirt were unfastened.

'Can I see some rings please?' Chris asked her, feigning interest and wiping the perspiration from his forehead.

In an instant she lost her plaintive look and was as bright and charming a salesgirl one could ever wish for. She leaned over the counter, pointing frequently at her beloved rings. Chris could see the ornamental clip in her hair and the bumps on her chest. A man in his forties, probably her father, entered the room from a backdoor. The young salesgirl instantly straightened her back and adjusted the shirt that floated about her breasts. As a distraction she brought Chris a glass of iced tea. Chris stared at the drink.

'Can I go to toilet please?' Chris pleaded to the young woman. She nodded and escorted him to the staff toilet. Chris emptied his bladder with several audible sighs of relief and a copious flow of urine that lasted a full minute. He unlocked the door. The young salesgirl was standing in front of him, smiling broadly. A mischievous thought occurred to him. She must have heard and imagined everything. On noticing her burning cheeks and cat-like eyes staring at him excitedly, he quickly returned to the sales room.

'I will be back with my credit card,' Chris lied to the man.

The man nodded and feigned appreciation. Chris made his way to his hotel. He arrived breathless, with tired feet and clothes soaked through with sweat. Pretty soon he fell asleep on his bed.

When Chris awoke the sun had set and it was time for the dark heat. Leaning sideways, on his elbow, he gazed through the high-rise window. All around, the great mass of the city had erupted into an explosion of lights, and below, still within earshot, the traffic oozed in a long slow-moving file. Chris showered and changed.

While sitting in the hotel lobby, he made some pretence at reading the *Bangkok Post*. Chris was waiting for a taxi to arrive, but it had to be a normal taxi with Thai passengers. He did not have to wait long and, to the annoyance of the waiting drivers outside, Chris approached the car and opened the door.

'Pat Pong please,' Chris asked, hiding his excitement.

'Ninety baht,' the driver replied.

'I paid fifty baht yesterday,' Chris scoffed, tongue in cheek.

The driver looked up at Chris with a bemused expression on his face, and then bent his head in thought.

'Today many traffic,' the driver muttered under his breath.

Chris pondered awhile, looking even closer at the waiting vultures, and out of pure spite he said, 'Okay.'

Chris stepped into the taxi and threw himself onto the backseat.

'First time in Thailand for you?' the driver asked, watching Chris in his rear view mirror.

'No, I have come here three times.'

'Why you go Pat Pong?'

'I want to go to Pat Pong – nowhere else,' Chris insisted, his voice suddenly harsh.

The driver grunted, dissatisfied, and remained mute throughout the rest of their journey.

They arrived at Pat Pong, which turned out to be two parallel side streets running off the main road. A line of traffic held them up, so Chris paid the driver and left him in the queue. He approached one of the side streets where the buildings, all of them bars or night-clubs, engulfed his eyes.

'Hello sir, you come inside sir,' a female voice called out.

Chris turned suspiciously to the voice. Three sweet-smiling women, two of whom sat on chairs outside the doorway of a nightclub, observed him curiously. One woman beckoned Chris inside.

'How much to go inside?' Chris enquired.

'No money sir – you come in for free.'

The woman stood up and opened the door. Waves of rock music rippled into the street. Chris stepped through the door and up a dim staircase. At the top of the staircase a chink of light waxed and waned around a corner. Inside the main room Chris stood and lingered awhile. Throughout was a pleasant sweet-smell of women's perfume, almost like the freshness of a spring morning. 'Hotel California' by the Eagles began to play and before his eyes came an exhilarating picture of women in glittering bikinis caressing and hugging chrome poles. They danced and gyrated to the rhythm of the music; music, which was homage to an American paradise, that was also decadent and addictive. Soon, Chris too was immersed in the experience and a gale of euphoria rattled through him.

'Mirrors on the ceiling, the pink champagne on ice. And she said, we are all just prisoners here, of our own device.'

It was all here, Chris reflected. Even more so, they were all in hedonistic Bangkok. It was a wonderful moment and Chris thought about the history of the place, imagining weary American GIs on R & R from the Vietnam War, seeking a ray of light in that dark episode of history.

Chris wended his way to a table near the stage. A waitress promptly came over.

'What you want drink sir?' she asked him.

'Large Singha beer please,' Chris answered and turned to face the agile dancers.

Watching them keenly, Chris came to the opinion that they were really good. He felt sure that they could get a job in a British cabaret. His beer arrived and Chris took a large gulp from the refreshing beverage. Suddenly he felt a warm, slender arm slide around his shoulders. Chris turned to face a young woman. She was everything a man could wish for, with dark silken hair, glowing sable eyes, and long legs.

'Hello, what your name?' she asked him, with a vivacious smile.

'Chris,' he replied.

'Hello, Clis,' she said softly, and held out her arm. Chris clasped her elegant hand and they shook. 'Clis, can I sit down?' she asked, throwing her head towards the seat next to his.

'Sure,' he replied and added, 'do you want a drink?'

She smiled, a lovely warm reassuring smile and said, 'I want beer please.'

Chris raised his arm and beckoned the waitress. The woman sat beside him and her short white skirt slid up her thighs. She wore a turquoise velour top with gold braid and a red number badge pinned above her petite, perfectly proportioned bosom. Chris glanced up at the seductive dancers. They too wore similar badges pinned to their taught bikini bottoms.

'Where you stay?' the woman asked him.

'President Hotel,' Chris replied.
'Oh! Number one hotel,' she commented.
Chris grinned and sipped his beer.

A man approached their table. He held a pen and a sheet of paper. The man was rather stooped, with a wrinkled face. He offered Chris the paper. Rather unwittingly, Chris accepted it. He studied it for a moment. It contained several names written in various handwritings.

'What's this for?' Chris asked him.

The man pointed a finger towards the stage and said mysteriously, 'Lady write your name.'

Perplexed, Chris peered at the woman sitting beside him and asked, 'What does he mean?'

'A lady write your name – it's okay,' she replied vaguely, while stroking his hand to reassure him.

Full of bravado, Chris grabbed the pen and wrote CHRIS at the bottom of the list. He handed the paper and pen back to the man.

'Twenty baht sir,' the man urged.

Chris grinned and paid him.

Clouds of dry ice wafted across the stage like a fogbank moving eerily towards a beach party and the dancers' backs glistened with sweat, evidence of the tremendous effort they were giving to their performance. Chris wondered how all of this could be free. To watch them back home would have cost a small fortune, he mused, and even then it would have been an inferior show.

'Clis,' the woman asked, 'you like ladies?'

'Of course,' Chris chirped.

She ran the end of her finger softly across his hand, and said, 'I happy you enjoy.'

The music stopped and the dancers retired backstage.

'The Power of Love' sung by Jennifer Rush began to play. A young woman full of passion and sensuality glided onto the stage.

'This song was number one a few weeks ago,' Chris said to his companion. She smiled back at him. The woman on stage wore white stockings and suspenders, which contrasted nicely with her raven pubic hair. Using both hands, she clasped a chrome bar and hugged it against her bosom. A stark-naked man with a twinkle in his eye and a fairly humorous face climbed onto the stage. He strutted up to the woman, held her hips, and eased his genital area against her buttocks. Amazed at the turn of events, Chris turned to his companion and they exchanged glances. Then his companion returned her gaze back to the couple. Chris peered around the nightclub. Everybody was captivated by the intensely personal events unfolding before their eyes. Even the waiters and waitresses stood watching. Chris could not believe it. They were actually going to make love in front of at least 50 strangers. The woman on stage turned round. An indulgent glance passed between her and the man. With her buttocks now pressed against the chrome bar she slid sensuously to her knees and, with passion and tenderness, demonstrated fellatio. The song intensified and the couple rolled around the stage like two playful puppies. Then, finally, she lay on her back and eased the man's tool inside her.

It soon became apparent that their lovemaking was in harmony with the song. There was a good deal of authenticity and beauty to it. It was no half-hearted affair, and it was essential that their union be blessed in the only way possible. The man would have to reach a sexual climax as the final notes of the song faded away. That's why everybody is watching, thought Chris. Would he manage it in time? Their expression of raw emotion gave way to a poetic conclusion as the song finally finished and so did the man, right on time. He withdrew and the audience leaned forward hoping to catch a glimpse of his spurting eruption. The couple left the stage to no applause whatsoever, not the most dignified of endings to a stimulating, almost spiritual performance.

Chris turned to his companion and asked, 'do they do it every night?'

'No – one night each week,' she explained.

'Is the woman his wife?'

She giggled and said softly, 'She not wife – it just job.'

With reverence, Chris gazed around the nightclub. Here true hedonists were finally sworn in, he thought, given the oath of allegiance so to speak, rather than aimlessly wandering around the world from bar to bar. Here nobody would ever make acid remarks towards a homage to that most basic of human desires, to reproduce, to copulate for the very existence of the human race.

Chris turned to his companion and said, 'I want to go to the toilet – can you watch my drink please?'

She nodded. While Chris stood at the urinals the lavatory door banged open, and to his surprise out stepped the very man who had just performed on the stage. He was now clad in a smart business suit and trotted off briskly with a very superior expression on his face. Chris grinned. After all, he thought, it was only a part-time job to pay the rent. This man was probably going home to a wife and five kids.

Chris returned to his seat. The dancing women had returned and, 'One Night in Bangkok' sung by *Murray Head* seemed an apt accompaniment. Chris's companion placed her hand next to his and affectionately rubbed it with her fingertip.

Chris peered into her eyes and reluctantly said, 'I don't want sex.' She looked at him in a gaze that questioned his sexuality.

'Clis,' she protested, 'why you sleep alone?'

'If you go with me do I have to pay you?' asked Chris, going straight to the point.

With an almost exonerating reply, she explained, 'No, you pay the bar three hundred baht and I go with you.'

Chris was sure she was a prostitute, but this, though she would not say in terms quite so explicit, was what she did for a living.

Chris shook his head and calmly said, 'I think it's better you sit with somebody else.'

On finally realising that she would have to relinquish all hope of going with him, the woman finished her drink and like a butterfly went off to roam around the room.

Chris ordered another drink and a warm arm hugged his shoulders.

'Hello, what your name?'

Chris turned towards the female voice. The young woman had the same, neat little figure as the previous woman, with good legs and high cheekbones. Her long lashes curled lazily over her brown eyes and she too had that instantaneous magnetic attraction which the warm-hearted could not refuse.

'Chris,' he replied with resignation, 'sit down here – what do you want to drink?'

With her teeth gleaming, the woman replied, 'Fanta please.' She sat down and whispered into Chris's ear, 'Where you stay?'

'President Hotel,' he replied flatly.

'Oh! Number one hotel,' she said.

The dancing women left the stage, hips swaying suggestively from side to side. The stooping man with a wrinkled face returned holding several large sheets of white card. He climbed onto the stage and a woman in her early twenties tiptoed behind him. She was naked, apart from a white straw boater hat. The music started again, it was Madonna singing 'Like a Virgin'. The man handed a smaller piece of paper to the woman and she read it. A large sheet of card was now placed onto the stage floor. The woman crouched down low and, with her sculptured nether regions poised over the card and knees almost drawn up to her chin, held a chrome pole. Chris curled his toes. The woman looked as if she was about to defecate, he thought. She's not going to take a shit, surely not, he asked himself.

The waiter returned with Chris's companion's Fanta. He placed the folded bill with the others.

'Thank you Kliss,' she said softly and gripped the bottle with such force that her knuckles turned white.

She wrapped her delicious, painted lips around the straw and sucked it in a suggestive manner. Chris saw her eyes widen.

Chris turned to face the stage. The man produced a thick felt tip pen from his pocket and handed it to the woman.

'God's teeth!' Chris exclaimed, as she carefully inserted it inside her feathery quill. With well-orchestrated knee movements and deep concentration she proceeded to write on the card, stopping occasionally to check her scrawl. The sheet of card was passed back to the man.

The man, now wearing an insolent grin and clutching a microphone, hollered, 'Lobert.'

The audience chuckled at his mispronunciation and then an uncomfortable silence fell. Finally a blond man held up his hand and the sheet was passed to him via a waiter. The woman stood up and rotated around the stage. Altogether, she wrote out several names, and they were each in turn handed out like the stone tablets bearing the Ten Commandments. By now it was becoming obvious that the woman was suffering from pain. Her face grimaced with each stroke of the pen. Chris cringed when his name was finally called out and, rather sheepishly, he too raised his hand. The poor woman pulled herself up with a prodigious heave. Her angry eyes followed the card around the room until it was handed to Chris. She had finished now and stood quite still, projecting a cold, forced smile to her final customer. Chris's name, being the last one, had hurt her far more than the others. He felt guilty now and could have crawled under the table. Under the coloured lights Chris stared at the stiff card. He could just make out the woman's child-like scrawl. The poor woman must have been exhausted, thought Chris and there was an air of sadness about her. The dancing women returned.

Chris drained his glass and said to his companion, 'I'm going now.'

'I want go with you,' she admitted, gazing at him with her youthful eyes.

Chris, fairly reluctantly, shook his head and left the amazing nightclub. On returning to his hotel, Chris sat on his bed drinking and watching the habitual kick-boxing on TV. In the clear light of his bedroom he gazed once more at the piece of card, focusing his eyes straight onto several speckles of blood.

'Oh God!' Chris yelled in disgust and threw it into the waist paper bin.

Chris shook his head sadly, asking himself why some poor people had to do such things to earn a living. This was the other side of Bangkok, the decadent side of the hedonistic coin. Nevertheless, it had hooked him and after two weeks in Thailand he returned home with an unexpected air of maturity.

'Daddy, Jintana did a poo-poo,' Chris's daughter's sweet voice echoes from the bathroom.

Chris had agreed to name their daughter Jintana because of the unusual sound of the name. However, it was his wife who loved its Thai meaning: Imaginativeness. Chris puts his old passport down and catches a glimpse of the next immigration stamp. For he did return to Thailand the following year. Chris was now convinced that it had been his destiny to return there. After all, if he had not returned his lovely daughter Jintana would never have been born. Chris holds his breath and wipes his daughter's bottom. He exhales slowly, and dresses her.

'Good girl,' Chris says, 'now go down the stairs and eat yer breakfast.'

Jintana's eyes tingle as she leaves the reeking bathroom, leaving Chris to wash his hands.

6

House Husband

Chris breathes a deep sigh of despair. Another mundane day as a bloody house husband lies ahead of him. However, as today is a Saturday his parental care and attention dovetails well with the other fathers on weekend leave. Chris shakes his head, sadly. He would never have predicted that after so many years since his first visit to Thailand he would be reduced to this.

With all this in mind, Chris recalls the events of one year ago that had led to this state of affairs. His daughter Jintana was in a fortunate situation. She had been exposed to two languages, Thai and English. In spite of this, his wife's mother tongue had completely taken over. At weekends he had found, to his horror, that Jintana could hardly understand him. One Monday morning he made a momentous decision. Chris telephoned his wife from work. He told her that his employer was to end his contract the following Friday. Of course, his wife knew that Chris was only temporary, but it still came as a shock to her. Afterwards, Chris sat down in deep thought. Perhaps it was going to extremes to meet the requirements of the problem, but in any case the decision had been made. In society as a whole, Chris reflected, one can have a perfectly conventional job with an unconventional lifestyle. However, the emphasis is placed on a regular job with a regular income, which essentially means working as everybody else does. Chris's secret project of providing 'father tongue' was far more worthwhile than any well-paid job. Besides, he was no longer interested in material things. But Chris had to redress Jintana's language problem. After all, children whose first language is not English almost certainly have problems when they first start school. You cannot learn to read and write without the language to back it up. Chris was determined that this was not going to happen to his daughter. The only trouble was, he could not bring himself to tell his wife that he had left the job of his own accord. Chris had never lied to her before and at the time he had felt terrible. So now, as he stands here as a fully-fledged house husband does, his wife is still in the dark as to why he has no job.

Jintana finishes her breakfast and Chris decides to take her to the children's park. They visit the park over and over again, with Chris always explaining the perennial wonders of daisies in springtime to the golden leaves shimmering on ancient boughs in October. Sitting on a swing, bright as a button in her blue summer dress and pink sun hat, Jintana soon realises she is alone.

'I want to go on the slide, daddy,' she says, pointing with a finger.

Chris continues pushing her, knowing that they will soon visit all the playground facilities like a dog marking out its territory. Jintana purses her lips and adopts a very tragic pose. But it is in the expression of her eyes, even more than in the colouring, that she is different from Chris. Jintana can also appear as though the world has abandoned her, just as her mother can. Chris weakens and they stroll towards the slide followed by the crisp images of their shadows.

'Jintana,' Chris says jokingly, 'try not to step on yer shadow.'

She looks at her feet and runs around the playground

shouting, 'I cannot do it! Go away naughty shadow. Daddy – help me!'

Chris smiles.

'Why don't yer try jumping up then,' he suggests.

Jintana briefly impersonates a kangaroo and then cleverly outfoxes her father by stepping into the shade.

'Daddy,' she says, 'look, my shadow – it's gone now.'

She smiles her lovely smile. Chris preserves a tactful silence, watching her climb the slide with his stiff, pricking eyes. Jintana's shadow follows her up the steps. To Chris's alarm, Jintana turns round as if to come down head first.

'Jintana,' Chris yells, 'be careful, yoh'll hurt yourself.'

To Chris's relief she turns round once more and slides down the correct way.

The playground soon fills up. There is an anticyclone nestled above the country, and it is a golden opportunity for parents to spend quality time with their children.

'Jintana,' Chris asks, 'do yer want a wee-wee?' His daughter shakes her head. 'Don't yer dare wet yer pants,' Chris says sharply, looking at her sceptically. Jintana continues to climb the steps once more. 'Cum on Jintana, have a wee-wee now.'

She slides down the slide, shuffles her feet and starts to perform her dance that is a tell-tale sign that she is about to urinate. It is a dance of such uncommon quality that Chris has often wondered whether an anthropologist should record it for posterity, just on the off chance that it is a throwback from evolution. Chris quickly escorts Jintana to a large tree trunk and she irrigates its roots. They return to the playground and Chris's daughter glances towards the paddling pool. Small children shout raucously to each other in an incoherent language that only they understand.

'Daddy, I want to go swimming,' Jintana informs him.

'Jintana,' Chris explains, 'yer cannot, 'cos I don't have yer swimming costume – cum and play on the swings again.'

Jintana agrees.

A short time later a voice sounds from behind Chris.

'Itz the fust time uv bin here – is it new?'

The voice is somewhat devoid of any emotion whatsoever. Chris turns round and sees a man peering at him over the top of his spectacles. He has a haughty expression on his pallid, almost grey face, which resembles scattered ashes.

'Yes,' Chris replies politely, 'it's about two weeks old – I watched them build it.' Chris wrinkles his nose and sniffs the air. 'Yer can still smell the glue under the safety matting.'

'Can yer,' the man replies, 'I con' smell no more – not since I went in 'osspital.' The man pauses a few seconds and then asks, 'How cum yoh watched em build it, are yoh unemployed?'

Such enquiries constantly prove to be a source of anxiety to Chris, if not embarrassment.

Chris hesitates, rubs his nose, and explains, 'I suppose I'm unemployed – but I don't claim any benefit. I'm what people call a house husband.'

'Ow'd yer manage ta live then?'

'Well, my wife has a part-time job,' Chris admits.

The stranger furrows his forehead and asks, 'Wer'd yer live – in a council flat?'

'No,' Chris offers vaguely.

The man observes Chris dubiously and awaits a further explanation. He has a disconcerting physical presence.

Chris recaps for a moment and rather reluctantly adds, 'I used to werk – but now I've paid my mortgage off.'

'Oh!' the stranger exclaims, surprised, and smoothes his unruly hair with his hands.

The stranger's eyes hold a faint suggestion of distaste and displeasure. Then, rather rudely, the stranger limps away without so much as a goodbye. Chris carries on pushing

Jintana and wonders what it would be like not to be able to smell.

A child walks in front of their swing and, in an instant, Chris is forced to hold back the push he is about to deliver. The child stands still, totally unaware of the danger. The child looks at his mother with large sad eyes, sad with an eerie sadness unnatural in one so young. His mother's gaze is elsewhere. She sits on a bench smoking a cigarette while chatting to another woman. Chris has seen this woman before. He recognises her brown roots growing through her gaudy blonde hair. She had been chain-smoking in this very playground a few days earlier. It was one of those episodes that from time to time occur unexpectedly, forming a sort of epitaph to someone. Jintana had seen her carelessly drop an empty cigarette packet onto the floor. Chris's lovely daughter had retrieved the litter, giving it back to the embarrassed owner. It was a great moment, as the litter bin was only two yards away.

'I want to go back on the slide, daddy,' Jintana insists.

Chris lifts her out of the swing and they return to the slide. Jintana climbs up the steps and stands still, with her gaze fixed on the children below. The sun filters through slats in the wooden fence, throwing stripes across the grass for children to leap over. Chris strains his eyes. Peering through the fence he sees several unleashed dogs, followed by their entourage of careless owners. On many occasions an unleashed dog has proved to be a menace to Jintana.

'It's all right – he loves children,' would be the usual reply uttered by a dog owner, shortly after Jintana had been knocked to the ground by an eager wet nose.

Chris looks at his watch. He waits a few more minutes delaying the bad news for his daughter and finally he says, 'Cum on, Jintana, shall we go into the town and look at the shops?'

'No daddy, I want to stay in the park,' she protests.

'It's time to go now!' Chris shouts in mock rage and picks her up, placing her into the pushchair before she can start a tantrum.

Chris wends his way to the town centre. It's strange how familiar every tree, every garden, and every squirrel has become, thinks Chris. In the town they pass a charity shop that sells second-hand clothes and well-thumbed paperbacks. A tiny girl stands in the doorway. Wide-eyed, she watches her mother sorting feverishly through piles of underwear. Other customers carry socks and several vests under their arms, perhaps enough for all their family and friends. They pass a greengrocer's shop with boxes of apples and oranges shining in the sunlight. Jintana licks her lips and mentally tastes the fruit.

'Yer can have an apple after lunch,' Chris informs her.

Above, the church clock strikes eleven. Chris turns his attention to a magpie, which struts about the old flat tombstones unconcerned by the turmoil of shoppers walking past. Beyond, he glimpses what used to be the maternity home. It is the place of Chris's birth, totally refurbished now and transformed into a small mental health hospital.

'Look Jintana,' Chris says proudly, 'that's where daddy wuz born.' His daughter's eyes follow Chris's finger straight to an upstairs window. 'Do yer understand? Daddy wuz born inside that house.'

Jintana's blank expression stares back at him.

Chris continues to stride past the building. 'Jintana,' Chris says jokingly, 'they might erect a plaque one day: *Chris Pepperdine was born here third of December 1959*, – huh! No blooming chance!'

Chris waits to cross the road, his brain sifting through philosophical ideas. Suddenly, it occurs to him that he could be one of those people who are destined to die on the same spot as they were born.

They cross the road and Chris increases his pace, defying

anybody to pass. In the end he careers along as fast as he can, with Jintana giggling as she bumps helplessly up and down. They approach a bus shelter with several people queuing out of line and blocking the pavement. Shame-faced, they are forced to retreat as Chris trundles towards their toes. Chris passes them, with a nonchalant expression on his face. Pushing a pushchair can be such fun, Chris admits to himself.

'Jintana,' Chris asks, 'wot do yer want for lunch?'

She squeezes her lips together in deep thought, and timidly says, 'Ham and brown sauce.'

Hope lights up her face. Chris nods in silent agreement.

Presently, they arrive home and Chris makes lunch. The familiar scorched crusts remain on Jintana's plate, which are always difficult for a child to desire.

'Jintana,' Chris says sharply, his fingers tapping rhythmically on the table, 'stop playing with yer spewn and put it back. Yer don't need a spewn to eat sandwiches.'

She returns the spoon to the cutlery drawer and seats herself at the table again.

'I don't want them, daddy.'

'You must eat yer crusts,' Chris insists, now standing straight backed with his hands akimbo.

Eventually Jinatana weakens and eats them all up.

After lunch, Jintana asks warily, 'Daddy, can I draw now?'

Chris duly obliges, as this is certainly to be encouraged. She starts scribbling on the scrap paper, which her mother has brought home from work. She's doing better now, thinks Chris. She's holding the pencil properly, instead of gripping it like her mother pounding chillies with a pestle and mortar.

A little later, Chris suggests, 'Yer can watch one cartoon, if yer want to.'

Jintana's eyes sparkle excitedly, but then she mysteriously

replies, 'I want *Bewdy beet.*' An unpleasant suspicion of *déjà vu* crawls up on Chris.

'Jintana,' Chris protests, 'I don't understand yer. Yer not talking to mommy now – tell me in English.'

'No! *Bewdy beet*,' she insists.

'I'll have to ask yer mom what it means when she cums home from werk.'

Jintana gets frustrated. Chris makes a quick note of her pronunciation on sheet of paper. Jintana loses her patience and walks up the stairs returning with the video *Beauty and the Beast*. Chris smiles.

'Jintana,' he explains, 'yer should say beauty and the beast – cum on, try it.'

His daughter sits down and says, 'Beauty and beet.'

Chris smiles again and allows her to glue her eyes to the television screen.

Approximately one and three quarter hours later the videotape ends and Chris suggests that they go into the garden. After several minutes of running around and teasing his daughter with the football, it is now time for Chris to sit down on the bench, exhausted. Suddenly Jintana runs onto the flowerbeds to pick up a pebble.

Chris jumps up and shouts in mock rage, 'If yer do that again we'll go back inside the house.'

She jumps back onto the lawn. As Chris expects, within seconds, boredom overcomes Jintana.

'Where is mommy?' she asks him, sadly.

'Today is Saturday – she's at werk all day. Fust of all, sit down on the bench and we can look at some things in the garden.'

Jintana sits down and swings her legs. Her eyes tingle with excitement. She knows what to expect, as they have played this sitting down while daddy has a rest game before.

'Where's the spider's web?' Chris asks her.

Jintana leaps to her feet and walks towards the fence, shouting, 'Here it is!'

Chris applauds her. His eyes scan their garden for something a little more difficult.

Chris catches his breath. A rare sight appears, hovering above the washing line. It is Chris's favourite insect, a wonderful dragonfly. Chris rises to his feet and silently beckons his daughter over.

'Look,' Chris whispers into her ear, 'a dragonfly.'

She observes it in amazement and, to Chris's astonishment, the insect lands on the washing line. This is an opportunity not to be missed, Chris decides, so he picks up his daughter and creeps towards the object of his desire. The brightly coloured dragonfly remains motionless as they approach. Jintana is silent, her eyes transfixed onto its beautiful abdomen and transparent wings. It is a true dragonfly, thinks Chris, as it is holding its wings spread out while resting, unlike the weaker damselfly which holds its wings high above its body. They are observing a design that has lasted millions of years. Its eyes and mouth seem almost human in appearance, such is Chris's admiration for this insect. Then, quite unexpectedly, the dragonfly turns its head towards Jintana and peers into her eyes, its thin mouth almost smiling.

'Jintana,' Chris whispers, 'look, he's smiling at yer.'

His daughter bursts into laughter, causing the dragonfly to rise and majestically fly away.

'Where's it gone?' she quickly asks.

'He's gone home – did yer see it look at yer?' Chris improvises.

'Yes – he smile his mouth,' Jintana says, happily.

Chris glances at his watch. It reads 5.30, time to have a drink of cider, he thinks. He returns to the kitchen and pours out the first of the day. Jintana follows him inside.

'Do yer want some more pop?' he asks her.

She picks up her beaker and shakes it suspiciously.

'It's empty daddy,' she explains and hands Chris the beaker.

Chris downs his pint with gusto like the actor Sir John Mills in the movie *Ice Cold in Alex*, and then prepares Jintana's drink.

The evening finally arrives. Looking out of his daughter's bedroom window, Chris sees the sun go down, the sky pulled thin towards the west in shades of pink. Chris carries out all the activities of bedtime, the brushing of teeth, the combing of hair and the reading of stories. Jintana follows the book with her intelligent, brown eyes, moving them keenly from side to side and down the page.

'Goodnight, Jintana.' Chris says and kisses her.

Jintana faithfully gives him a huge hug and asks, 'When will I see mommy?'

'Tomorrow,' Chris replies, 'tomorrow is Sunday and we are all going to yer cousin's christening.'

Jintana's expression is blank.

'Goodnight, daddy,' she says softly.

Chris extinguishes the light and descends the staircase.

Presently, Chris decides to check for any messages on the telephone answer machine. To his astonishment, there is a message spoken in his wife's language. It disturbs Chris. It is the distraught voice of a Thai woman whom he cannot recognise or understand. Chris exhales slowly. An aeroplane shatters the sultry silence as it flies overhead. Chris sits down with his pint of cider and awaits the return of his wife.

7

Cupid's Sting

Tomorrow, Chris reflects, his Buddhist wife who was born more than 7,000 miles away will attend a christening service in an English church, all because he returned to Thailand, many years ago. A small tear springs from his eye and he recalls his second trip there. It was a trip full of emotional awakening.

The tropical sun bore down its wrath. Chris shook his head sadly. He could not understand why he was the only tourist to have chosen the three-day tour. Perhaps he had made a bad choice by booking from a glossy brochure back in the UK. Most of his fellow travellers had booked one-day tours from their Bangkok hotels. Now Chris was quite alone on a stifling mini-bus, whilst the others were enjoying an open-windowed train journey. Chris gazed wistfully through the tinted window, unaware that the adventure of his life was about to begin. Pretty soon, he forgot the inadequate air-conditioning and sat back, watching the distant mountainous jungle slowly reshape the emerald vista. His journey to the upper part of the River Kwai Noi valley had begun to hold his interest. The mini-bus gained altitude and Chris's ears popped. Then, the driver negotiated a sharp left-hand bend and, below, the idyllic view took Chris's breath away. It was his first sight of the river meandering through the jungle, cutting its path as it had done for so many centuries. Somehow the river had begun to work its enchantment on Chris. They continued along the serpentine road, occasionally glimpsing a few bamboo thatched houseboats floating on the river. In a perceptive flash Chris wondered about those families. The river was their source of food and highway. They must have lived like this for hundreds of years, thought Chris. Modern consumerism eluded them. They were floating free in history.

'Driver,' Chris asked, 'when do we arrive at the hotel?'

Rather carelessly, the driver turned his head away from the road and peered at Chris through his smeared bifocals. To Chris's horror, the road ahead seemed to suddenly disappear around a sharp bend.

'Ten minutes,' the driver replied, and paused.

His lips slowly parted, as if to say something else. Chris suppressed an overwhelming urge to point a finger towards their impending doom. Instead he gave the driver a swift double nod and smiled in a friendly fashion. It worked, as the driver now turned to face the road just in the nick of time. The driver's face stared out of his rear view mirror like a china doll. Garlands of dead flowers hung like ponytails around his reflection, flowers that unified the chipped and worn Buddha standing on his dashboard. Chris shook his head and cursed under his breath. Next time, thought Chris, I will leave him alone to concentrate on his driving, as his dilapidated Buddha and shrine looked as though they were about to run out of good luck. The only religious possession this driver had of any value, mused Chris ruefully, appeared to be his tonsure bald patch.

Half an hour later, the mini-bus suddenly slowed down for no apparent reason. A narrow lane came into view on their left-hand side. They turned off the main road and drove along it. They were heading towards the river gorge now, with its verdant hilltops towering high above them.

Rather ominously, a yellow traffic sign depicting a truck plunging comically down a ravine greeted them. With all this in mind, Chris hoped the driver knew what he was doing. The traffic sign proved to be a gross under-estimate of the gradient, with Chris's clammy hands gripping the underside of his seat and buttocks clenched in nervous pain. Somehow, he avoided sinking his front teeth into the driver's dashboard. Chris's sense of doom lightened a bit as they levelled off and the brown river finally came into view. Then, before Chris's gaze and surrounded by a lush teak forest, came the River Kwai Village hotel standing proud and sublime on the left bank of the river. Hotel staff clad in deep blue uniforms slept in the shade of trees. Those that were working, walked with a sort of slow dawdle blissfully unaware of their arrival.

The driver stopped the mini-bus and slid the door open. Chris inhaled the sweet scent of tropical flowers. All around, squawks from invisible birds filled the air in complete harmony with a chorus of crickets. Chris followed his luggage to the reception. A teak table carved from a huge tree trunk formed the centrepiece of the lounge. In the guise of a peacock, several branches had remained intact and in a fanlike fashion spread out along a redbrick wall. This relic of the forest must have been hundreds of years old before it was felled, reflected Chris. In admiration he brushed his fingers along its exotic patina.

A toucan stood on the reception desk, proudly displaying its large and colourful beak. Chris observed the bird closely. There was no chain around its leg and, with its wings clipped, it was free to wander around the hotel terrorising any nervous guest. After checking in, Chris was informed that lunch would be served as soon as the one-day trippers had arrived. Chris decided to take a leisurely stroll around the grounds. A pebble-dashed concrete footpath with a primeval-looking bough handrail led him to the swimming pool. Here, a natural waterfall drained out of the jungle and meandered its way through a leaf-green rock garden. Chris stood awhile, listening to the melody of the rippling stream and watching the Japanese koi gulp air. This hotel was just what he needed after the pollution and noise of Bangkok, he thought. More importantly, the hotel was not busy. In fact, he could not see any guests at all. Perhaps they were on a trip. Chris passed a menagerie of playful monkeys, fish, parrots, mongoose and cockatoos. In the distance butterflies danced across the open space of the hotel and the feathery jungle edge.

Chris entered the jungle view restaurant. All the tables were neatly laid out with chequered vinyl tablecloths and gleaming cutlery. The floorboards creaked as he crossed to the parapet. Below, and within earshot, he could see the brown river in between the gaps of huge trees. There it was, rushing down the gorge at an awesome speed and yet, despite its ferocity, Chris was in total awe of its natural beauty.

He had nearly walked full circle now. In the distance Chris could see the reception area. A quaint bar separated the restaurant from the lounge. It intrigued him, as the counter was made from a huge tree trunk sliced in half. Chris was drawn to it like a butterfly to a flower. The bar was unattended, so he sat down and waited for a member of staff to arrive. Before his eyes, rising up from behind the counter, was a young Thai-Chinese woman with a heart-shaped face and a radiant smile. A mystical sensation of perfection enveloped Chris.

'You want drink sir?' she asked softly.

In an instant, Chris gazed into the bronze windows of her soul. He saw a kind soul, full of goodness and no guile. Information from his senses flowed to untapped neurones in his brain. Emotions and motivation were permanently forged. Chris knew he would happily die for this woman.

He had met his intended partner for life. Chris was looking at his future wife. So this was it then, thought Chris, the moment you read about in books and see in movies. Love at first sight, Cupid's sting, and it had happened to him, the moment which poets, psychiatrists and philosophers all try to explain.

'Singha beer, please,' Chris said cheerfully.

She was raven-haired, with a bob haircut that was held back on one side with a girlish hair clip. Occasionally, her fringe fluttered in the breeze from an overhead fan.

'What is your name?' Chris enquired, aiming at a cheery casualness.

'Salinee,' she replied, whilst pouring out his beer with dexterous hands.

Chris entered her response into his memory and replied, 'my name is Chris.'

She smiled again, showing her gleaming white teeth. A thought occurred to Chris: he would have to remember how to pronounce her name properly, so he tried his luck.

'Sally knee,' Chris said, tremulously. She glanced sideways and peered at him through her lashes. Chris hesitated, and asked, 'Have I said your name correctly?'

'Yes – you say my name.'

Chris drank his beer and watched her restock the bar with an owl-like gaze. The scent from the exquisite garden wafted in through the open windows. Chris knew he was in love with this woman, even though she was a complete stranger. This was a new emotion for him and he pondered on it. What if she were married, engaged, or had no feelings whatsoever for him? Whether it was divine intervention or not, Chris had an overwhelming feeling that his guardian angel would ensure they would get married one day.

A loud and authoritative Thai voice interrupted his thoughts. Salinee put the crates to one side and checked the bar counter for cleanliness. More shouting could be heard from the reception and kitchen areas.

'What is happening?' Chris queried.

'The tour bus is come now,' she explained.

Chris carried on drinking and observed the hotel swing into action. He gazed through the window and at that moment a tour bus came hurtling into view after negotiating the 'clenched buttocks ride'. As the noise grew, the sleepy calm of his jungle retreat was lost. Thirty or so tourists piled off the bus and promptly formed a queue outside the lavatories.

A tour guide wearing a gleaming, unsullied white shirt clapped his hands like a good-humoured headmaster and hollered, 'Free traditional Thai dinner is now served in the jungle view restaurant.'

The queue dispersed and the sound of rubber flip-flops smacking across the wooden floor resonated around the room. Bursting bladders would have to wait, as finding a decent table had now become top priority. The guide's excellent English, plump figure and well-tailored clothes suggested a well-bred upbringing of some kind, thought Chris.

'Chris,' Salinee urged, 'you must eat tour lunch now.'

Chris glanced at the thickening crowd forming around the tables and joined them.

Two fat Dutch women garbed in flowered cotton frocks sat opposite Chris. Consumption of the hot Thai cuisine was varied. The more experienced tourists ate all of their green and red chillies. However, these two Dutch women soon spat them out and gulped large quantities of water. Chris's eyes tingled with suppressed laughter as he helped himself to the chilli fish sauce. Peering towards the bar, Chris was appalled to see men drinking and talking to Salinee. They had finished their meals and were on the prowl, he thought. It suddenly occurred to him that this is what it must be like every day. The love of his life was a sitting target for any wolf. A shudder ran down his spine. All he wanted was to get up and scuttle back to her. Chris leapt to his feet and walked towards the bar, dodging several galloping waitresses in the process. Salinee was working hard, serving drinks and fending off advances with polite repartee. Chris deliberately kept his distance from them and waited his turn to order another beer. The gang continued to be a more dominant force, but eventually Chris made eye contact with Salinee and she replenished his drink. Pretty soon the hot chillies began to take effect so, using a technique Chris had picked up from a fellow tourist, he carefully paddled his tongue in the cold beer.

Presently, the tour guide clad in a gleaming white shirt cried out, 'Everybody, please finish your drinks and follow me down to the river. We are taking a short boat ride.'

Chris took a seat and watched the entourage descend several slippery steps towards the riverbank. Chris shunned the vigorous pace and loudness of the crowd in favour of spending more time with Salinee.

'Chris,' Salinee observed, 'why you not going on trip?'

Chris looked at her face. She looked genuinely concerned.

'I want to stay here with you,' Chris said impulsively, adding, 'I can go another day – I'm on the three day tour.'

Chris had laid down his first statement of interest for her. She passed it by with a slight twitch of her nose and showed no visible signs of disconcertment. Perhaps she had misunderstood, thought Chris, as her English was far from perfect.

'You stay here three days?' she asked.

'Maybe longer. I like it here – I like you.'

She continued cleaning the bar counter.

A young man, who appeared to be the hotel gardener, had caught Chris's attention. Chris had seen him glance at

Salinee several times through the bar window. He was clocking her, thought Chris. With all the bitterness of a teenager in love Chris felt jealous. This gardener had been watching Salinee in a lascivious manner. But most importantly, he would remain here after Chris had returned home. Chris instantly disliked him and he wanted to shed some light on the state of affairs manifesting inside his head.

'Sally knee,' Chris asked, 'do you live around here?'

'No – Kanchanaburi,' she replied quickly, sudden pride in her voice.

'Where's that?'

'One hundred and fifty kilometres south.'

'Do you have a boyfriend?' Chris boldly asked her.

'No – I never have a boyfriend.'

A flourish of trumpets echoed inside his head. It had been a wonderful reply. Not only had she told Chris she was unattached, but also she had inadvertently told him she was a virgin. It was just what the doctor had ordered. This truly was a great day and Chris consumed Salinee's beer like a thirsty mosquito. The day-trippers returned with dishevelled hair and moist clothes. Soon, they left for Bangkok and the quirky jungle noises returned to stimulate Chris's senses. Pretty soon, the beer was rising in him, so he thought it prudent to return to his room for a nap.

The sun had set when Chris woke up with a gripping hunger pain in his stomach. It was 7.15 and he rubbed his hands in anticipation at spending more time with Salinee. In an effort to concentrate on his image, Chris put on his best clothes. He felt pleased to have had the insight to pack a tie. Chris knew that it was far too hot to wear it, but he was prepared to suffer to enhance his chances. Full of bravado, he unrolled the lemon-yellow tie and cracked it like a whip.

As he approached the bar, Chris could see Salinee in her

blue uniform sitting behind the counter. However, to his annoyance, Chris was not the only guest staying that evening. Two elderly English ladies sat at a table in bored conversation with a middle-aged American woman.

'Hello, Sally knee,' Chris said cheerfully.

'Hello, Chris, you sleep?'

'Yes – can I have a beer please?'

Salinee glanced at Chris's tie and said, 'You are smart!'

Feeling embarrassed, Chris gave a sideways glance towards the three women. They continued to talk to each other.

'Why do you think I am clever?' Chris enquired, jokingly.

Salinee looked puzzled and promptly produced an English/Thai dictionary from beneath the counter. She passed it to Chris. He found the word 'clever' and pointed out its meanings: smart, intelligent. Chris was playing games with her.

She shook her head vigorously and explained, 'Because you have tie. Nobody wear them – it too hot!'

Chris apologised and showed her the many meanings of the word 'smart'.

The sweet and sickly fragrance of fraudulent toilet water soon wafted towards the bar. Chris wondered fleetingly which of the three guests were wearing it. The two English ladies appeared to be sisters. They were both bony women with lop-sided smiles, and each had a deep dimple in her chins. They possessed all the hallmarks of affluent widows spending their inheritance. The American woman wore spectacles and her long, thick eyebrows, which almost met over her nose, gave her the solemn gaze of a magistrate.

'Sally knee,' Chris asked, 'can you turn the fans up to full speed please?' She obliged and the smell retreated.

A waitress by the name of Apinior joined Salinee and Chris at the bar. She was a short woman in her early twenties with black hair, cut in a neat bob that framed her round, chubby face. Chris had noticed her working earlier. She was plagued by her own anxieties, thought Chris, and her job appeared far too much for her to cope with. Chris brought her and Salinee a drink. Apinior looked at Salinee and gave a deep sigh. Perhaps drinking was a chore as well.

'Apinior,' Chris enquired mischievously, 'have you been working hard today?'

'Yes,' she replied.

Somehow, Chris did not believe her and turned to face Salinee who promptly wiped a smirk from her face. Perhaps Salinee and Chris had formed the same opinion. Hard work was not Apinior's forte. Apinior continued to sit close to Chris, as if by some magical process Chris might absorb her attentions directed towards him.

The evening ripened and the constant drone of the blades rotating above Chris's head hypnotised his mental perception. There was something about those ceiling fans, he thought. The room and everybody in it appeared to blend into the background, leaving Salinee and himself alone. Nevertheless, the drab rock band, which consisted of three waiters attempting to capture the essence of western rock music, would soon hit a wrong chord, plunging Chris back into the real world. They were awful, having learned their lyrics and chords from pirate music cassettes. Apinior finished her drink and left.

The American woman joined Chris, perching her substantial figure gingerly onto the edge of the barstool. She was a severe-looking woman by the name of Judie. To Chris's relief she was not the person wearing the offending perfume. Chris brought Judie a drink. The two English women had abandoned her a short time ago making a timely retreat to their rooms. She now had only Chris for her conversation.

'Chris,' she said, 'do you remember Watergate?'

'Oh, let me think,' Chris said absently.

'C'mon Chris – you ought to remember Watergate.'
'Well, just about,' Chris said more alertly.

Her eyes glowed through her pink-rimmed spectacles. She was excited now and lifted herself up onto her elbows.

'Well, I was seriously involved in Watergate,' she said cheerfully, adding, 'mah job was as a personal secretary for the key attorney in the investigation.'

'Were you really?' Chris remarked, with arms crossed over his chest and hands tucked into his armpits.

'Yeah,' she said, and added, 'President Nixon ought never to have resigned. I guess people think he was a manipulative politician.'

A thought entered Chris's head. She must have been working on the president's defence team.

Chris was not convinced with her argument, so he snapped, 'All politicians are manipulative – that's how they climb to their positions in public life. It is also why the public tends not to trust any of them anymore – because of scandals such as Watergate.' She shook her head vehemently. 'C'mon Chris – mah job was to sift through the evidence. Hey – I saw stuff that was held back.'

She continued to remonstrate. Chris now understood why the two English ladies had retired to their rooms so early.

Through his torpor the woman eventually glanced at her watch, saying, 'Jeez – I must go to bed.' She rose from her seat, her eyes gleaming malevolently. 'Hey Chris,' she whispered, 'be careful – all the girls here have got Aids!'

She gave a sideways glance towards Salinee, so as Chris understood whom she was referring to.

'I don't think so,' Chris replied humbly.

'Sure they have – mah doctor told me.'

Chris just stared, convincing himself that it was difficult for a virgin to catch it.

Judie had gone now and Chris was delighted to be alone

with Salinee. 'Sally knee,' Chris asked, 'how many hours do you work each day?'

'I start ten o'clock in the morning and finish twelve o'clock at night,' she calmly replied.

Chris looked concerned.

'This is a bloody Victorian sweat shop,' Chris scoffed. She had not understood his comment, so Chris pointed out the meaning of 'Victorian' in her dictionary. She smiled shyly. Rather mischievously, Chris ordered several cocktails just to observe Salinee's wiggle whilst she fused the mixture inside the cocktail shaker. His primeval male instincts were hard to suppress. Finally, Salinee declared that the bar was closed and Chris proceeded to watch her lock up the booze. She handed him a purple orchid used for garnishing the cocktail glasses. Chris allowed his nose to nestle inside the honey-scented flower. Chris pondered awhile. Why had she given him the flower? He asked himself. What did this mean? The alcohol took over and Chris spoke on behalf of his penis.

'Sally knee . . .' Chris said, and hesitated a moment, 'will you come to my room?'

'No!' she replied sharply and promptly walked away with a fiery brow.

She was quite simply furious. Chris cursed his stupidity and trudged back to his room in shame.

8

Staff and Clientele

The following morning, Chris awoke to an unfamiliar dawn chorus of squawks and chirps eddying from the enormous block of forest. The rooms in the hotel were simple, painted in soft restful pastels and fairly plain. They complemented the lime-green natural surroundings outside. Chris drew back the curtains and gazed into the gorge. Overnight fog had formed and drained down the surrounding slopes back into the river. The fog lay a few inches above his elevated ground level, and even the sun's radiation had been unable to disperse it so early in the morning. Nonetheless, most of the high-level vegetation was now bathed in a halation of salmon-pink light reflecting back from the fog's upper surface. In a strange and eerie way, the jungle view restaurant cast an enlarged shadow through the many layers of water droplets. A coloured corona surrounded this shadowy outline, like a developing Polaroid nestled on top of the fog.

Chris took a shower and strolled to the restaurant. He eyed the motionless ceiling fans hanging above the bar. The bar was still closed and there would be no sign of Salinee until ten o'clock. Chris felt empty and emotionally exhausted. In the distance he could see the American woman eating alone. Sitting at some distance away from her were the two English ladies, carefully avoiding her ostentatious conversation. Chris meandered through the tables and chairs, waving cheerfully over his shoulder and seating himself far away with alacrity. Suddenly, it occurred to him that this very morning he was to embark on his second day tour. Chris was keen to apologise to Salinee. But, he would be travelling up the river when she came on duty. Not only that, he wanted to be back in time for lunch so as to protect her from the new male arrivals.

Chris's waitress was the lackadaisical Apinior.

'Apinior,' Chris asked, 'what time does my tour finish?'

'Umm . . .' she hesitated, adding, 'maybe you want to go with somebody?' her eyes gleaming excitedly.

Feeling slightly irritated, Chris replied quickly, 'yes – I want to see Sally knee.' Chris saw Apinior wince visibly.

'You come back afternoon,' she said gloomily.

Perhaps Apinior had expectations to go with him, he thought.

Chris finished his awful, synthetic-tasting sausages and walked over to the reception. This morning, a different woman was on duty. She had an oval, almost solemn face with vivid black eyes and jet-black shoulder-length hair. Unlike the restaurant staff, she wore a name badge and appeared far more competent than the previous person had. Chris glanced at her badge.

'*Yuwadee*,' he said, 'good morning – can you tell me what time I go on my tour?'

She glanced rapidly through her itinerary and raised her eyebrows in an intrigued expression.

'Nine thirty,' she replied and added, 'your guide's name is Terapat.'

'Thank you,' Chris said, still wondering what had intrigued her so much.

He peered at his watch and it read 9.20. Chris waited 20 minutes. The fog cleared and Chris saw the tiny shape of a man running towards him. He too wore a name badge and possessed a certain sartorial eloquence. Terapat was a man in his early thirties, with pouting lips and a strong belief in his own abilities.

'Mr Pepperdine,' Terapat urged, 'please, we go now.'

He led Chris down the steps to a long-tailed motor boat and a cross-looking skipper. The vinyl-canopied boat had room for about 20 people. For all that, on this day Chris was the only passenger. The skipper was dark skinned, in his mid-thirties, with a thin moustache and possessed a jugular vein that visibly swelled each time he inhaled a cigarette. Chris sat down and the six-cylinder Chrysler engine roared into action. Chris glanced out over the stern and was treated to the sight of a large spume of spray rising majestically into the air. The ten-foot long propeller shaft had engaged with the river. Soon, they were travelling upstream to visit the Kaeng Lava Cave, and see the exotic Sai Yok Waterfall. Quite soon, Chris's eyes were attuned to the silky reflection of the water. In spite of this, he soon realised that every time they took a bend the river sprayed his face and shoulders. Earlier, and to the amusement of the skipper, Chris had insisted on squatting at the front of the boat. Now Chris knew why the skipper had cast him an insolent grin.

After 20 minutes or so they arrived at their first stop. An overgrown jetty was the only indication that humans had been there before. Terapat pointed a long finger aloft, towards a dark and ominous entrance to a lava cave. The black hole was a few metres below the crest of a hill and was surrounded by thick vegetation. At first sight Chris wondered how they would manage to reach their objective. Chris followed Terapat along an invisible footpath that only he recognised. They were half-way up when Chris glanced back and realised that this was potentially as dangerous as it could get. If either of them fell they were hours away from a hospital. They reached the cavernous opening and Terapat produced a battered household torch from his unmanly-looking shoulder bag. Chris felt uneasy about the whole situation. They eased their way into the thick veil of darkness and were met by an intense heat, a strange, eerie heat, as if from hell itself. An odd odour hung around, like damp unwashed clothes. Terapat's torch was energised and in an instant the requirement for mountaineering helmets was realised. Chris waited anxiously, but Terapat produced no safety equipment whatsoever. They had only their skulls to protect their brains. Chris stooped lower as they walked beneath razor-sharp rock formations. It occurred to Chris that if the batteries failed they would be in deep shit. Terapat said nothing. He just guided Chris with exaggerated arm movements and eye gestures. Chris's guide possessed an unnerving self-assurance. They stopped and Terapat pointed his finger towards black fungus hanging from the walls. Chris examined it more closely and saw that it was shimmering.

'Oh no!' Chris whispered, as he suddenly realised his mistake.

Hundreds of eyes stared back at him, reflecting the torch beam like glow-worms. Leathery-winged fruit bats hung from every nook and cranny, occasionally stretching their wings like broken umbrellas. Any moment now, thought Chris, the bats will overwhelm them in a cacophony of flapping wings and wild squeaks. However, to Chris's surprise they stayed put. They were, of course, the most obvious inhabitants of this odoriferous terrain, but somehow Chris had not expected them. Terapat shone his torch into Chris's face and he gave Terapat a mute look of anguish. To Chris's astonishment, they eventually passed through the jagged chain of rocks and re-emerged into the bright sunlight totally unscathed.

'I think you not enjoy the cave,' said Terapat, astutely.

'It was okay,' Chris insisted.

They made their way back to the boat. In a futile attempt

to cover over some of the cracks appearing in his machismo, Chris once again chose the front two seats to sit on. A stifled chuckle was heard from the skipper as Chris sat down. The skipper started the engine and they were away. Chris braced himself and felt a warm, sticky substance spread along his hand. Chris surveyed it suspiciously. It was bat excrement, smeared along the seat by his shoes. Now Chris understood why the skipper had chuckled. He felt foolish, but said nothing. Chris slowly manoeuvred his hand over the side and submerged it into the fluvial waters.

At first sight, the skipper had annoyed Chris. But as their journey continued, Chris finally had to admit to himself that he envied him. Chris also wanted to skipper long-tailed motor boats up this river. Around more bends and in between high walls of bare rock, their boat sliced its way through numerous layers of geological time. The reverberating drone of the Chrysler engine followed them as it broke the jungle tranquillity. Just at that moment, the skipper cut the engine down and they drifted under some overhanging rock formations. The skipper was keen for Chris to observe the rocks and with exaggerated hand movements he took on the guise of a geologist.

After the cave, Chris had prepared himself to be thoroughly disillusioned on his arrival at the waterfall. However, it turned out to be idyllic, not a waterfall of great height, but the last statement of a small tributary cascading majestically over hippopotamus-sized rocks. Nonetheless, the usual tourist traps were there to spoil its natural setting. A thatched houseboat lay moored to the riverbank, complete with restaurant and bar. Chris ordered a Singha beer, asking Terapat and the skipper if they would join him. Terapat drank an orange juice, whilst the skipper declined and went swimming. It was the only time Chris had seen him without a cigarette. Chris could see him splashing and diving in the water with all the enthusiasm of a mermaid.

He really did love this river, thought Chris. Terapat and Chris ordered rice and chicken curry. Terapat sat opposite Chris, and watched Chris gaze at the timid waitress's cleavage as she bent over.

'Maybe I can help you!' Terapat said.

There was a wistful note in his voice. Chris looked at him with a stern eye, wondering what he could possibly mean. The words 'help you' had somehow irritated Chris. Chris said nothing and brushed away a group of annoying flies hovering above his food.

'Shall we go swimming after lunch?' asked Terapat smiling affably.

Chris peered towards the roaring transfusion. It looked inviting, but he felt uneasy about Terapat's sexual orientation.

'No! I have no swimming costume,' Chris explained.

Terapat's eyes dilated and a self-satisfied grin appeared on his face.

'It does not matter – nobody will see us behind the rocks.'

'Yes, but you can,' Chris rapped.

'I don't mind – we are all boys together,' said Terapat, still grinning.

'No, I want to stay here and drink,' Chris protested and ordered another Mai Thai cocktail.

To Chris's annoyance Terapat remonstrated monotonously about Chris's lack of participation in swimming. Finally, it was time to go, so Chris made a quick visit to the toilet. He had been spoilt by the hotel facilities. The toilet there was rural in style. Sitting at floor level, it lay like an upturned crab shell stripped of its guts by a scavenging seabird. The participating party was required to crouch down and flush with water scooped up from a nearby bucket.

Presently, they set off on their return trip. Chris looked

aloft at the hills around him. A flock of birds beat a silent course across the darkening sky. Perhaps they knew a storm was brewing, he thought. It was the month of May and moist air had risen, causing a strong probability of monsoon rainfall. Chris peered anxiously at the dark clouds that appeared to be getting denser and heavier with each passing second. Suddenly the breeze veered, advance notice of what the birds had foretold. This was the rainy season and rain it did, not English style rain, but tropical rain, which had an incomprehensible force that made Chris appreciate why ancient cultures worshiped the power of weather. Those civilisations had been afraid and so was Chris. The river swelled before his eyes and the visibility diminished to an unsafe level. The verdant hills now looked rather gloomy and sinister. Chris could hear distant thunderstorms growling to each other. The skipper, of course, had seen it all before and continued to open the throttle to full speed. At first, Chris thought he was merely showing off, but he continued heading into the gloom like a *kamikaze* pilot. Chris feared they might hit some rocks he had seen on their way upstream. After all, he reflected, the skipper was only human. The torrential rain bounced off the turbid river and Chris's face. Then, quite suddenly the skipper tucked the boat in close to the riverbank. Chris was convinced they would strike a hidden rock. His feet felt wet. The boat was collecting water with the enthusiasm of a sponge. Maybe they were sinking. To Chris's horror the skipper appeared to go mad with the rudder. For no apparent reason, he made several jerks to the left and right in a sinuous fashion. Perhaps he had X-ray vision, thought Chris, or some rocks had been spotted. Then, Chris could just make out the shape of a structure through the rain. He sighed with relief. They were back at the hotel. The skipper had gained Chris's full esteem. The skipper's ken of the river was inspiring. Sunken rocks, hidden banks and a fast approaching snag had all been negotiated with a skilful jerk of the rudder. He had a profound and respectful understanding of the river's awesome power.

On entering the hotel Chris walked straight to the bar. Chris felt as though he had returned to a place that was good for him. Salinee sat with a bemused expression on her face. Several plastic buckets surrounded her. Each had been carefully positioned beneath a hole in the corrugated roof. They were filling up fast. Chris looked at her and she stared at his water-drenched body. They both burst into laughter at each other's predicament.

'Hello, Sally knee,' Chris said, 'can I . . .'

His voice trailed off. He could see that Salinee had cupped her hand round her ear in an attempt to magnify his voice. The noise of the rain pounding against the roof echoed around the room. One could easily have mistaken it for a calypso steel drum band. Actually, it even sounded better than the hotel band, thought Chris.

He raised his voice, yelling above the noise, 'Can I apologise for my behaviour last night?'

'That's okay,' she hollered back, adding, 'I think you drunk yesterday.'

'Yes,' Chris admitted, and was quite surprised at how forthright she had been. He paused and added, 'can I have a Singapore sling please?'

Chris watched her shake the mixture in rhythm with the deluge. She poured out the cherry-red drink into a long tall glass and Chris held out his hand in anticipation.

'Chris – I not finish,' she said vaguely, watching his face closely.

'Sorry,' Chris replied, bewildered. She hastily garnished his drink with a lemon slice and orchid. 'Can I leave my drink here and come back after I've changed?' Salinee nodded.

Chris went to his room, changed, and returned to the

bar. Salinee was still there, so too was the hotel gardener sitting next to Chris's seat and cocktail. Chris gazed at him uneasily. He was a young man in his early twenties and Chris just knew that his charming good looks would bring him success with women. His fleeting glimpses towards Salinee had convinced Chris that he had a flame burning for her.

'The rain has nearly stopped now,' Chris said to Salinee, in an upbeat tone.

The gardener glanced outside and saw several staff resuming their duties. He decided to leave.

Chris tapped the side of a red bucket with his fingernail, and commented, 'This bucket is nearly full – shall I empty it?'

'Yes please,' Salinee replied.

Chris threw the water out of the window. A wicked thought entered his head. It was a pity the gardener had not been working below. Presently, Yuwadee came over and sat at the end of the bar. She spoke to Salinee in Thai, and then they both gazed at Chris searchingly.

'Sally knee, how old are you?' Chris enquired with interest.

'Twenty-three,' she replied, and quickly asked, 'how old you?'

'Twenty six – but I've had a hard life.'

Both women missed his jest completely. He would have to use a simpler style of humour in the future, he thought, perhaps similar to his childish dictionary joke. Then quite unexpectedly, out of the corner of his eye the toucan appeared with its beak only inches away from Chris's bare legs. Chris was completely taken aback, as he was sure it would sink its yellow beak deep into his ankle. He gazed at the bird with the deepest suspicion. The bird examined Chris's feet and stepped clumsily around the barstool.

Finally, it walked off and disappeared under the forest of chairs.

'What do you think of Terapat?' Chris asked. Both women's eyes met each other's and their eyebrows wrinkled in unison. Chris spoke again, 'Let me rephrase my question. Does he have a girlfriend?'

'He likes the man,' Salinee replied, cheerfully.

Chris nodded in agreement and said haughtily, 'I thought so.'

'Do you like Terapat?' Yuwadee asked him.

Suddenly, Chris realised what had intrigued her first thing that morning. Yuwadee knew that Terapat would try his luck.

'I like women,' Chris explained, frowning defiantly. He turned to face Salinee and rather cheekily said, 'I like you.' Her cheeks blushed with embarrassment. Chris continued with, 'God did not create Adam and John in the Garden of Eden.'

Both women looked puzzled. The two Buddhists did not understand his biblical comment, or his mordant British humour.

'How much is it to stay here per night?' Chris asked, glancing at Yuwadee.

'One thousand two hundred baht per night,' she replied.

'Sally knee,' Chris queried looking at her searchingly, 'how long is it before you go back home?'

'I go on Sunday.'

'Wonderful,' Chris said enthusiastically. He paused.

'Yuwadee,' Chris declared, 'I want to stay until then – I want three more nights here please.'

The two women exchanged glances.

'You can book tomorrow,' Yuwadee replied, with a huge grin on her face.

'Will the toucan bite me?' Chris asked cheerily.

'Yes – if we ask him,' Yuwadee quickly responded and both women laughed.

'Do you have many guests staying tonight?'

'Two men,' Yuwadee replied, adding, 'it is the rainy season – we are not busy.'

Chris felt uneasy and picked up his glass. He held it with his finger and thumb, tilting it slightly. The condensation dripped onto the wooden bar counter. Like a magician, Salinee swiftly produced a cloth and wiped it dry. Chris drank the glass empty. Tonight would be interesting, he thought. He now had an opportunity to observe a typical night with men sitting at the bar.

The time passed quickly. It was six o'clock and the sun was low. The restaurant manager had set a video running. From the bar Chris could hear a familiar tune. David Lean's movie *The Bridge on the River Kwai* had been requested by one of the guests. Chris slid off his barstool and peered into the lounge. An elderly man sat alone, glaring at the screen in an affronted fashion. Chris returned to his seat, his curiosity deeply aroused.

'Sally knee,' Chris asked 'do many guests request this film?'

'Every night – when busy season,' she replied.

'Ah,' he said. The cocktail board caught his eye. 'I want a different drink this time. I want to try a Grasshopper.' Salinee rattled the cocktail shaker to the tune of 'Colonel Bogie'. Chris visualised the scene in the movie, a scene in which a soldier's worn-out boot flops about, as he marches on the parched soil. Salinee poured the thick emerald liquid into a champagne glass. It made a colourful contrast to the view outside. The sun's last rays had now turned into an orange quilt, tucking the tropical forest in for the night, leaving them to swelter under a high tog rating.

The leather-faced old man approached the bar and

ordered a beer. He was English, and Chris grabbed the opportunity to return to his Black Country accent.

'Have yer bin enjoying the film?' Chris asked him.

The stranger lit up a cigarette and placed it in his mouth. It waggled as he spoke.

'Bloody marvellous lad – but it's not accurate.'

'My name's Chris. I'm going to eat soon – do yer want to join me?' Chris watched him with anticipation. It came as somewhat of a relief when, after a pregnant silence, the stranger finally shook Chris's hand and said, 'My name's Jack – let's go!'

They entered the jungle-view restaurant and Jack demonstrated his tropical ken by saying, 'There's a strong breeze blowin' – so there'll be no mosquitoes.'

'The river is swollen tonight – can yer hear it?' Chris commented.

'Oh aye, I hear it all right.'

Jack forced a smile onto his lugubrious face.

'Wuz yer a prisoner of war here?'

Jack looked at Chris and saw that he was sincere.

Jack sighed reminiscently and replied, 'Oh aye – but I wish I weren't.'

Their waitress came over and they ordered a selection of Thai dishes.

'You know, when we were working on t' railway all we dreamed about eating was fish and chips.'

'Wot did the Japanese give yer to eat?' Chris asked, wondering.

'Nowt, we never could understand why they wouldn't give us more food. If they had fed us well, we could have worked quicker. We were well and truly buggered. When we arrived at t' camp, they immediately put us on half-rations.'

'Wot wuz that then?' Chris asked in puzzled amazement.

'A ball of cooked rice with a pinch of salt,' Jack explained.

'Wot,' Chris cried with some alarm and dropped his jaw in sympathy.

'Did yer get any black market food?'

'Some of t' Thai's helped, though some of 'em took advantage. One day some daft sod swapped a bloody good pair of boots for a bunch of bananas. He never did get any new 'uns.'

Their meal arrived and they shared the various dishes. Jack flicked his cigarette ash onto the wooden floor and continued with, 'Today in Kanchanaburi, near t' bridge – I saw tee shirts, postcards, and books all celebrating t' film.' He stabbed the television screen with his finger and added, 'I've seen t' film many times. But there's no way t' Japs would have allowed us to take over and build t' bridge on our own terms.' He shook his head vigorously and said, 'I bet thee believes we could.'

'No, no,' Chris replied in good humour, 'but without the film yer story wouldn't have bin told. Probably a quarter of the world's population has seen it. Even some of the Japanese kids must have seen it by now.' Jack looked thoughtful as he considered Chris's comment. 'Just take a look how many Japs cum to this hotel for a day trip,' Chris insisted, adding, 'look how many yer saw in Kanchanaburi?'

Jack looked at Chris and spoke softly, 'I watched 'em walking slowly around t' cemetery today. They were all young uns, none of 'em was born before the war.'

Jack shrugged his shoulders philosophically.

Chris interrupted negligently with, 'The world has always belonged to the young.'

Suddenly, Jack uncrossed his long bony legs and looked across at Chris with smouldering eyes.

'Not my generation,' he said and continued with, 'those names on t' gravestones are engraved with such precision that nobody would dare question their authenticity. In fact, most of t' remains have been randomly collected from funeral pyres of dozens of bodies.' He paused, and as an afterthought added, 'Good lads, bad uns and odd-ball types, all mixed together.'

Jack's lips curled in a fragile grimace of distaste. It had been a lachrymatory comment. Jack's eyes filled and Chris stared at him in silence. They had both finished their meals, and there was nothing more Chris could say to this sad, old war sage. Chris excused himself and left Jack to his own thoughts. The river continued to rush past below him, like time itself.

Chris returned to the bar feeling less than wonderful. Jack's words had evoked images as realistic as watching a scratched black and white newsreel and when his eyes pooled with tears it was as though the film had stalled, scorching the celluloid into brown-hued, curling remnants of a distant memory.

Salinee was talking to the other guest, a young flaxen-haired man approximately Chris's age. He had deep blue eyes and a well-groomed moustache. In fact Chris was envious, as he was a good-looking bastard. Chris sat down and detected a foreign, European accent. Chris's first impression of the guy was that he was a single man on the prowl for sex. He was right, as most of his attention was obviously focused on Salinee. Chris knew enough, in short, to know that the only way he could deliberately scupper his plans was to pretend he and Salinee were a couple.

'Hello, my name is Chris.'

Chris extended his arm in friendship, and they shook hands.

'My name is Youst,' he replied.

'Where are you from?' Chris queried.

'The Netherlands,' he replied without a hint of pride.

'I'm English,' Chris said at once.

'I know, I can er . . . what you say – hear your voice.'

Youst turned to face Salinee.

'Here you are,' Salinee said and passed Youst a glass of beer.

She sat down and proceeded to write out his bill, placing it with the other half dozen or so. It was obvious that this guy could drink, thought Chris. Chris decided to watch him very closely, as he might begin to behave badly towards Salinee. Then Chris remembered how badly he had behaved the previous evening. He felt guilty once more. Youst and Chris brought each other drinks and talked about the women of Bangkok and Pattaya. They secretly toasted the recognition of their similarities to each other.

'Apart from Pat Pong, have you been to Soi Cowboy?' Chris asked him.

Youst searched his memories and replied, 'No, where is it?'

'It's in Bangkok – any taxi driver will take you there. I was there last week...' Chris's voice trailed away and he added, 'It made a nice change from Pat Pong.'

'What did you see?' Youst asked, his eyes tingling with interest.

Chris glanced at Salinee and suggested, 'I will tell you later – I do not want to say anything rude in front of Sally knee.'

Youst stared at Chris with a puzzled gaze, hoping he would elaborate.

'When are you er ... what you say, go back Bangkok?' Youst asked.

'I'm staying here a few more nights with Sally knee,' Chris explained, pointing a finger to Salinee.

Youst was nonplussed for a moment, but rather strangely he did not appear resentful. He glanced at Salinee. Chris knew he desired to emulate his expectations and it was not long before Youst left to talk to Yuwadee in the reception.

'Sally knee,' Chris asked, 'can you tell me about the Death Railway Tour? I'm going on it tomorrow.'

'The tour is good. The train it go slow and you can see many things,' Salinee explained vaguely.

'Good, so I can take a lot of photographs then.'

Salinee nodded. Every 20 minutes or so, Youst would return to the bar and refill his glass. He would wink at Chris and then return to Yuwadee. On one occasion he commented how awful the band was. This brought huge grins to Salinee's and Chris's faces.

Presently, it was time for Salinee to undertake her daily stocktaking duties. Chris drank his beer and sat in deep thought. In these days of air-conditioned jumbo jets running in harmony with exotic tours of far-away lands, a meagre draughtsman from England can easily find himself sitting in a bar surrounded by a tropical forest. This does not necessarily mean that that person is of great wealth or importance. Nonetheless, it appeared to Chris that it was his great fortune to have been born in these modern times. His fate at meeting Salinee would never have been realised a few decades ago. For Chris, these thoughts were quite sobering.

Chris continued to drink and talk to Salinee until the band left and she closed the bar. A woman from the kitchen came to meet Salinee, looking about 55, short and fragile with a long, serious face. She glared at Chris very directly and her expression was hostile towards him. She had come to chaperone Salinee back to her room.

'Goodnight Chris,' Salinee said softly and they both departed.

Chris's heart sank. He was alone now and worried about the bad impression he had made. His stupid antics on the previous night had caused concern to Salinee and some of the staff. He would have to work really hard during his remaining time here, to even gain a slight foothold. Chris knew that every move he made, every gesture, would be watched. He knew enough to know that even his own body language could create a bad impression.

Feeling totally deflated, Chris passed the reception desk and saw Youst bending over the counter. He was whispering into Yuwadee's ear. Frustrated at his own lack of progress, Chris decided to take a long stroll through the electrically illuminated rock garden. Chris stood and lingered for a few minutes, listening to the tumbling waterfall and watching the moths gather round the garden lights. The footpath teemed with nocturnal life. Beetles, cockroaches and lizards scampered into the relative safety of the dark undergrowth. Presently, Chris entered his room and switched the air-conditioning off. He was eager to allow the river, waterfall, and jungle to lull him into a deep, primitive sleep.

9

Death Railway

A room maid's trolley disturbed Chris's slumber, as it trundled passed his door. It was 7.30 and Chris's entire body lay beneath a thin coat of sweat. He turned the air-conditioning on and took a well-needed shower. Whilst under the shower, he could just make out a couple of red spots on the back of his legs. They were new blemishes. Thirsty mosquitoes had taken advantage during the night. Chris quickly reached for his daily anti-malaria tablets. Suddenly, it occurred to him that he had not taken a single tablet since checking into the hotel. He had been too preoccupied with Salinee. Chris quickly threw a pill down his throat.

Outside the weather looked fine, a clear blue sky showed no sign of yesterday's deluge. The sun had cleared the hills and was changing from the hazy yellow of early morning to the white heat of day. The restaurant was deserted. There was no sign of Jack or Youst. Whilst sitting down at a table, Chris sniffed the morning air like a bloodhound. He decided to avoid the sausages by ordering some good old-fashioned bacon and egg. Apinior served his breakfast and presented him with a plate of fried egg and square cuts of cold tinned ham.

'Apinior,' Chris asked accusingly, 'where is my bacon?' She looked at him with a puzzled brow and pointed towards the processed ham. 'Okay,' Chris agreed, as he did not really want to get involved in an argument.

After all, ham was from a pig, he thought. Perhaps the menu was incorrect or something had gone wrong during the translation. Chris's knife flashed in the morning sunlight as he stabbed the fried egg. An exotic butterfly caught his eye. It flew across his table and landed on a high-backed chair. It waited a short time, resting and flexing its wings slowly. Suddenly Chris felt a gust of wind and the butterfly was off. It flew over the parapet and into the gorge below.

Youst arrived bleary-eyed, his chiselled chin unshaven. They smiled their greetings and Chris saw Yuwadee arrive in the reception.

'Come and join me,' Chris urged.

Youst sat opposite, and sipped a glass of orange juice. Chris put aside his food and gave Youst his full attention.

'How did you get on last night?' Chris asked him.

His triumphant smile of success had intrigued Chris. Youst winked a bloodshot eye and gave Yuwadee a hurried glance that told Chris she had been the subject of a successful pick up.

'You did okay then.'

'Yes, we er . . . what you say – hanky panky.' Chris grinned. As a passing thought Youst added, 'what about you and Salny, did you . . .?'

Chris interrupted, saying, 'Sally knee is a good girl and I'm prepared to take a long time to win her heart.'

This simple statement, with such off-the-cuff sincerity left Youst nonplussed. To Chris's immense joy and satisfaction, he had used his own abysmal lack of success to pour scorn on Youst's one-night stand. Youst sat in silence with his mouth agape. Finally, Youst reached into his pocket and produced a crisp business card.

Chris recoiled and hesitated a moment.

'Why do you take these on holiday?' Chris asked, detecting a gesture of superiority.

Youst took a deep breath and sat with slumped shoulders.

'One day, I want to give a card to a good girl,' Youst replied, in a forlorn voice.

His voice had caressed the words 'good girl'. Perhaps he too was hoping to meet somebody like Salinee, thought Chris.

Youst continued with, 'If it does happen – will you write and tell me?'

Chris took the card and mischievously replied, 'Okay. By the way, your guide today will probably be Terapat.' Chris kept a straight face, adding, 'He is a nice man. You should take your swimming costume because he knows a secluded place to swim near the waterfall.'

'Er . . . what you say, secluded?'

'Secluded means, peaceful and quiet,' Chris explained.

'Thank you – I like swimming.'

'That's okay,' Chris replied and stood up, adding, 'I have to go now and get ready for my railway tour.'

Chris left with a huge grin stretching his face.

Yuwadee accepted Chris's deposit for the extra nights, totally unaware as to what Youst had informed him. Chris watched her keenly as she wrote out his receipt. He had been wrong about her, he thought. She was not like Salinee after all. Yuwadee informed Chris that a guide would meet him on the train. Until then the skipper of the long-tailed motor boat would escort him to Lum Sum railway station.

A short time later Chris went down to the riverbank. The boat was waiting for him with its engine already running. Once again, the skipper greeted Chris with a steely gaze. Chris stepped aboard with a robotic stumble that rocked the boat from side to side. He faced the skipper with a foolish grin. The skipper cast a malevolent stare in his direction. This time Chris sat near the stern, close to the skipper's bandy legs. Chris had invaded his space, and the skipper produced a glare of derision that persuaded him to move forward two more places. In his eyes Chris would never be at home on any boat, especially his. Then, the skipper suddenly pointed towards the river and set off without any warning. In a reflex action, Chris successfully grabbed the brim of his straw hat before it flew into the river. Chris placed it under his seat. They were travelling south now, and the sun's resplendent reflection kept pace with them as it skated across the river's brown, copious surface. Once again Chris found it an exhilarating experience to invade the steaming humidity of this mosquito-infested jungle. Chris's feelings for the river had changed too, in a strange way it had become a companion that had guided him to Salinee. On the riverbank Chris could see huge chunks of stone uprooted by ancient trees. They passed a small settlement of floating, bamboo houses. Four children waved, as if they knew of their arrival before Chris did. Chris waved back at them, vaguely.

They turned into another bend and ahead of them Chris could see white water flowing over distant rocks. Perhaps a century ago or even last week a violent landslide had occurred here, he thought. They were at the mercy of the constant reshaping of the gorge. It can happen any time, just as lightning can strike without warning. The skipper throttled the engine down and he surveyed the scene very carefully. Maybe the rocks had fallen recently, Chris thought. The skipper turned the boat through a complete circle and then decided to proceed, weaving in and out of the hazard like an eel. More floating houses came into view and Chris reached for his camera. A couple of children seized the opportunity to imprint themselves onto his film. They bubbled with enthusiasm and waved with angelic smiles that no warm-blooded tourist could resist. Chris obliged with several exposures and if it were not for the tiresome clicks of the shutter he could have easily run out of film.

Then before his eyes came the precarious-looking railway

track standing high above the riverbank. The wooden viaduct dominated the countryside for miles. Then Chris remembered Jack, the World War Two soldier. He tried to imagine having to construct such a commanding structure along the contours of the river, sometimes only inches away from the sheer rock face. All this was done with only a ball of rice for sustenance. So it seemed quite reasonable to suppose that the structure could collapse at anytime. Chris was amazed it was still standing after all these years. In spite of this, Chris decided it must be safe. After all, he reflected, they test the construction every day by running a daily train service. He too would have the opportunity to test the structure later that morning, as he was due to return along the very same railway line. Chris looked at his watch. An hour and a half had passed sweetly by. Chris refrained from asking the skipper how much further they had to travel, as by now he considered him a master of tantalising concealment. Sure enough, for no reason whatsoever the skipper cut the engine and ran the nose of the boat against the riverbank. The skipper clambered onto the grass and moored the boat to a tree.

'You go with me,' the skipper insisted.

Chris climbed out and followed him up a trail that had been trodden into the hillside. The absence of thick vegetation led Chris to believe the trail was used quite often. He was correct, as it soon led them straight to Lum Sum railway station.

Lum Sum railway station was a gross disappointment. Crudely constructed a few metres next to the railway track, it consisted of a couple of wooden benches standing under a weather-beaten roof. It had probably stood here for decades, thought Chris, providing a gateway for the indigenous river people to trade along the railway. A woman aged about 30 sat waiting, her left breast exposed to the hot breeze. She grinned broadly, showing a row of uneven teeth blackened by years of chewing betel leaves. The woman reeked of poverty and hopelessness. However, her angelic baby suckled with contentment as it drank from nature's elixir of life. Chris could see the baby was much loved. Their life was bleak, but family life is close and affectionate here, whatever the circumstances.

Seeking an opportunity to demonstrate his English, the skipper pointed a nicotine-stained finger towards a small hole penetrating the railway track.

'Bullet hole,' he explained.

Chris strolled over and slid his little finger through the rusty hole.

'Is it Japanese or an Allied bullet hole?' Chris asked him.

The skipper frowned and shrugged his shoulders philosophically. Chris smiled to himself, as he realised what a silly question he had just asked. How on earth could the skipper know the answer? Chris ran his hand through the long grass that surrounded the track. Even the rotten sleepers were losing their battle against the encroaching vegetation. Looking aloft, Chris could see the cloudless blue sky through his sunglasses. Thank goodness for the projecting brim of his hat, he thought. Chris returned to the shelter and its heavenly shade. The baby had drunk its fill and fallen asleep. Its mother had now slipped her breast inside a shabby blouse. Chris found the poverty unsettling and he was discouraged. He feared for Salinee and her family, for poverty can bring about political change in the shape of another *coup d'état* or even a bloody revolution.

They waited and waited. Everything was quiet as if crushed by the overwhelming power of the sun. The train was late and Chris could see that the skipper felt uneasy. By now, the skipper had smoked several cigarettes whilst pacing around the shelter. Chris guessed he was eager to go back to the hotel and put his feet up. From aloft Chris could see a cloud of smoke, a lazy cloud that drifted slowly to one side, its unclean vapours blackening and disturbing the peace and serenity of the blue sky. Chris stood up and walked onto the tracks. In the distance a bright light shone from the centre of the railway line, above it a veil of thick black smoke belched high into the sky. The light grew larger slowly and spoke with a muffled pant that beat regularly in the vast silence. Closer and closer the black iron horse came. Chris felt rooted to the spot, hypnotised by the growing light. Now the thump of the steam engine reverberated along the track. Then suddenly, there was a loud whistling sound and Chris was tapped on the shoulder. He turned round to see the worried face of the skipper urging him to get off the track. Chris decided to step back and return to the shelter. A black gleam crept in front of them. It stirred and like a pent-up breath released by a serpent from hell, hissed and lurched to a sudden halt. Inside her heart she was burning fiercely, a single fire, and from its summit the mournful, sinister black smoke ascended from the funnel. The shining steam locomotive had arrived.

A man stepped off the train and walked towards the shelter. His shirt was a pure unsullied white and Chris recognised him immediately. He was the very same tour guide he had seen at the hotel. The guide spoke to the skipper and held his hands together in the traditional Thai greeting.

The guide turned to face Chris and asked, 'Are you Mr Pepperdine?'

'Yes,' Chris replied.

He handed Chris a railway ticket. Chris stared at the erect, dark-haired man with his sonorous, well-educated English. He motioned Chris forwards with a commanding gesture.

'Come this way please,' he urged.

Chris followed him up two steps, and the metal handrail

was hot to the touch. Inside, the carriage was full but not overcrowded. A seat had been kept for Chris. However, Chris soon realised that he was on the wrong side to view the river.

'Please stay here with the rest of my tour,' the guide insisted and added, 'if you want to see the river you can stand up and take photographs through these windows.'

Chris nodded back at him.

Suddenly, the locomotive gave out a loud blast of her whistle. There was a hiss of steam and a few sparks flew past the window. The train jolted and trembled as it rolled forwards. Chris looked back towards the wooden shelter. A young woman had met the baby's mother. Garbed in a rather pert, pink dress, she looked totally out of sorts with her current surroundings. Chris smiled as he remembered Wanna and how easily the young women from poor families can feel obliged to seek work through prostitution. This was the hidden agenda behind Thailand's thriving tourism. Single men, who had failed in their quest for love, were easily drawn into a vast labyrinth of hedonistic adventures. Chris also had failed and, he guessed, so too had Youst. But now Chris had stumbled on Salinee, it was a golden opportunity to put his life in order. Chris looked again towards the mother. She hugged and kissed the younger woman. Perhaps she was her younger sister returning home to fill the family coffers.

Chris's tee shirt fluttered incessantly around his arms. The carriage windows were all pushed down allowing a life-preserving wind to blow as they rolled along. He felt relaxed and at peace. Chris leaned back and the hard wooden seat creaked. There was no upholstery and his thighs stuck to the flaking yellow paintwork. The passengers were mainly Thai with a scattering of tourists. An old Thai man aged about 70 sat opposite. He was sick looking with an unnatural blackness around his eyes. His head lay on his wife's shoulder and as he coughed she put her hand over his mouth. Pensive, her face without expression, the woman's eyes shone like black lights as if she knew her husband was dying. Chris too stared at her without expression, focusing onto a disgusting green liquid sloshing inside a polythene bag. The old woman sipped the drink through a straw and to Chris's surprise, she offered him some. Chris refused with a polite shake of the head.

The sounds of excitement began to echo all around. Slumbered stirrings changed into panicky movement. Tourists reached for their cameras and leaned out of the windows. It was not until Chris stood up that he noticed the river below them. The train was now on the wooden viaduct. Chris hastened to the vestibule and looked out of the carriage door. They were travelling along a slow bend in the track, following the contours of the river. Dozens of heads could be seen peering out of the windows, their necks craned as if waiting to be guillotined. Chris too peered out and looked down into the ravine. The brown river flowed below him. Chris happened to glance through the opposite door and saw a wall of silvery rock gliding past the window. Chris could almost reach out and touch the folds and fissures. The sun splashed light off the bare rock and cast strange shadows down the sides of the rock face. It seemed as if he had come straight up against a mountain. The train slowed down to a crawling pace. For some unknown reason, Chris felt compelled to stare at the wall of rock instead of the idyllic river valley. Strange and puzzling holes had caught his gaze. Then Chris realised that these were not natural rock formations, they were in fact man-made, not ornamental, but construction holes. Each one had been cut deep into the grey rock by some poor Allied prisoner of war. There was no carved graffiti up here. No 'Jack was here 1942' written in jest. Chris shivered, as they almost appeared symbolic, peeping out of the rock like human skulls. The holes staring back at him, sadly.

The rotting viaduct creaked below their immense weight. This was why the driver had slowed down. They were about to perform the Thai railway's safety test. The carriage swayed to the left and then back again. Chris could hear more creaking below the bogies. The train whistled a mournful bleat. Chris shivered again, for he had the feeling that he was desecrating numerous graves. He looked back towards the following carriage, and it too swayed in sympathy. It was an unnerving moment but eventually they reached solid bedrock and the train gained speed. Chris sighed with relief. The viaduct had successfully passed the safety test and everything was okay for tomorrow's train. He reached for his camera and photographed the rapidly disappearing construction.

On returning to his seat, Chris could see that the old man was now fast asleep, totally unaware of the excitement all around him. Soon, the atmosphere in the carriage became relaxed and contented, with everybody sprawling around on his or her seats. Chris joined them, briefly closing his eyes when, suddenly he was tapped on the shoulder by a well-dressed wiry figure. Anticipating the ticket collector, Chris looked up to see a bejewelled Thai man with dozens of Rolex watches. He handed Chris a gleaming timepiece and he sat silently holding it for a short time. Feeling slightly annoyed at having been disturbed, Chris shook it gently and listened for any defects. He knew it was a gimcrack copy, but Chris was enjoying leading him on. The salesman looked down at Chris and began to fret, brushing his brow with the back of his hand. He glanced at the other passengers and was acting more nervous all the time. The salesman was aware that everybody in the immediate vicinity had sat up to take notice. Finally, after Chris had mulled it over in his mind he shook his head and handed it back to him. The salesman looked cowed and unhappy. Chris had questioned his wares in front of everybody. Now Chris felt ashamed and uneasy.

Hoping to disassociate himself from the salesman, Chris quickly peered around for his tour guide. Chris saw him, he was grinning self-consciously and with a great deal of difficulty he manoeuvred himself towards him. A badge declared his name to be Harry.

'Hello Harry,' Chris said, 'I'm not going back to Bangkok today. I want to stay at the hotel until Sunday.'

'That's okay,' Harry replied flatly, adding, 'I will tell the office in Bangkok to reserve your seat on the tour bus.'

Chris strained his ears to hear his words above the locomotive. Harry uncoiled himself from the chair and brushed his trousers with his hand. He grinned and drew out a shagreen wallet, fumbling inside for a piece of paper.

A puzzled frown pinched his forehead as he asked, 'Why do you want to stay up here – it's more exciting in Bangkok?'

'I like talking to Sally knee.'

'Oh! I see,' Harry said and he made a note of Chris's revised itinerary.

'Harry, your English is excellent.'

'Thank you, I had an English teacher when I was a child in Singapore,' he explained haughtily.

'Was you born in Singapore?'

'Yes, but my mother and father are Thai,' he answered quickly, adding, 'They worked in an Englishman's house.'

Chris nodded and returned to his seat. Chris could not help admiring the sight before his eyes. The Thai countryside rolled past his window like an outrageous back projection in a low-budget B-movie.

Eventually, Chris arrived back at the hotel and he made his way straight to the bar. Salinee was working hard, but she still made the effort to smile back at him. Chris ordered a beer and watched the tourists take their places in the restaurant.

'Chris,' Salinee asked, 'why you not eat?'

'Okay, I will come back to see you later.'

Chris ate his lunch with Jack. In the morning Jack had felt unwell and had now decided to return to Bangkok that afternoon. Chris thought it prudent not to mention the death railway tour. They shook hands and Chris returned to the bar.

Harry announced the boat trip and the tourists gathered round.

'Why are you smiling?' Salinee enquired, as she gazed at a wry grin developing across Chris's face.

'I'm just watching them walk down the slippery steps,' Chris replied.

'You want somebody to fall down?' Salinee asked with concern.

'No!' Chris said quickly, shaking his head vigorously, 'but if somebody does fall down the steps – I'd like to see it.'

He held his arms out in a gesture of honesty. Salinee glanced through the window. At that very moment a gingerly-footed tourist miraculously regained his footing. If only that arched spine, the flying feet with those elaborate facial and arm gestures could have been captured on film, thought Chris. Salinee laughed aloud, and then stifled her mirth by thrusting a hand over her mouth. She turned to face Chris. Chris smiled broadly, to acknowledge that he too had seen the incident. Her face was frozen with embarrassment. She sat down to organise more bills.

The hotel was temporarily void of guests. Youst, the Dutchman, would not return for half an hour. Yuwadee joined Chris and Salinee at the bar. The two women exchanged smiles.

'Hello Yuwadee,' Chris said softly, instantly remembering the comments Youst had made during breakfast.

'Hello Chris,' she replied and looked at Salinee in an enquiring gaze.

The two women then proceeded to stare at him. Chris sensed something important was about to be asked. Yuwadee nudged Salinee and she reached under the bar counter. Salinee produced her English/Thai dictionary and placed it next to Chris's beer. He raised his wet glass and sipped the beer with reverence.

'What's the matter?' Chris asked.

'Chris,' Yuwadee asked, 'what is hanky-panky?'

Chris's eyes bulged towards the edge of their sockets, and he gulped some more beer.

'You want to know what hanky-panky is?' Chris asked in a disbelieving voice. The two women nodded in agreement. Chris pushed the dictionary across the bar towards Salinee. 'I don't need to look at the book,' he declared, 'it means to have sex.'

The two women blinked at each other in disbelief, and then shook their heads slowly.

Chris stared at Yuwadee and asked, 'Who said they want hanky-panky?'

She rubbed her chin with her hand, and hesitated for a short moment.

'Youst, the Holland man,' she explained and continued with, 'he kept asking me for hanky-panky all evening.'

The shadow of a smile moved across Chris's face.

'Did you have hanky-panky with him?' Chris asked with a knowing twinkle in his eyes.

Yuwadee blinked at him in disbelief.

'No! I am a good girl,' she protested in a defiant tone, showing irritation for the first time.

Chris turned to Salinee and said, 'The women who work here – far away from the cities, they are not the same as those working in Bangkok or Pattaya – are they!'

Chris shook his head to himself.

The two women exchanged glances and Yuwadee said, 'We are good girls – not prostitutes.'

Chris nodded in agreement and drank some more beer, whilst harbouring the thought that Youst was a lying bastard.

The heat intensified and the welcome breeze from the ceiling fans increased his faith in modern technology. Here he sat, hopelessly dependent on an electric ceiling fan. The faint stutter of a motor boat could be heard in the distance, growing nearer and louder as it bounced along the gorge.

'This must be Youst and Terapat arriving,' Chris said.

He was curious as to what had happened between Youst and Terapat. Chris stood up and peered out of the window. The engine stopped and Youst strode up the steps like a man marching into battle. His face was stern and motionless. Chris watched him as he went straight to his room. Presently, Youst returned with an overnight bag and beckoned Yuwadee over. They chatted awhile and Youst appeared to check out. Chris watched with a puzzled gaze as he approached the bar. Youst ordered a beer and insisted on paying cash.

'Did you enjoy your trip?' Chris enquired, with his eyes blinking innocently.

'No!' Youst replied brusquely, and added, 'I check out now, and er . . . what you say, I go to Bangkok with the many people.'

Chris saw something in Youst's face he had never seen before. Youst was angry and utterly disgusted.

'I thought you were going to stay one more night and do the train tour tomorrow,' Chris commented.

Youst shook his head and said in exasperation, 'I want to go Bangkok and go away from . . .' he paused and gazed around the hotel.

He learned over and whispered into Chris's ear, 'Terapat is er . . . what you say, a homo.'

Youst nodded to himself. Chris shook his head in sympathy.

Youst continued with, 'I could see his er . . . what you say – his big dickey when we go swimming.'

'My God,' Chris cried, shaking his head and holding back an irresistible urge to burst into laughter. 'I think you are right to get away from here,' Chris said coyly, adding, 'if I were you I would go to Bangkok.'

The day-trippers returned, and Youst finished his drink. Youst shook hands with Chris and he said softly, 'Good luck, I hope it er . . . what you say, it happens for you and Salny.'

'Thank you,' Chris replied and waved goodbye.

Chris sighed with relief, as he was secretly glad to see the back of him.

Presently, the tour bus left and once again Chris was the only guest staying that night. He mulled over the joke he had played on Youst. All sense of time vanished. Chris felt uneasy. Perhaps he was wrong about Youst. He had not had sex with Yuwadee after all. Youst was probably lonely, in search of love, just as he was. Chris felt guilty and remembered how Youst had brought his business cards on holiday. What was it he had said, 'One day, I want to give a card to a good girl'. Youst was lonely, thought Chris. Those damn cards were burning a bloody hole in his pocket, waiting for a decent woman to take one. Chris felt ashamed at his treatment towards Youst, for he now saw his obvious despair.

10

Extra Time

With only three more nights left at the hotel, Chris felt with increasing pessimism that the clock was ticking away a surreal, almost borrowed time. Time, which in the context of the universe as a whole was an insignificant point in duration. Nonetheless, in the context of Chris's life it would be a monumental period. He would have to utilise the opportunity to its full extent if he were to win Salinee's heart.

Chris heard a man's voice through the open bar window. Salinee leaned out and spoke Thai. Chris stood up and saw the gardener working below. Salinee threw several chunks of ice into a polythene bag, filled it with water and secured it with an elastic band wrapped tightly round a straw. The gardener held out a grimy hand and she passed him his drink.

Chris returned to his barstool and mournfully said, 'I think that man likes you.'

Salinee smiled and explained, 'He is married.'

Chris shrugged his shoulders and spread his hands in resignation.

'I still think he likes you,' he added.

Salinee said nothing, giving Chris the impression that as far as she was concerned that was the end of it. He felt more at ease and decided to say no more about the irritating gardener.

Yuwadee returned with Apinior. They both joined Salinee and Chris at the bar, where they all shared an afternoon of decorous merriment. Occasionally the English/Thai dictionary would be produced in an effort to clarify the obvious. Chris came to the conclusion that if he were popular with Salinee's friends, it would greatly enhance his own chances of success. He knew the tone to adopt when talking to them. Chris pulled out all of his best jokes. Not adult jokes, but girlish, silly jokes, as if, like the television character Sergeant Bilko, he charmed the women with a golden tongue. In the kindest way, the three women would turn to face him with candid expressions. The fact was that their thoughts towards Chris lay hidden behind those bright eyes.

Some of the staff had gathered round the video and set it going. *The Deer Hunter* was playing. Chris went to the toilet, passing the television screen on his way, and on his return he froze like one of Salinee's ice cubes. Chris could see the actors Robert De Niro, Christopher Walken, and John Savage all drifting down a river. In the scene, strange and deformed rock formations had caused concern as the three men drifted underneath the crags. The overhanging rocks were the very same Chris had observed during his bat cave tour. He remembered how the skipper had pointed them out to him and at the time Chris did not understand why. Bubbling with excitement Chris rushed back to the bar and asked the three women, 'did they film *The Deer Hunter* on this river?'

'Yes, they stayed at this hotel,' Yuwadee casually answered.

'Sally knee,' Chris enquired, 'did you see the actors?'

'No, it was eight years ago,' she declared, 'we all still at school.'

Yuwadee and Apinior left to talk to a couple of waitresses. In the distance, Chris could see the four women chatting awhile, occasionally glancing in his direction. The awful thing was to understand only too clearly that he was the subject of vivacious gossip.

The smell of oriental food awoke his hunger senses.

'Sally knee,' Chris observed, 'if I order my food now, can the kitchen staff finish early?'

Salinee smiled at his suggestion.

'Yes, they can finish early if you eat now.'

Chris narrowed his eyes and sat with slumped shoulders as he read the Thai menu. It offered nothing plain, so he pretended to have difficulty in choosing a meal.

'Sally knee,' Chris asked, 'can you eat with me and help me choose?'

Half-believing she would turn him down, Chris observed her reaction with trepidation.

'Yes,' she agreed in a small voice.

At once Chris was in a happy schoolboy mood. He straightened his back and looked across the room. They made the decision to sit near the stage. Hoping to impress Salinee, he threw caution to the wind and ordered the hottest noodle soup. Pretty soon, Chris suffered in silence with his tongue twisting and lolling round his mouth as if he had chewed a wasp. The spotlights threw colours onto his face, which must have resembled some grotesque figure, of sorts. Fairly discreetly, he washed away all vestiges of chilli seed with several gulps of beer. The band had stopped playing, and from outside the sound of crickets began to serenade Salinee and Chris. They exchanged small smiles. It was obvious that they shared the same love of nature. Chris glanced towards the lounge and saw a sea of faces watching them with great curiosity.

'Sally knee,' Chris asked, 'do you like western rock music?'

'Ah! Live Aid,' she replied dreamily.

'Oh, yes, that was last summer – did you see it up here?'

'No, I see Queen in my home,' she told him cheerfully.

They had both finished eating and the bill arrived. It seemed incorrect, so Chris showed it to Salinee.

'I want to pay for your food as well?' Chris declared.

'No Chris! I am staff – I do not have to pay.'

'Oh! I understand,' Chris paused awhile, adding, 'Is your room free?'

Salinee nodded and explained, 'We have low money – but we have many tips and free food.'

Chris raised his glass but it was empty.

'Can I have another beer please?'

Salinee grinned and said, 'I think you want eat same as me – but it too hot for you.'

She stroked the back of his hand to console him.

'I enjoyed eating with you,' Chris commented.

Salinee's reaction was one of acute embarrassment.

Her cheeks reddened and she quickly said, 'I have to work now – I will get you another beer.'

Chris followed her like a metallic tack leaping towards a magnet. Again, with the aid of the English/Thai dictionary they talked until Salinee closed the bar. Once again Salinee was chaperoned safely back to her room by the woman from the kitchen.

With the ceiling fans now idle Chris sat there awhile, peering through the window at the star-filled sky and listening for sounds in the darkness outside. He sniffed the air and there was a strong odour of flowers. The gardener had done a good job, he thought. Back in his private kingdom of bedroom, Chris was so hot that he had to tear his clothes off and prance about under the air-conditioner. When he returned to his bed, sleep came easy to him.

In the morning Chris realised he had time on his hands. Salinee would not be seen until she opened the bar at 10.00. It was 8.45 and the heat was already uncomfortable. The shimmering swimming pool beckoned him. With the bravado of a bungee jumper, Chris leapt straight into the cool water. When he opened his eyes, he peered at the black figure of a bird walking along the footpath. It was the dreaded toucan. It stood still briefly and in an almost lemming-style jump leapt over a small rock onto the grassed garden. Chris closed his eyes, submerged his head and floated on his back. The liquid disembodied cries of birds extinguished like a doused flame. There, in the tremendous silence, Chris could imagine floating in the depths of outer space. Eventually, he slid out of the pool to succumb to his immense wish to stretch out under the burning sun. The rippling stream softened all his senses and he fell asleep with a beatific smile on his face.

Hot and bothered, Chris awoke panting like a domesticated dog lying too close to a gas fire. The sound of splashing water had woken him up. It intrigued him, as the hotel staff could not use the swimming pool. Bleary eyed, Chris peered at the pool in search of some connection between the moment before he fell asleep, and this moment of waking up. It took awhile before his organs of vision were attuned to the glare of the water. Chris was horrified to observe the toucan drowning before his very eyes. There it was, flapping its wings erratically and plunging its beak skywards in an attempt to stay alive. Chris sat up in alarm and jumped into the pool. Wading as quickly as he could through the heavy water, his legs like concrete, he cupped his hands like a wicket keeper and scooped the bird to safety. The toucan shook its wet feathers, bent over and waved its ruffled bottom at Chris. Then, it calmly shuffled its way towards the hotel leaving a trail of steaming footprints along the hot footpath. None of the staff knew what had happened. Chris decided dutifully to report his heroics.

He showered, and returned to the reception. In the lounge, looking every bit like Cleopatra on her barge, Apinior lay sprawled out along a cushioned couch. She caught sight of Chris at a distance, smiled and put her magazine down. He approached her and pointed a finger towards the toucan.

'Apinior,' Chris said shrilly, 'that bird fell in the swimming pool.'

She shifted slightly on her couch and tilted her face towards his.

'Don't worry,' she said cheerfully, 'he always keeps swimming until somebody sees him.'

Chris faced her with a foolish grin, then turned and strode towards the bar. Salinee was peering through the window frame in a bored gaze. In the guise of a violinist, she showed her bowing technique by vigorously filing her fingernails.

'Good morning, Sally knee,' Chris said cheerfully.

Salinee looked his way and their eyes met.

'Hello, Chris, you are late today.' He looked at his watch and saw it was 10.40.

'I rescued the bird from the swimming pool,' Chris said with a half-smile.

'The bird fall into swimming pool many times,' she casually replied.

Chris's eye twitched and he gave a deep sigh through his puckered lips.

'Can I have a cold beer please?' he said in a disgruntled tone.

'Yes, sir, I have many bottles for you.'

Salinee proudly opened the door to the refrigerator. He felt seduced by the sight of so many cold beers stacked high on each shelf.

'Are all those for me?' Chris cheekily asked.

'You are only guest here,' she replied with a wry grin, adding, 'I think you enjoy beer.'

Chris sat down and wiped the sweat from his brow.

'Can you turn the fan up please – I'm too hot.'

Salinee adjusted the controls and the lethargic whine increased to a deep humming noise, as if a helicopter lay hovering above their heads.

'Ah! That's better,' Chris said and sipped his beer.

The morning passed quickly. In the heat of midday, the air outside vibrated like strings on a harp. The landscape distorted into strange and unfamiliar shapes. In the distance treetops stood decapitated above their trunks. It all seemed as surreal as a melting clock. Chris ran his finger down the glass, disturbing the condensation that had formed on the outside. He took another drink. The cold beer felt good as it ran down his throat. It was his reward for saving the bird's life, he thought.

Suddenly, Chris could hear several loud voices shouting and laughing from outside. Chris craned his neck but he could see nothing. Then, the laughter and shouting appeared to come from below the restaurant. Salinee and Chris stood up and hurried across the wooden floor, her flip-flops clumping as she ran. They peered over the parapet. Several waiters had gathered round a flourishing bush. Some held stones while two others probed the undergrowth with large sticks. Another waiter held a bright red plastic bucket. It was the same bucket used by Salinee to collect the rainwater. The men all chuckled with enthusiasm, as if on a schoolboy fishing trip, of sorts.

'What is happening?' Chris asked Salinee.

She stood quite still, unblinking.

'They want to catch a cobra,' she whispered.

A shiver ran down Chris's spine. More laughter could be heard. Then, suddenly one man leapt sideways and dropped his stone. He yelled out to the others and pointed a finger towards the long grass. Chris's eyes widened as he saw the snake for the first time. The waiters gathered round. They hurled stones and beat it with their sticks. The helpless snake jerked as each blow struck its body. After a short period it lay dead. The waiters congratulated each other with soft blows to arms and shoulders. One waiter gleefully picked it up with his stick and dropped it into the bucket. There it lay, with its beaten body curled up like an anti-mosquito coil. Chris could see that the expression on Salinee's face had now changed from concern to disgust.

'What is happening now?' Chris asked her.

'They want to eat it,' she grumbled.

Having had no notion of what they was going to do with it, Chris recoiled in horror.

'They'll eat the cobra!' Chris asked, shrilly.

Salinee nodded and explained, 'If they eat the cobra, it gives the Thai man power for sex.'

In a strange way Chris felt sorry for the snake. He knew it had crossed the invisible boundary between jungle and hotel, but to be dealt with in such a cruel manner by those barbaric waiters caused him to shy away from the subject.

As an afterthought, Salinee added, 'If you eat garlic – it is good for sex.'

Chris grinned and cheekily said, 'I love garlic.'

Salinee's vacant expression told him that once again she had not understood his joke.

During the afternoon Chris found himself browsing through the souvenir shop. Like most single men, he found the essential problem of washing the few clothes he had brought with him insoluble. The only answer he could think of was to purchase more clothes. Chris held up a silk dressing gown monogrammed in the accepted oriental fashion of a dragon with Chinese lettering.

Apinior, the perpetual worrier, strolled over and asked, 'Can I show you the waterfall go into the river?'

She had a look of appeal on her face.

'Is it that waterfall?' Chris asked, pointing a finger towards the rock garden.

She nodded, and gazed at him with ventilating eyelids.

'Okay, let's go,' he replied.

They both walked past the bar.

Pensive, her face puzzled, Salinee asked Apinior, 'Where you going?'

Her voice had crackled with her first sign of emotion.

Apinior fumbled for an answer, 'umm – we . . .'

'We are going to see the waterfall,' Chris said bluntly.

Salinee's eyes lingered on both of them. They continued on their way, down the slippery steps towards the river. A nagging feeling entered Chris's head. Salinee had spoken English when confronting Apinior. He could tell that she was uncomfortable with their activities, but by speaking English, Chris surmised that she had wanted him fully to understand.

They reached the riverbank. Here, butterflies were in abundance. Their blurred shapes would briefly vanish, only to reappear, clear-cut, on a flower. Chris gave a backward glance to see the outline of the hotel shimmering in the hot, hazy air. Salinee's rueful face peered down at them through the open window. Chris brushed aside his concern and followed Apinior along the grassed riverbank. A dilapidated barbecue table lay abandoned under the shade of trees. They were out of sight now and the repeated cast of Apinior's glance fell on Chris furtive and swift. They walked into the shadows and a timbered footpath came into view. They stepped from log to log, with a slow and cautious walk. The air tasted stale and damp, as it filtered through the deep, dark foliage. This was no ambrosial heaven, Chris thought. Slowly, the concentrated calm was broken by the continuous clamour of flowing water. Then up they climbed like a restless cloud, elevated by an archaic footbridge. Standing there, Chris looked up towards the picture spread out in front of him. There were no glistening stones here, he thought, no finely polished rock face, just a sombre darkness of earth and water standing in solemn isolation amongst ancient trees. Chris peered through the slats beneath his feet. The wash of the waterfall sent a swift froth along a black slime. Apinior leaned against the handrail and began to fidget. She ran her hands on each side of her, low down. Her downward glare wandered right and left, eventually her eyes lingered on Chris's loins. No words were spoken. When her gaze finally rested on his face she pursed her lips and looked at him with lowered eyelids. A hint of sexual desire showed in Apinior's eyes.

'It's nice,' Chris commented, and quickly suggested, 'shall we go back now?'

Apinior looked astonished and her round soft cheeks quivered.

'You want to go back now?' she said, openly displaying her disappointment.

'Yes, I want to go back to Sally knee.'

They returned after only 20 minutes, thus giving a clear message to Apinior that he was not interested in her. Besides, Chris was determined that such a consideration would not find fertile ground. He feared what Salinee might think if they spent too many hours cloistered in the shadows. They arrived back at the bar and Chris bought Apinior and Salinee a drink to iron out any differences between them.

The afternoon matured and, to the surprise of everyone, a black Mercedes pulled up parallel to the bar window. It had a Bangkok number plate. Chris wondered what business it was that brought such a car to this hotel. They all stared into the tinted windows to see who was at the wheel. At that instant, the door was flung open and out stepped a western man. The stranger made his way to the reception.

'Do you know who that is?' Chris asked Salinee.

She shook her head and spoke to Apinior in Thai. Apinior stood up and casually walked over to the reception area. In the distance Chris caught sight of his face. The man grinned, opened a large briefcase and took out a business card. Apinior stood close, she was eavesdropping on their conversation. Salinee and Chris watched keenly as she returned. To Chris's irritation, he could barely hear, for she whispered, afraid she would be overheard.

'He is American, he want to stay one night and look at hotel for conference,' she explained.

Chris nodded to show he understood.

The sun was now setting and, like a gleaming krugerrand, the sky had turned to a disc of gold. Below, the fast moving river drained out of the jungle. Watching it, Chris felt a sweet, smug satisfaction that he was here to witness it all.

Time passed quickly and the American guy eventually came to the bar.

The lean, wiry man sat down and said to Salinee, 'Hello, gal, Singha beer please.'

'Are you staying here long?' Chris asked him.

'Ain't sure – maybe one night. I'm looking at the hotel facilities for a possible conference in November.'

'You're not a tourist then.'

The stranger grinned, shook his head and explained, 'I live and work in the north of Thailand. Near Chiang Mai.'

'How long have you lived there?' Chris asked.

'I came to Thailand in sixty-nine. I love the oriental way of life, I first experienced it in Saigon.'

Chris's eyes lit up.

'Was you in the Vietnam War?' he asked.

'Yeah,' the stranger said sadly.

'You don't look old enough to have been in that war.'

'I'm forty five – the orient is kind to your body.'

A broad smile stretched his tanned face.

Chris turned to Salinee and said, 'Look at him – he's forty five.'

Salinee looked genuinely shocked as she examined his youthful good looks.

'Oh! You look young, sir,' she said cheerfully.
'Thank you,' he replied in a whisper.
'Were you a conscript?' Chris asked.
Chris's lips started to form his expected answer of yeah.
'No! I was already a soldier,' he replied. He squirmed on his seat and fumbled for a cigarette, adding, 'Somehow, I managed to survive the war.' With a burning look in his eyes he abruptly said, 'Dammit, there was no way I was letting them send me back. I had no other option but to leave the army.'
'America had no chance of winning then,' Chris said negligently. The American frowned. Chris hesitated, and as an afterthought quickly added, 'What I mean is – if the army regulars didn't want to go back, then the draftees couldn't have had the heart to fight.'
The American looked at him square in the eyes and replied, 'Yeah, yeah, I know – y'all can say that, but our government wasn't prepared for that jungle. Everything we had that was made of leather turned green and rotted away.' He was enlivened now and began to make facial expressions as he spoke.
'Charlie dressed like peasants, we couldn't tell em apart. Their sandals were even cut out of truck tires.' The stranger sighed and took a drag from his cigarette, 'We all expected to whip their butts, but it didn't happen. Goddammit, we had the finest computers in the world sifting through the intelligence, but command didn't listen to the GIs who were doing the actual fighting.'
Chris interrupted and opined, 'It was not until the public protests and demonstrations made the news that your government admitted to the real story, which was that you where actually losing the war.'
The man gave Chris an impatient glare, shook his head and protested, 'They didn't admit to it until years after the war had ended.' He hesitated a moment, wrinkled his brow

and said, 'Oh, the hell with it. Hey, why ain't you in Bangkok enjoying the boom-boom girls?'

The American had successfully changed the subject.

Chris glanced at Salinee and explained, 'I'm staying up here to talk to Sally knee – I want to get to know her.'

The American gave Salinee a slow, lingering stare. She was now trying to ignore their conversation by working on some paperwork.

'I have some advice for you, young man,' the American asserted, 'I have a oriental wife and if you want to keep her happy just give the gal a home.'

Chris nodded in agreement and considered his comments for a moment.

'How much green did you pay to fly here?' the American asked him.

'About eight hundred pounds,' Chris replied.

'Jeez, that's about one thousand two hundred bucks. Now that's expensive.'

The American finished his beer and glanced at his watch. He saw it was 11.30.

'I'm going to my room now,' he said and beckoned Salinee with his finger. Salinee gave him a pen and indicated to a dotted line. He scribbled his signature on the bill. 'Goodnight,' the stranger said and shook Chris's hand.

Chris was left with the happy thought that his oriental wife had probably reshaped him for the better.

11

Chaperone

Chris's last evening at the hotel had arrived. Whilst sitting on a barstool with his arms crossed over his chest, Chris found himself staring at the ceiling fans. Those long rotating blades, forming a perfectly round shape that stood out with a transparent, almost motionless solidity caused him to reflect awhile. Reflect upon the ridiculous fact that he had not spent a single moment alone with Salinee, apart from in the hotel bar and restaurant. Tomorrow they would both depart for their homes, which under normal circumstances would not have been a problem, except that in their case, they just happened to live more than 7,000 miles apart. It was a cruel and ludicrous joke, one that Chris thought he did not deserve. That apart, Chris was not sure if Salinee had any feelings whatsoever for him. Chris shook his head sadly.

'Chris,' Salinee observed, 'what is the matter?'

He straightened his neck and reached for his glass of beer.

'Sally knee,' Chris admitted, 'I feel sad. Tomorrow I have to go home and I will not see you for a long time.'

Salinee stroked his wrist, sympathetically.

'Sally knee, I want to write to you. Will you give me your address please?'

Salinee shook her head and hesitated a short moment.

'It is better you write to this hotel,' she replied, warming to his suggestion.

Like a cardsharp, Salinee quickly produced a thin cardboard beer coaster advertising the hotel and bar. She turned it over and with her black ballpoint pen wrote down her name and address. She passed it to Chris with a polite smile. He studied her insecure handwriting. She had written down the hotel's Bangkok office.

'Who will bring my letters up here?' Chris enquired, wondering.

'The tour guide,' she replied vaguely.

'Do you mean Harry?'

'Probably.'

'How do you pronounce your surname?' Chris asked with a puzzled brow and offered, 'is it Tin can?'

'No! It is Tinkran,' she said firmly.

Chris grinned.

'Can I have a piece of paper? Chris suggested, 'I want to give you my address.'

She tore out a page from her notebook and passed it to him. In his best handwriting Chris wrote down his home address.

He passed her the sheet of paper and, being fairly pedantic asked, 'Can I see you write it out please?'

'I can write it,' she replied, in great surprise.

After a short pause she resumed with, 'If you write to me – I will write to you.'

Chris smiled broadly.

'Sally knee,' he said, 'I wanted us to go somewhere together, before I went back home.'

She gazed into his eyes and paused a moment in deep thought.

Finally she whispered, 'We can go to the Hindard hot spring tomorrow morning.'

Chris gave her a deep, thankful stare.

'Yes please – thank you,' he whispered.

Salinee highlighted a possible barrier by suddenly asking, 'Can you ride a motorcycle?'

A knowing twinkle came into his eyes.

'Yes, I have a motorcycle at home,' he replied quickly. 'But whose motorcycle can we use?' Chris observed, wondering.

'We can go on a waiter's motorcycle, but you must pay him some money,' she explained.

'Okay, I will pay anything to go somewhere with you.' Her suggestion had in it the entire elements dear to Chris's heart: Salinee, a motorcycle and a natural spring.

'Will we have any helmets?' Chris enquired. Salinee shrugged her shoulders.

'Oh! See what . . .' his voice trailed away. Chris paused for a few seconds in deep thought, and resumed with, 'Whatever you do try and get a helmet – even if there is only one for you.'

Salinee smiled and quickly said, 'Yes, sir.'

'What time will we go?' Chris challenged her, 'because I have to be back to catch my tour bus.'

'Ten o'clock,' she replied and made her way to the lounge. She returned soon after, and explained, 'The waiter wants three hundred baht for his motorcycle and fifty baht for one helmet.'

'That's okay,' Chris said and insisted, 'but I want you to wear the helmet.'

Salinee nodded and topped up his glass.

Fifteen minutes passed by, whereupon Terapat was at Chris's side with an uncharacteristic, wry grin on his face. Chris had hardly had sight of him, ever since his failed seduction of Youst had shown his true colours. Chris could see he had something on his mind.

Terapat leaned over and whispered to Chris, 'Are you going with Salinee tomorrow?'

'Yes, we are going to the Hindard hot spring,' Chris replied with sudden pride in his voice.

Terapat's face changed to one of solemn concern.

He sighed and said, 'Salinee is a lady who wants only one man in her life, so don't take her into the bushes.'

'No, I won't do that,' Chris protested at once.

Chris wondered how he knew so quickly that they were going out. Then he realised that Salinee had confided in Terapat. It had become glaringly obvious that Terapat thought himself an agony aunt of sorts, always keen to help his female colleagues in their personal relationships. Chris guessed that the women trusted him, his sexuality posing no threat towards them.

Later, Chris was once again reminded of his foolish, bad behaviour on that first evening. The woman from the kitchen had now arrived. Her ashen-grey face looked weary and exhausted from her hard day's work. Chris felt sorry for the woman. She had obviously stayed up late until Salinee closed the bar. Instinctively, Chris glanced at his watch and sure enough it was nearly eleven o'clock.

'Goodnight Sally knee, I will see you tomorrow.'

Chris emptied his glass and strolled back to his room.

Pretty soon, he lay on his canary-yellow bedspread masturbating and in a self-contradictory fashion yearned for his final day to arrive. He had an intense desire to be with Salinee and, after he had finished, sleep did not come easily. He was perfectly aware that juggling melancholic thoughts with romantic mistiness would plunge him into a bottomless spiral of insomnia. But juggle he did, long into the early hours, only eventually to founder through a state of inactivity known as sleep.

Chris's last day had unfortunately arrived and, with deep anxiety, he sat in the lounge waiting for Salinee to show her face. Chris glanced at his hands. They were trembling slightly, so he quickly hid them inside his pockets. Chris was wearing short trousers and a tee shirt, and with no helmet or gloves he would soon break every motorcycle safety rule. Chris shook his head sadly and bit his lip. Nobody can travel 7,000 miles and take no risks at all, he thought. Anyway, a date spent with Salinee was worth it. Chris's eyes wandered over the room, up and down. In the end they settled on the front page of last week's *Bangkok Post*. The main photograph showed a child aged no more than eight. There he stood, at the kerbside in Bangkok, quite alone, with his mother's dead body under the wheels of a car.

'Good morning, Chris,' Salinee said softly.

Chris looked up and gaped: her mere appearance was like a balm to his early morning nerves. This was his first sight of her out of uniform. It was like chocolate to a child's palate. She wore a flowery brown shirt and dark denim jeans. A thought entered his head: today he must take plenty of photographs. After all, it was his last chance to obtain her image.

'Hello, Sally knee, you look nice.'

'Thank you, we must go now,' she pointed a finger outside.

In the distance Chris caught sight of Apinior and the nauseatingly suave gardener. There was a long pause. Not a word was spoken. Chris felt uneasy. The recognisable appearance of their hotel uniforms were nowhere to be seen. The gardener's face wore an inspired and keen expression. A large penny dropped inside Chris's head and his heart sank, which was no wonder, since he now realised they would not be alone. Salinee would have two chaperones joining them. Chris turned his eyes back to Salinee. Any date with Salinee, even with two chaperones was better than nothing at all, he thought. Chris decided to make the most of it and keep her happy. They strolled over and Chris greeted the two intruders with a forced smile. After all, he had no choice but to put up with them. To Chris's further disappointment, it soon became apparent that Apinior was to ride with him. Salinee had now placed the helmet over her head and straddled the gardener's sporty motorcycle. Apinior and Chris were left with a disappointing trial motorcycle, complete with torn seat that exposed its yellow foam stuffing. Chris placed the only protection he had over his head, his sunglasses, and peered at the gardener's face. The gardener conveyed an impression of being completely safe and secure leaning against his dream machine. Chris watched with a malevolent stare, as the gardener smoothed his short black hair with his hands and zipped up his leather motorcycle jacket.

Chris kick-started the two-stroke engine and the exhaust pipe cried out at full volume. It is a Thai faculty, thought Chris always, to remove the unnecessary mufflers as soon as a motorcycle has left the showroom, thus, transforming the machine into a screaming cyclone. Apinior straddled the seat and wrapped her arms tightly round Chris's waist. The gardener thumbed his electric start button and threw Chris a glance over his shoulder. In an instant the gardener sped off around the corner and up the 'clenched buttocks ride'. He had caught Chris by surprise and would have been satisfied with his swift exit. Chris followed in hot pursuit, convinced the gardener would make a concerted effort to pull away and embarrass him in front of Salinee. Chris banked left and then right. He surprised himself by naïvely selecting the wrong gear, causing the motorcycle to stutter to an abrupt halt. The severity of the gradient began to drag the two of them towards the river. Apinior leapt off, allowing Chris to dig his heels in and stabilise the motorcycle. Chris cast an eye at Apinior. She raised her eyebrows, questioning his competence.

'Sorry! Not a very good start,' Chris said humbly and grinned foolishly.

After several attempts he started the engine and they

finally made it to the top, where the gardener waited, dryly amused.

'Are you okay?' Salinee hollered.

Chris nodded and they set off again. There was no traffic on the main highway, so Chris soon anticipated a pleasant ride. Chris decided to take up a positive, more central position in the left-hand lane. He gazed ahead. What Chris saw pleased him. By riding near the hard shoulder, thus adopting a more conservative position, the gardener had put Salinee's safety first. In a profound, almost symbolic vision, her red helmet gleamed in the morning sunlight like a red cherry waiting to be picked. Chris inflated his lungs, determined to return and claim that cherry.

Half an hour passed and Chris soon found out that, unlike riding a motorcycle in Britain, here the dry tropical air evaporates the sweat forming on your face far too quickly. In spite of this, as soon as it has gone any fall in speed and your sweat glands open up to fulfil the cycle. One thing does remain the same though, Chris observed. Just as in Britain, insects still insist on spreading their internal organs across the lenses of your sunglasses.

They were travelling north-north-west, following the river valley. The morning sun was still behind them and Chris could see their shadows racing along the tarmac. On passing a large wooden bus shelter, he caught a brief glimpse of a woman and three small children sitting in the shade. The children's ill-fitting clothes, perhaps hand-me-downs, suggested they came from a large family. In the distance, a large advertising hoarding showing three scantly dressed Thai women wielding machine guns appeared from nowhere. Soon, Chris saw that it was an artist's impression of a Thai movie. The advertisement promised revealing glimpses of the glamorous women, but in reality, the movie would only feature very hostile female fighters, albeit they would not be clothed in a very sensible way for combat.

They rode past the advertisement, which instantly brought a wide grin to Chris's face.

Ahead of them, the brake lights on the gardener's motorcycle lit up. Chris too slowed down and followed them onto a gravel car park. Smells of cooking greeted them. It was a small ramshackle village and market, selling fruit, drinks and food. After parking the bikes on their side-stands, they all strolled over the uneven ground towards a shop. Cold soft drinks were rapidly consumed by each of them. They stood and lingered awhile; a large and dusty white sheet caught Chris's eye. It was held taught by a rusting framework and seemed to dominate the entire scene. Chris wondered what it could possibly be used for. Perhaps a sunshade of sorts, as it appeared to be the focal point of the whole market. The sheet fluttered in the slightest of breezes and the sky made a blotch of glorious blue in the tattered right-hand corner.

'What's that?' Chris asked Salinee, his voice a nudge.

'For the movies,' she replied.

Then Chris quickly realised they had come to a small dilapidated drive-in cinema.

'They watch movies on that!' Chris exclaimed, pointing an accusing finger.

Salinee said nothing and, apart from the slight twitch of her nose, remained quite still. Chris wanted to ask a battery of questions but time was short. They returned to their motorcycles and when Chris sat down his sweaty thighs fried against the hot seat. He leapt off immediately and fairly comically blew on the black vinyl. Apinior giggled, girlishly.

They rejoined the road and Chris noticed that in the short time they had stopped the temperature had increased as if on a logarithmic scale. The ferocious sun seemed to have transformed their surroundings into a furnace. Ahead of them, the heat of the day appeared to force up the tarmac and created the illusion of a vast expanse of shimmering water. The illusion kept pace with them and, like a rainbow, always out of arm's reach. Heat rose from Chris's air-cooled engine and passed up the inside of his thighs. It was too hot, so he began to open and close his legs in an insinuating rhythm. Apinior must have noticed, as Chris felt her grip his waist even tighter.

The gardener beeped his horn three times and pointed towards the road. Through the heat haze Chris could just distinguish the vague outline of a dead animal. Chris moved towards the centre of the road and slowed down to a crawling pace. Numerous flies circled and covered the light brown fur of a dog. As the motorcycles approached the corpse, the horrible flies dispersed, temporarily curtailing their need to plant eggs into the soft decaying flesh. Sickened at the sight of such a distasteful scene, Chris refused to take one last look in his wing mirror. At least he wasn't condemned to stare at their raisin-like bodies and that poor dog, he thought. Suddenly, a loud air-horn bellowed from behind. Chris glanced at his wing mirror and paled. A large bus was hurtling towards them at great speed. It gave him another, much longer blast like a large ocean liner arriving in port. Chris veered off the road onto the gravel, finishing only inches away from a ditch of foul-smelling water. The bus hurtled past, with the conductor hanging precariously from the open door. He turned his head to face Chris and hollered several words in Thai. The conductor's face told Chris they were words of rebuke. Chris inhaled a lung full of diesel fumes and was immediately aware of the reason why the gardener had not taken up a central position in their lane. It seemed to Chris that these huge buses had them wholly at their mercy, believing that they owned the roads; nothing ever stands in their way. Chris now saw no reason to differ from the gardener's judgement. He returned back to the road, firmly intending to follow the gardener's rear wheel.

The jungle-covered hills around them gradually increased in height as they neared the Burmese border. The road meandered, and then cut back away from the direction they should have been going, forcing the sun to briefly scorch Chris's face. Finally, to his relief they turned back again and the sun was behind them. It was like riding through an elaborate tapestry of marvellously rich shades of green. The trees and creepers clung to the hills like a long beard, never to be shorn.

The motorcycle ahead slowed down and indicated left. Chris followed and they turned off the road, passing a small sign in Thai and English. They had arrived at Hindard hot spring. Half a dozen Toyota pick-up trucks stood parked in the shade of trees. Both motorcycles joined them in the relative darkness. Here, alongside dead grasshoppers, the gritty floor was still damp with the strong odour of sodden leaves and twigs scattered about Chris's feet, the last remnants of a great hosing of rain. The earth steamed where the sun's yellow beam peeped through the leaves and caught a patch of damp soil.

It was a Sunday and a few Thai families ate lunch outside a small, dilapidated shop. They stepped off their motorcycles and the four of them stood quite still, their eyes staring ahead, piercingly. A lean mongrel dog had welcomed them with a rather ominous growl. There it stood, in a stand-off position, with eyes aflame and a haughty snarl on its face. On hearing the gruff voice of the shopkeeper shout crossly, the canine menace pricked up its ears and walked away with its tail between its legs. Still mumbling obscenities, the man waited and then spat at his dog. The shopkeeper had missed and calmly stretched out a leg to rub out the spit with his sandal, only inches away from a customer's table. Undeterred, the customer continued to eat.

The reverberating sound of water, which rises and falls

quickly, could be heard beneath a concrete footbridge. Chris walked over and stood on the footbridge. Salinee and the others followed. Beneath them the angry brown foam of a stream had crumbled the muddy banks, exposing a network of tree roots. A small branch, hanging by a thread after the deluge, suddenly fell into the wash, sending up a splash of water. They all watched as it was carried away below them, only to re-emerge a second later from the other side. Women's and children's laughter could be heard in the distance. They walked closer, and now Chris could clearly see people's heads and upper torsos. They were sitting in rudimentary concrete baths, which had been constructed in a jungle clearing above hydrothermal crevices.

Chris placed his hand into the clear salubrious water and opined, 'This is too hot for me.'

Salinee looked disconcerted and turned sulky. For a moment everybody seemed to have lost his or her tongue. A half-smile lingered on Chris's lips and he quickly stripped off to his swimming trunks.

'Oh all right then – let's get in,' he cheerfully said.

Salinee and Apinior undressed down to baggy shorts and shirts. Chris had hoped they would have worn swimming costumes, but it was clear to see that all the other Thai women wore similar shorts and shirts. Chris began to realise that he was observing the genuine Thai article, not the revealing sexy beachwear worn by the prostitutes of Bangkok or Pattaya. This was the more traditional and discreet approach to courtship.

The hot mineral spring water soon overpowered Chris. He had no intention of becoming a boiled lobster, so retreated to the concrete ledge and dangled his feet in the water. To his surprise, the gardener never ventured in. He had returned to the motorcycles after watching the women undress. So this was Chris's date with Salinee, bathing in a public bath and surrounded by the jungle. It was certainly different, thought Chris.

Time was short, so after half an hour they decided enough was enough. On retracing their journey back to the hotel, they passed the flattened ribcage of the dead dog. Towards the centre of the highway, torn meat, fur and muscle now lay scattered along the tarmac. Very soon, the traffic would eventually destroy all traces of the canine beast together with any grey-white maggots. Chris looked skywards as the sun dimmed. Clouds had formed in the distance. Rain perhaps. Chris began to worry, as he certainly did not desire riding through a deluge of monsoon rain. His motorcycle backfired, adding more worry. What would happen if they broke down? Chris thought. He would miss the tour bus back to Bangkok and then, once again, he realised that a more important thing was about to happen. Very soon he would be saying goodbye to Salinee. Chris's heart sank. All that day, from time to time, he had confronted the same agitation of mind: How to say goodbye to a loved one? Chris had never been in love before. He had seen it many times in movies, of course, and would laugh aloud as his mother reached for the tissues, but this time it was he. How would he handle it? Chris glanced in his rear view mirror. A distant shower scratched a grey, slanting stripe above the hills. Now Chris's attitude towards the jungle changed. Until then, during his brief duration here, he had considered himself an integral component of it. But now the jungle seemed to distinguish itself from him, allowing Chris to memorise it as a whole entity, forever engraved in his brain.

Pretty soon, they arrived back at the hotel. The tour bus had already arrived and the new guests and day-trippers ate their lunch in the restaurant.

'Sally knee,' Chris said, 'thank you – I enjoyed that. Before I go can I take some more photographs?'

'Yes, we can meet here,' she replied and walked quickly towards her room.

After checking out Chris ate a sandwich at the bar. Salinee was off duty now and had been replaced by a smiling waiter. The bar lacked the same atmosphere, triggering a horrible scenario in Chris's mind. What if he had come here when Salinee was at home? He could have gone back to Bangkok without ever meeting her. Chris shuddered at the thought of it and began to wonder about all of those indiscriminate changes in his past that had shaped his life. They were commonly known as luck. Nevertheless, this so-called luck, whether it is good or bad, was now manifesting into an uncharacteristic whirligig.

At last, and not too soon, Chris saw Salinee walking towards the reception. She had changed her clothes and was now wearing white trousers and a red and white striped tee shirt. Chris finished his drink and met her.

Yuwadee joined them, and suggested, 'Shall I take your photographs?'

'Yes please,' Chris said cheerfully. He turned to face Salinee and enquired, 'Where shall we take them?'

Salinee looked round with a puzzled gaze, a tell-tale sign that she had never had her photograph taken there before.

'Over there, next to the flowers,' she replied.

Salinee and Chris stood next to each other as Yuwadee held the camera. Their arms hung straight down, motionless, as if they were a couple of mannequins. No body contact was made. After two clicks of the shutter Salinee moved and returned to Yuwadee. Chris felt disappointed, as he was quite prepared to stand with Salinee until his roll of film had completely finished.

They stood around awhile, waiting until it was time to go. With Chris's hands now sweating profusely, he gazed into Salinee's eyes.

'Sally knee,' he said, 'I will come back to see you again.'

'Goodbye, Chris,' she replied.

They parted and Chris joined the other tourists on the air-conditioned bus, thus saying goodbye to that deep transparent smell of trees, flowers and river. The driver started the engine. It was the noise Chris had been dreading for days. Chris was depressed by the way in which, before their departure, he was allowed to sit and wait, in a forlornly hesitant manner. Chris wanted to press his face against the glass that separated him and Salinee. It was an agonising wait, but eventually the driver set off and Chris waved to Salinee through the window. They turned the corner and she was out of sight. Chris was travelling now, putting distance between them, a lot of distance, oceans and continents between them. He felt sick and bereft at the thought of it.

12

Air Mail

Chris arrived back home in a state of apprehension. Pretty soon, he placed Salinee's framed photograph beside his bed and banished all vestiges of Wanna's image into a gimcrack paper wallet. Chris was pleased that he had decided against meeting Wanna in Pattaya and had stayed with Salinee those extra days. This way, Wanna would never know of his return to Thailand. However, with Salinee's new photograph in mind, Chris's parents still knew nothing of his intentions towards her. Nevertheless, Chris did detect some disapproval from his father. His father was a proud, hard-working middle-aged man, who quite often would remind other family members that his shatterproof safety spectacles were issued free from work, as if a perk, of sorts, for his efforts.

One morning he entered Chris's bedroom with a cup of tea, and with a scornful snigger said, 'Do yer know that if yer have any kids – they'll be half-caste.'

He had meant it as a joke and was merely acting out the role of wise old father. But there was enough seriousness in his joviality to cause discomfort. Chris took the hot cup of tea from his father's rough, work-worn hand and gave his comment no credence whatsoever. Chris listened as the back door was opened and then locked. His father had begun his early morning walk, which a doctor had recommended to aid his phlebitic legs; legs, which now resembled a well-matured, blue cheese, due to standing in front of a lathe for years on end. Chris drank his cup of tea and Salinee stared out at him from the picture frame. The artistry of the photograph was flat and amateur, but it did capture a moment in time, a record of their only date and the last few moments they had spent together. Chris glanced at his alarm clock. It was six o'clock and Salinee would be working in the bar, possibly serving the lunchtime day-trippers. At that moment, Chris could imagine the squeak of her cloth, as she wiped a cocktail glass.

Chris dressed and set off for work. He had a mission now, a mission to earn as much disposable money as possible. At work he was as lively as a squirrel gathering nuts, cracking as much overtime as they would allow him to do. However, rather disturbingly, Chris found that during his lunch breaks he would wander aimlessly around the town with a sense of superiority. He felt different from the rest of the crowd. He had been up that river, into the depths of the jungle and had fallen in love with a woman born thousands of miles away. Chris had found his destiny, but had still to fulfil his dream. He had a strong overwhelming urge to shout and tell all of them what had happened to him. He refrained from doing so, but common sense did not prevail. Chris came to the absurd conclusion that it was their fault that they were unaware as to what had happened to him. It was they who were walking around wearing blinkers, carrying on in their petty ways. They would all remain blind, never to experience the delights of that mystical river. He would pause on the street, outside a travel agent and then hesitate inside a newsagent's shop.

Enough was enough, thought Chris. It was time to write a letter. After all, he had now waited four days since writing to Salinee from his Bangkok hotel. Chris brought a pack of air mail envelopes and writing paper. Those inanimate sealed packages were his only source of communication and, unfortunately, he would have to rely on complete strangers to deliver them. Chris shook his head sadly and insisted that he calm himself down. He was not the only person to have found himself or herself in a similar position. Other people had relied on the post for many years to foster a relationship. In spite of this, Chris would still require his letters to be hand-delivered by the tour guide, probably Harry. Harry might decide to open and read them himself, and after a good laugh with his mates in a bar might throw them away. Chris shook his head again. He was becoming paranoid. Chris decided to write a letter that very night.

Two weeks elapsed and there was still no reply from Salinee. Paranoia had set in once more and Chris had become increasingly isolated. Each evening he was immured in his bedroom drinking and listening to the Pink Floyd or Elton John. With the air inside his room reeking of cider and new leather from a motorcycle jacket, Chris was afloat in a musical bubble. He felt helpless, like an insect trapped in a web of his own making. Putting thousands of miles between him and Salinee, and feeling a weaker sun against his skin, had forced his confidence to sink to rock bottom. From England, their precarious relationship appeared even more fragile, like a nest of eggs on a cliff face: one bad storm, someone's seductive smile, and he could find himself up the creek without a paddle.

Then one evening, Chris arrived home to be greeted by a bluish air mail envelope. He held it up, and instantly recognised the insecure handwriting as the same written on the beer coaster.

'It's from Sally Knee,' he said, half-aloud to his parents and went up the stairs to his room. Chris opened the letter and read her reply, blinking a little faster than usual.

20/6/86
Dear Chris.
  I am happy when I got your letter again because before I got letter form Bangkok and I hope you received my letter. I thank you very much for photograph. Could you give me your photograph please? What did you photograph in your bedroom? I think you are work hard some me. I hope you and your family are in good heath and everything suceess for you.
  Sincerity your.
  Salinee

A puzzled frown pinched Chris's forehead, as he tried to decipher her awful grammar and spelling. With each sentence he picked up traces of her accent as if she were in the very same room. However, what did she mean by the question: 'what did you photograph in your bedroom?' Chris scratched his head trying to fathom it out. If somebody else were to read this letter, thought Chris, they might assume he had photographed himself naked in the privacy of his own bedroom. Was Salinee merely voicing a reasonable question, or was it a contrived request for such an intimate photograph? Chris read the sentence again. She might have expected the chief emphasis to fall on any one of the seven words. Half an hour elapsed and Salinee was still saying, '*What* did you photograph in your bedroom? ... what did *you* photograph in your bedroom? ... what did you *photograph* in your bedroom? ... what did you photograph in your *bedroom?*' Then it dawned on him. She had misunderstood a sentence from his letter. In it, Chris had commented that he had placed her photograph in his bedroom. He shook his head, sighed, and read her letter again. Chris's heart sank. There was no sign of romance or affection in her words whatsoever. She had simply replied to his letter out of pure politeness. But wait a moment, there was a sentence that instantly raised his spirits. Chris read it again: 'Could you give me your photograph please?' He placed the letter back inside its envelope and with supreme confidence wrote a number one in the top left-hand corner.

From that moment on, Chris wrote two letters to Salinee each week. The texture of the air mail writing paper became so deeply ingrained as to seem an innate part of his fingers. Then once more there was silence, a silence like the grave. Chris seemed entirely alone in his frustration and distress. But he remained assiduous and diligent. He painstakingly continued to express his feelings and affection in a constant stream of letters. Chris was conscious of the weakness in his own knowledge of the subject, so he sought advice on the style and content of love letters. Chris chose a work colleague named John. John was a married man in his early thirties, inclining to baldness. There was an expression of pure benignity on John's face, as he gazed over Chris's letter under the fierce strip lights. John's piscine eyes were wide, their pale blue exactly matching the colour of the air mail writing paper. He appeared to be a good choice, as Chris considered him to have a mild and gentle temperament with the ability to respect other people's frankness. Nonetheless, the faintly crooked smile that went with his suggestions should have warned Chris of things to come. The whole episode turned out to be a huge mistake. To Chris's horror, John had memorised his letters and told all and sundry, thus making Chris the laughing stock of the office. With thunder-flash eyes and a severe frown, Chris stood back and remained mute, making a sorrowful appraisal of John.

Revenge came sweet though, by a stroke of irony, that astonished the office as much as it astonished Chris. John's meek and naïve disposition proved to be his Achilles heel. One morning, John came into the office looking morose and unsociable. His whey face soon sought advice and he confided in another man who was considered by many to be a cross-grained person, well versed in bigotry. It proved to be a bad choice. Very soon, John too became the laughing stock of the office, only more so. Apparently, John's wife was having an affair. The lover had been allowed to move into their house and was shagging the wife on a regular basis. All this was happening whilst John was forced to sleep in the spare room. The lover had literally got his feet under the breakfast table. Chris failed to understand how John could tolerate such goings-on. It was the best example Chris had ever come across of somebody taking the piss. But it certainly brought the message home to Chris. He would never trust anybody from work again, wherever he was working.

Four weeks elapsed and there was still no news from Salinee. The letterbox failed to regurgitate any reply. Chris would see postmen and postwomen everywhere, delivering letters with the urgency of creeping ivy. Why was Salinee's reply taking so long? Perhaps he had opened his heart too soon and frightened her away, he thought. On the other hand, Harry the tour guide might not have delivered his letters at all. Chris experienced emotional turmoil and wanted to forget his troubles in drink and sleep. One hot night, whilst he slept with the window open, Chris dreamt that an aeroplane had been hijacked abroad. All of his letters were on the aircraft. For several days the aeroplane lay on the airport runway, surrounded by Special Forces. His whole love life was in the balance, totally at the mercy of crazed hijackers. Chris woke up sweating, and worrying that he might be going insane.

Then to Chris's joy her second letter arrived. The creased and tattered envelope had all the marks of serious travel on it. Inside his bedroom Chris cast an eye over her reply.

23/7/86

Dear Chris.

I hope you are in good health too. I sorry, you didn't get my letter but do not worry. You can tell me, when do you came back again. Because I can changeable off my friend, but I can't work off Friday – Sunday you know. Now I study English in Open University you know. Sometime I not understand, I ask Terapat (your guide before). I will write you more in my next letter. Thank you.
  Sincerily yours.
  Salinee

This letter meshed exactly with the theme that was running in Chris's head. In one resounding chord, it pealed notes of victory. His diligence appeared to have paid off. Salinee had suggested that she wanted to take time off work and go somewhere with him. Also, her spelling and grammar had slightly improved. Chris gathered that she was now making a serious effort to get it right. Perhaps that was why she had started her English course at the Thai Open University. Chris wrote a number two in the top left-hand corner and decided to pay the travel agent a visit the next day.

In an attempt to declare his unconditional love for Salinee, no price was considered too high. Mindful of the fact that Salinee and Chris would travel elsewhere for a short break, he decided to pay through the nose and chose a tailor-made, three-week holiday at her hotel. Chris wrote to Salinee informing her of his travel plans. For the first time in his life, Chris would jeopardise his family Christmas by flying out on Boxing Day.

13

Heed the Eyes of Argus

A small quantity of beer spilled over Chris's knee as the aeroplane shook like a flapping flag. With a foolish grin on his face Chris glanced at the ferret-faced man sitting next to him. Neither he nor his mother had noticed Chris's mishap. The man was about Chris's age, in his late twenties, and Chris wondered why he was taking his mother to Thailand.

'Has yer mom bin to Thailand before?' Chris asked him.

'No,' the stranger replied, 'I want her to meet my girlfriend in Pattaya.' In an instant Chris remembered Wanna. The stranger sighed, unhappily. 'I wanted my girlfriend to visit England last summer,' he resumed after a pause, 'but she couldn't get a visa.'

'Oh!' Chris raised his eyebrows in surprise. 'Wot wuz the problem?' Chris asked him.

The stranger straightened his back, drew his stomach in and threw out his chest. Chris listened carefully.

'Because she works in Pattaya,' the stranger said, 'you know – in a bar.'

The stranger's voice had emphasised the word 'bar'.

There was a brief silence and then Chris admitted, 'I want my girlfriend to visit England one day. Do yer think she might have a problem getting a visa?'

The stranger shrugged his shoulders and replied, 'Depends if she's got a proper job.'

'Yes,' Chris nodded, 'she werks at the River Kwai Village hotel.'

'You shouldn't have a problem then,' replied the stranger and he continued to study his magazine. Chris peered over his shoulder. Inside the magazine, a colour photograph of the King and Queen of a Thailand regarded Chris and the stranger with a chilly, marital gaze.

'Wot are yer going to do?' Chris asked.

'Well, if my mum meets her it may help to get the visa.'

He turned round to face his elderly mother. The woman was fast asleep, her wizened face expressive, with lips curled in grimace. In fact, she looked quite dead. The flight had been too much for her, thought Chris. Perhaps the whole trip would be an ordeal. Chris sensed an air of desperation in the stranger's actions and he feared for his own future.

'When do yer fly back?' Chris asked.

'In three weeks – on flight TG917.'

'Great! That's my return flight,' said Chris. This offered a unique opportunity for Chris to meet him again and find out how he had fared. 'I'll see yer both at the airport then,' Chris said, 'by the way my name is Chris.'

'My name is Martin.'

They shook hands.

With only one day in Bangkok, Chris curtailed his plans to sleep off the jet lag and decided to adorn Salinee with a bouquet of flowers. Like a medieval knight in a strange land he roamed the *sois* (avenues) in search of a florist. Elaborate shopping centres seemed the obvious choice. However, Chris repeatedly drew a blank. Thailand's obsession with flower arranging haunted him. He could see garlands of white jasmine flowers in every vehicle and department store and yet Chris could not find a single bouquet. He decided to try one last store. But inside, Chris soon learnt that they also had only garlands. He began to despise the bloody garlands and the way they were made.

A few children sat at a table, noses down, and with the patience of a surgeon they carefully intertwined the bell-like petals. They were of school age and should have been doing their homework rather than fiddling with petals, he thought.

He gazed round the store again. Here and there were such curiosities as elephant tusks carved into sailing boats, each one sadly representing a dead elephant. In amongst the paraphernalia Chris saw, to his delight, a single small bouquet lying on the floor. He approached it and touched the leaves. Chris's heart sank. They had the texture of cloth. He continued to study the flowers. The entire bouquet consisted of man-made fabrics.

'Do yer have some fresh flowers?' Chris asked the pretty sales assistant.

A look of surprise and astonishment came across her young face. Chris had forgotten to speak the Queen's English.

'I do not understand sir,' was her quiet reply.

'Sorry,' Chris resumed, 'can you tell me where I can get fresh flowers in a bouquet?'

The magnitude of his question proved far too difficult for her to fathom. A manager in a dark suit was quickly brought to him. He was very short, even for Thai standards, and yet broadly built with a round face. The puzzled sales assistant withdrew, with a mixture of embarrassment and bewilderment.

'Do you want fresh flowers sir?' the manager asked Chris.
'Yes.'
'I think you will only find in import warehouse, or market,' the manager explained, his expression warming sharply into a vindictive grin.

Chris made no attempt to conceal his anguish.

'Oh no!' Chris exclaimed and gave the man-made bouquet a glance of mute entreaty.

Chris walked outside feeling totally dejected. The manager's advice meant that he would need to travel through the time-consuming traffic, towards the river and bustling markets. Outside, in the unremitting hullabaloo of Bangkok, it was no wonder that he decided to give up his quest. Chris stood awhile under the blinding heat of the midday grill, with sweat oozing from his skin, like a saturated sponge dripping life into the dust of a desert. For some inexplicable reason his eyes were drawn to a small alley across the road. A strange calm possessed him. Chris experienced a strong illusion of *déjà vu* and felt compelled to cross to the other side. Crossing the road offered a tremendous challenge. Putting safety first, Chris walked to the nearest traffic lights and crossed when the Thai pedestrians considered it safe. Like a syringe drawing off fluid, a perfumed smell mingled with the tingle of chillies to suck Chris into the alley. Street vendors cooked for suited office workers as they sat at rickety tables on the pavement. The suction increased and tore the soles of his shoes away from the ground in a brisk trot. Chris was excited now, using his sense of smell like a bloodhound. To his left, Chris could see a dilapidated small block building with no door, just an open space with an old rag pulled across the top. The honey-scented odour tempted him to probe the puzzle behind the cloth. Chris peered inside and saw a marvellous uncontrollable profusion of red, blue and yellow. His face lit up like a child enraptured by birthday gifts. Chris had found his florist.

The next day had arrived and Chris found it hard to get out of bed, even though this was the day he had yearned for. This was the day he would see Salinee again. From his hotel window the polluted sky was purple-red around the newborn morning sun. He struggled to eat breakfast and rather sleepily boarded the mini-bus that would take him to Salinee. During his journey, Chris began to recognise subtle changes *en route*, such as the completion of a new highway that would now provide easy access to the bottle-green jungle. His fairytale was about to be shared out like slices of birthday cake. Perhaps Salinee's appearance had changed too, he thought. What would she look like after seven months? Maybe a different hairstyle, if so, he would have to admire it. Chris tried to visualise her face in his mind and to his horror he failed miserably. Chris had actually forgotten what she looked like. He felt ashamed and embarrassed. Moreover, Chris was travelling thousands of miles to visit a woman he could not recognise anymore. He began to panic. What if he gave the bouquet to the wrong woman? Chris was a detective now, fretful at his own ability to search his mental impressions. In desperation, Chris methodically searched through the many fragments of facial features hoping to compose them into an identikit. He was still searching his memory when, to Chris's anguish, they suddenly turned off the main road and approached the 'clenched buttocks ride'. Soon, very soon, he would arrive at the hotel. But would he be able to recognise Salinee? Chris felt a warm rush of adrenaline surge round his body as they levelled off and the hotel came into view. He marvelled at the beauty all around, pleasing, green and solitary. A female member of staff with a bob haircut and blue uniform walked along the driveway. In passing, Chris noticed with excitement a familiar wiggle. Was it Salinee? He asked himself. The driver was keen to get out of the mini-bus and sped by. Chris craned his neck and peered at her shrinking face. It was nothing like her, he thought, no radiant smile or girlish hair clip. How could he have been so wrong? His memory was really bad, or perhaps, it was just sheer fear and anxiety, he thought.

The mini-bus stopped and the driver opened the sliding door. The familiar scented essence and sounds brought a warm glow to Chris's heart. Now he had arrived and was only seconds away from her. To the driver's surprise, Chris totally ignored his luggage and hurried towards the bar clutching the sheathed bouquet. There she was, standing like a daffodil in an unfamiliar yellow uniform, three men sat drinking around the bar, invading her space like encroaching weeds. They had the touch of lust round their eyes and mouth.

'Hello, Sally knee,' Chris said softly, 'these are for you.'

He gave her the flowers.

'Thank you,' Salinee whispered.

She seemed embarrassed and hastily placed them under the counter.

'Sally knee, I've missed you,' Chris said with no hesitation.

The three men sitting at the bar turned to each other in astonishment and then pretended to ignore their conversation by drinking in total silence. Chris had successfully checked back the unwanted vegetation like liquid weed killer.

'What's that?' Chris said in a derisive tone, pointing an accusing finger.

'It my number badge,' Salinee explained.

'So your name is number six,' Chris said angrily. Salinee's face changed and Chris could see that she too felt the same as he. 'Let me check in and I will see you later,' Chris resumed.

Here he was again, thought Chris, the image of the hotel was the same, but the difference was unfamiliar members of staff. Yuwadee sat waiting behind the reception desk. In the lobby, there was usually some woman bent double in the middle of the floor, sweeping with a short home-made brush. These cleaners would even pick up the droppings from the toucan to leave a spotless passage for all barefooted guests. Nevertheless, on this occasion several other female members of the staff had gathered around, each of them curious to take a glimpse at the stranger who had come to see Salinee. Chris could hear them gossiping like schoolgirls and forging their very own opinions about him.

'Hello, Yuwadee, do you remember me?' Chris asked smiling affably.

'Of course Chris,' she replied cheerfully, 'we have a nice room for you away from the reception and near the waterfall.'

'Great!' Chris exclaimed.

It soon became obvious that the hotel was quite full. Guests lay sunbathing around the swimming pool and strolled back and forth between the bar in their swimwear. All the restaurant staff still retained their blue uniforms, but they too had now acquired number badges. Chris felt that the management had been totally insensitive. After all, the women now looked like the Bangkok bargirls who by law had to display their number. It was bad news. Salinee might now be approached or propositioned by men assuming she too was a prostitute.

Chris returned to the bar. To his delight it was empty now, with the other guests lounging about the pool.

'Sally knee,' Chris asked, 'Can I have a Singha beer please?'

'Yes,' she said, 'yes.' She had sounded fairly distracted, as if thinking of something else. Chris was about to sit down when she said, 'Chris, can you say my name better?'

Chris was quite surprised to find that he had been saying it incorrectly.

'How do you say it then?' Chris asked with a puzzled brow.

'Sa ... linee,' she explained with a short pause to emphasise the 'L'.

'Sar-linee, Salinee – is that correct?' She gave Chris a double nod.

'Yes, you can say now,' she replied, impressed.

'You told me that before,' Chris said haughtily.

'Now everything different,' she said softly.

Chris drank his beer.

'How long have you had to wear these horrible badges?' he asked her.

'Two months – nobody likes them,' she explained, shaking her head sadly and adding, 'the waiters fight who is number one and number two.'

Chris grinned. The number badges had fuelled discontent between the staff.

'Try and lose yours if you can,' he said with a wry smile.

A man came to the bar and ordered a beer. Chris watched the man keenly. He took a sip from his drink, glanced at Chris and Salinee, and then returned to the swimming pool.

'Chris,' Salinee asked, 'tomorrow can you see my mother?'

'Where is your mother – in Kanchanaburi?'

'No, she stay with my sister near here. She must see you before I go somewhere with you.'

'When shall we see her?' Chris asked.

'I will meet you in reception, five thirty tomorrow morning.'

'Okay,' Chris said and gulped some Dutch courage.

Chris was not looking forward to getting up so early, however, things were certainly changing for the better, and changing faster than he could have hoped for. Tomorrow, he was to meet Salinee's mother. What would she think of him? Chris asked himself, would she put the mockers on the whole thing?

It was still dark when Chris awoke the following day to his cacophonous alarm clock. This day would be a pivotal day, he thought. He had the fear that if Salinee's mother disliked him, then that would be the end of it all. Chris had long suspected that Salinee was the type of woman who would never cross her parents' wishes. He decided to put on long trousers and a smart short-sleeved shirt. The reception and hotel had relapsed into a peaceful silence that was occasionally broken by the call of a cockerel or the squawk of a cockatoo. A night porter lay fast asleep behind the reception desk. Chris sat down to stare at the driveway, as much as the sparse light from the stars would permit. Salinee arrived sleepy-eyed and yawned like a baby.

'How do we get to your sister's home?' Chris asked her.

'It's not far, we can walk,' Salinee urged.

'Can we see where we are going?' he asked, putting up a possible barrier.

'The sun come up soon,' explained Salinee.

Chris looked towards the east, a plum-purple fire blanket had began to douse the starlit sky. They both set off. Very soon, the gradient of the 'clenched buttocks ride' took its toll. After maybe 15 minutes or so, Chris stood at the top, puffing and gasping the dry and fiery air.

'Chris,' observed Salinee, 'are you all right – you look terrible?'

The morning sun was now scorching and he was parched with thirst.

'I'm okay,' Chris croaked, adding, 'it's a high hill to climb in this heat.' He followed her until two tyre tracks appeared on the left-hand side of the road.

'We go down here,' she explained, pointing her finger.

Chris was surprised to see the forest of big trees gradually diminish to create an open stretch of cultivated land.

'How old are these farms?' he enquired.

'The same as the hotel,' she explained.

'So when they built the hotel did they clear part of the jungle away too?'

'Yes.'

The sky had now turned gentian blue and the faint hum of a motor vehicle forced its way through a thin veil of tamarind trees.

'Are we getting near the main road?' Chris asked her.
'About one kilometre,' Salinee replied and added, 'we are nearly there now.'
'Bloody hell!'
Chris cursed as he tripped and nearly fell over a rigid water pipe. Chris followed it with his eyes until it was lost under the baked mud and grass. All around the pipe he could clearly make out the shape of human footprints, as if sandals had stepped into wet concrete, and where the water had flowed across the earth it had left a wrinkled groove like a dried-up miniature riverbed.
'Chris,' Salinee urged, 'be careful.'
'I thought it was a snake,' Chris replied jokingly. Salinee's face remained serious, so he hesitantly asked, 'Are there any snakes here?'
Salinee gave Chris a double nod and said, 'Of course.'
With haste, Chris stared at the ground around his ankles.
A dog began to bark and Chris peered into the distance. He could just make out the outline of a dilapidated wooden shack. They walked closer. In a compulsive desire to show concern for its owner's welfare, the dog approached them with intermittent growls. Salinee and Chris were forced to shield behind a Toyota pick-up truck half-laden with tamarind fruit. A woman's voice hollered from inside the shack and the dog ceased barking. The gaunt mongrel approached the truck, sniffed the tyre and urinated against the hubcap. An elderly woman walked outside and sat on a rickety tin stool beneath a canopy. The early morning sun sent rays low, lighting up her shapeless light-brown dress. She watched Salinee and Chris and remained motionless from amongst the large cooking pots and plastic containers strewn around her feet. Chris approached solemnly, stepping over a dead lizard and following Salinee as in a two-man procession.
'This is my mother,' Salinee declared.

'*Sawasdee krap*,' Chris uttered softly and placed the palms of his hands together.

Salinee's mother gave Chris a short nod and turned to face her daughter. They spoke to each other in their own language. It needed little imagination to understand whom they were talking about. Her mother's wrinkled face was full of colour and animated, with a mass of black-grey hair falling over her shoulders. Chris sat down. Pretty soon the dog could not resist the opportunity to probe Chris's groin with its soiled nose.

From what Salinee had told him, her mother would be an apt judge and jury. Her mother had seen every human characteristic throughout her veil of years. In spite of this, Chris could not take this wisdom for granted, nor could he underestimate this woman's maternal prevalence. She was the keeper of the family purse, an authority to be listened to and obeyed. Chris watched her mother as she gazed through her spectacles at him, with unseeing eyes, as if trying to make up her mind. Chris wanted to show her that he had no guile, but how could he do this without speaking to her? Chris came to the conclusion that he would have to rely on visual communication alone. His only asset was to fix a smile onto his face. But it needed to be a good smile, a classic smile that the most fastidious person could not resist. Chris searched his memory and chose the mouth of the *Laughing Cavalier*. It only served to bemuse the poor woman, who continued to chew her betel leaf and its nutty contents. She was literally chewing Chris over in her mind. Would she spit him out or find him a palatable relish? Chris asked himself.

A gruff voice resonated through the thickets. They all turned round, and saw the rather ungainly, burly outline of a figure whose large head and neck had been wrapped up tight in a protective cloth. It was a young woman, looking rather peasant-like in the classic sense. She approached

Salinee with a broad smile and gave Salinee a huge hug. At first glance, thought Chris, she was an ugly woman. The vision evoked was more than absurd. She was heavily built, with soiled toenails and had a curious cast in one eye. In fact, she was cockeyed, with the rare ability to order food from a menu whilst simultaneously selecting a drink from the cocktail board. Salinee, always cheerful, seemed to smile longer than usual.

'Chris,' Salinee said, 'this is my younger sister.'
'*Sawasdee krap*,' Chris said to her sibling.
'Hello, Kris,' her sister replied, eyes rolling uneasily.
Chris was startled.
'Oh!' He exclaimed, 'you can speak English.'
'Only little bit.'
Chris nodded and returned to his mute, whimsical smile, allowing himself to become the cynosure of all eyes.

Half an hour passed rather slowly, as if the earth had stalled in its rotation.

Finally, Salinee suggested, 'We go see my brother now.'
'Where does he live?' Chris asked, wondering.
'Not far, my sister can drive us. Can you say goodbye to my mother.'

Chris waved to their mother who was still peacefully chewing away. An optimistic thought entered his head. At least she had not spat him out.

The three of them stepped into the sealed, fruity aroma of the pick-up truck, whereupon they joined the main road and drove a short distance until they turned onto a grassed track, which cut its way through moss-green trees and shrubbery. The uneven track jolted and threw everybody about like a food processor. The track led them towards a range of verdant hills that seemed to grow ominously close. Now, the thick limbs of jungle trees stretched above their heads, with their burden of parasitic creepers and ferns bending them to breaking point.

It seemed only by chance that a coffee-coloured teak house loomed out of the greenery. They stopped and stepped outside into a hot, peaceful hush. The narrow trail had been broadened considerably and the jungle in front of the house had been laid bare, creating a small clearing no larger than two tennis courts. This was a scene of pure serenity: picture postcard material, thought Chris. The house was new, with no moss or traces of weathering. The hand-sawn planks of wood were chiselled and joined together with such precision that the whole construction was a pleasure to the eye. A slight gust of wind briefly kissed Chris's face and the faint chime of a bell interrupted the silence. In his mind, Chris visualised a chrome wind chime glinting in the sunlight. He approached the house and more chimes resonated through the still air. Chris peered around the corner, and saw his mistake. Two cinnamon-brown cows stood grazing and each had a tin bell round their neck. However, the seemingly ubiquitous flies were there to spoil Chris's picture postcard. There they were, scattered about their hindquarters and crawling all over the baking cowpats. A bell chimed again, as one of the cows decided to observe Chris with its large, brown eyes.

Everybody discarded their footwear and walked up three wooden steps. Inside the house Chris could see a bald-headed, saffron-robed monk squatting on the finely polished floor. His shaven head was buried deep in a pink-printed scripture of sorts. All about the room was a wonderful assortment of wooden furniture, a polished chair that could adjust in all manner of positions, book rests, and a wooden bed. Salinee and her sister sat on the floor. Chris too sat down, with his feet purposely pointing away from the monk. On the far wall hung a huge photograph of an important monk surrounded by his dignitaries, and next it was a slightly smaller photograph of the King of Thailand. The monk coughed and adjusted his robe. The wise expression in his eyes was that of a dolphin. He spoke in a soft voice to the two women. Chris remained quiet, conscious of avoiding a social gaffe.

'This is my brother,' Salinee explained.

Chris's eyes opened wide in total surprise at her revelation.

'*Sawasdee krap,*' Chris said softly.

The monk stood up and lit a cigarette and then he offered Chris one. Chris shook his head and Salinee explained in her own language that he did not smoke. The monk's face expressed regret. Soon, the formal ambience transformed into a casual and jovial affair, with the monk periodically rendering his two sisters into uncontrollable fits of laughter. His smile with dimples, thought Chris, was reassuring. They sat and talked for an hour, until two women from the village arrived with a large bowl of cooked rice and several dishes of vegetables. Salinee suggested that it was time to leave and they discreetly slipped away. Chris turned round, to see plates of food spread about the floor beneath the two photographs. Incense sticks had now been lit. The greyish smoke calmly rose towards the wooden ceiling, brushing the face of a large, golden Buddha. The two women knelt and prayed, whilst the monk blessed his and their food. Chris smiled.

Salinee's sister drove them back to the hotel, just in time for Salinee to open the bar at 10.00. Chris was her first customer and, after taking a huge gulp, he posed the vital question.

'Salinee,' Chris asked, 'what did your mother say to you?'

Salinee's lips began to form her reply, but then she hesitated and thought awhile. Chris sipped some more beer.

'She told me,' said Salinee, 'that if I cannot find a Thai man then I can go with you.'

Chris could see a happy flicker of triumph in Salinee's face.

'She said that?' Chris asked.

Salinee nodded and added, 'She also said don't kiss you on the mouth.'

Chris grinned and asked, 'Where shall we go next week?'

'I want to go to Chiang Mai,' she quickly declared.

'Okay,' Chris replied and hesitated a few seconds. He continued with, 'Why doesn't your mother want you to kiss me on the mouth?'

'She's old,' Salinee replied vaguely.

'Yes, I know – but you haven't told me why.'

Salinee paused in deep thought and then replied, 'She doesn't want me to catch Aids.'

Chris sat in silence, with his mouth agape.

14

Golden Triangle

Three days later Salinee and Chris arrived in Thailand's second city, Chiang Mai, just in time to witness those magical 15 minutes when the sun's early rays coat this gracious and unhurried northern town in a golden green light. Nonetheless, the sun soon cuts high across the unpolluted sky like a butcher's knife and the moment is lost until the following morning. Here, Chris was pleasantly surprised to see that the rush hour was a poor imitation of Bangkok's pandemonium. Built on the banks of the Mae Ping River, which flows through several air-conditioned, verdant valleys in the Himalayan foothills, Chiang Mai seemed another country apart. After spending the night huddled against Salinee, Chris now realised the advice given by Terapat to be correct. Whilst at the River Kwai Village hotel, Terapat had suggested that Salinee and Chris take the overnight bus rather than an aeroplane. 'It is the best way to get to know each other,' he had insisted to Chris. At the time Chris had considered any advice pitched by a homosexual to be inappropriate, but Chris now believed that Terapat's sexual orientation had given him a unique insight as to how a woman like Salinee ticked. She was a virgin and would remain so until married. Last night's cuddle on the bus was the closest Chris would get.

The bus pulled into Chiang Mai's bus station and Chris watched the shapely legs of two women depart with their luggage. The two women glanced at Salinee and then at each other. Chris saw both women's eyebrows lift. Chris also gave Salinee a glance and wondered if the women considered Salinee to be a prostitute. Chris had followed the women's movements keenly, ever since one of them had pinched his bottom on the courtesy mini-bus. Salinee and Chris were being transported from the travel agent's office to Bangkok's main bus terminal. The bus was full and Salinee and he were forced to stand up and grab the overhead handrail. In an attempt to claim as much territory as possible Chris had stood with a wide gait. Then, quite unexpectedly he felt a delicate hand grasp his buttocks. It was innocent enough, thought Chris, apart from the embarrassing girlish giggles that soon followed which instantly raised eyebrows from the other Thai passengers. The two cheeky women had broken a Thai social taboo. This action in itself had placed them amongst the realm of prostitutes. Having no desire to cause a commotion, Chris had said nothing and remained quite motionless. Chris had some inkling of what the women would look like long before he even set eyes on them. His guess was correct. They were both good-looking and aged about 20. Both women had bobbed hair, like Salinee, but in their case they wore the tight, figure-hugging dresses usually associated with the bars and massage parlours of Pat Pong. Salinee knew nothing of the incident and when they had arrived at Bangkok's main bus terminal she was still none the wiser. A few hours later, whilst on the air-conditioned bus bound for Chiang Mai, Chris had informed her of the incident. To his surprise, Salinee had simply passed the incident off with a smile and a 'good-for-you' comment that had rendered him speechless for several minutes. However, now that they had all arrived in Chiang Mai and were about to go their separate ways, Chris still could not help thinking whether they thought Salinee to be a prostitute.

Salinee and Chris took a *samlor* (trishaw) ride to their hotel. The tricycle rider was a man in his sixties, lean and fragile looking. In spite of this, he had calf muscles the size of ripe mangoes that could propel customers about town as if in a racing chariot. They arrived at their hotel, and Chris tipped the sweat-streaked rider a generous 50 baht.

Inside the hotel, a frosty receptionist peered at Salinee as they approached her desk. There was an uncomfortable silence as once again she glared at Salinee very directly and her expression towards her was unfriendly. She checked their reservation with a steely gaze. Not for the first time, Chris was forced to wonder if she considered Salince to be a prostitute. Salinee and Chris confirmed their booking for two separate bedrooms. At first sight Chris was pleased with the hotel, but even more pleased when the receptionist was forced to display her *volte-face* as she handed them separate keys. A porter showed them to their rooms and he too was left with a puzzled expression on his face as Salinee and Chris separated in the corridor.

There was no time to lose, so their first day was spent visiting the Doi Suthep Monastery. Here, a series of steep hairpin bends flank the temple and the scenery en route was spectacular. Standing at the top, high above the city, Chris could see the metropolis as if from a cloud, with the airport runway being the most dominant feature, a sure sign that Chiang Mai's ancient walls had developed cracks that the outside world could now infiltrate, thought Chris.

Later that night, Salinee and Chris paid a visit to the night bazaar where the heady whiff of cooking from street braziers intertwined with the sonic beat of full volume pop music: altogether, a heraldic and brazen display of imitation clothes, cameras, film, watches, videos, and hand-painted umbrellas.

'Salinee, ' Chris observed, 'all of this is for tourists; I

would like to see the locals living as they did before the airport was built.'

'Yes, ' Salinee agreed, 'I see tour in hotel, we can go to golden triangle and see hill people.'

Chris's eyes tingled and he asked, 'Is that where the poppies are grown for opium?' Salinee smiled and said nothing. They continued to walk around the city. Chris writhed when the occasional Thai man or woman openly stared at Salinee. Chris had realised early on that it seemed an impossible ambition of his to wish these people could look at her without raised eyebrows. In the meantime, Salinee took it all in her stride, whilst Chris, looking on, was all too conscious of the smirks. Back at the hotel he kissed Salinee goodnight outside her door. It was their first kiss, just a peck in fact but it was an important moment. The first step on the ladder, thought Chris.

The following day after breakfast, Salinee made a huge fuss about purchasing a bag of sweets. She had tried the hotel shop without success and in desperation strolled outside into the busy street, leaving Chris to watch out for the arrival of their tour bus. Chris was irritated and annoyed at her actions, as he knew the bus was late. Ten minutes elapsed and she finally returned clutching a polythene bag of boiled sweets. Chris sat in his chair, motionless, his arms crossed with a guidebook on his knee, and stared at her with faint grimace. Salinee could see he did not approve.

'Wot a palaver, where have yer bin?' Chris moaned.

Salinee stared at him nonplussed and said, 'I don't understand what you say.'

In his anger he had returned to his Black Country accent.

Chris passed it off by saying, 'Can I have a sweet, please?'

'Only one, ' she replied and added, 'I buy for the hill children.'

'Oh!' Chris exclaimed, feeling intensely embarrassed.

Presently, the mini-bus arrived with several other tourists

already on board. They travelled northeast gaining altitude all the time. Occasionally, fresh mounds of earth on the asphalt proved that landslides were not uncommon. They follow the serpentine road through fertile valleys, and onto a dirt track that redefined the words 'rut' and 'hole'. It ran across the mountains like a roller coaster and transported everybody back in time to when the western world knew very little of the indigenous population.

A small pocket of nomadic people belonging to the Karen hill tribe had settled and built a tiny village hemmed in by the mountains. Salinee and Chris disembarked and, in an instant, the gamy smell of fried chicken mingled with the noxious rancidity of pig excrement crept up everybody's nose. All the tourists stood round the fire and watched the orange flames licking the wok until the wood smoke got in their eyes. In a nearby pasture, protected by a single roped fence no higher than six inches above the ground, grew the white opium poppies. Their guide was quick to explain that although they still grew the poppies, the King of Thailand had now urged the hill tribe people to cultivate coffee, tea and garlic. Chris saw none of these crops.

The people of the village all wore traditional hill tribe costumes of dresses and scarves, embellished with colourful embroidery of indigo and red. These people were so remote, and yet so charming, that they even spoke to Salinee in an incomprehensible language. The women of the village spent much of their time weaving their colourful cloth on back-strap looms as they sat outside crude shacks.

An old man, slim and delicate like a withered runner bean, also sat outside with a curious-looking pipe. A tarry residue lay dormant in a small charred container. It was opium residue, and the tourists' slow-smiling guide quickly explained that anybody could try some if they wanted to. A young, Japanese man stepped forward as if warming to the idea. There was a *kamikaze*-like impulsiveness in his curiosity.

He must have had mixed feelings, thought Chris, because he passed his tongue over his lips several times. However, the swift words of rebuke uttered by his wife soon made up his mind. The Japanese man gave the old man a backward glance and turned the offer down with a scornful snigger. The old man watched them with rheumy eyes. Watching the old man, filled Chris with a strange melancholy that was sweet and fearful at the same time. Chris also refrained from sampling the opium.

They continued on their tour of the village, where the children offered everybody gimcrack trinkets with a sad-eyed performance designed to loosen the tourists' wallets. Chris looked around the shacks and saw their mothers' eyes, gazing ahead eagerly, hoping to weigh up their children's success. In spite of this, Salinee's presence was to change all of that. A keen-eyed toddler had spotted the bag of sweets and in an instant Salinee and Chris were surrounded by hordes of children. Pandemonium broke out. Salinee and Chris perambulated around the village like the Pied Piper, with the children following one after another. Chris was proud to be with Salinee. He felt like a World War Two soldier liberating a town and offering confectionery to its kids. It was strange that something so practical and down to earth should have resulted in such a feeling that would last with him for months to come. The rest of the tourists watched enthralled. Some gaped in amazement as the extraordinary scene unfolded before their camera lenses. The photographs they took that day, Chris reflected, would show the children for what they really were and not a fabricated scene put on for tourism.

During the following days Salinee and Chris spent their time on tours that under normal circumstances a single man in Thailand would have avoided. Chris found himself appreciating Chiang Mai's art and craft villages, with hand-painted paper umbrellas, bronze ware, cotton and silk woven on antiquated wooden looms and teak furniture expertly carved before their very eyes. Chris was mellowing in Salinee's company.

On their last day in Chiang Mai they paid a visit to an elephant camp. There, the elephants and handlers demonstrated the ancient technique of forest clearance by dragging huge logs about with their trunks as if picking up matchsticks. Later that evening, Salinee and Chris strolled towards the river and watched the water flowing down country. The ornate globe streetlights that decorated the city shimmered in its waters. They passed a large, opulent house, almost European in style. In fact, it could have been classified a mansion back in the UK, Chris thought. This lonely house faced across the river and its large garden came down to the footpath near the water's edge.

'Chris, ' Salinee asked, 'is your house like this one?' Chris smiled.

'No, my parents are working class – they have a small house, ' he replied, with elaborate nonchalance in his pride. 'You can come to see me in England if you want to. I will pay for your air ticket.'

'What about my job?' Salinee asked.

'You can take a holiday.'

'In Thailand we have no holiday, if I come I must leave job.'

'I'm sure you can get your job back, you work harder than the rest of them.'

'Did you know Yuwadee go to France soon?' Salinee said.

'Really!' Chris exclaimed in total surprise.

'Yes, she has French boyfriend.'

'Wow! You see – if she can do it then you can.'

Salinee smiled and later they returned to their hotel. Chris kissed Salinee outside her bedroom door and once again they parted like shy teenagers.

15

Unexpected Guests

Salinee's four-day leave had ended, and they returned to the River Kwai Village hotel in time for the New Year celebrations. A huge party, with a professional cabaret, had been arranged around the swimming pool. Chris had caught a glimpse of all the cabaret stills on a poster inside the reception, lovely women with feathered headdresses, dazzling smiles and glittering gowns. That evening the dark sky was spangled with myriads of tiny pinpricks and the emerald rock garden had changed to a moonlit one, bathed in silver. The party was packed with people, all of them happy, relaxed and warm at their tables. The vibrant cabaret enthralled everybody, with elaborate costumes and gorgeous dancing girls. Salinee's makeshift bar was located next to the graceful footbridge spanning the rippling stream and the alcohol flowed like the frothing water itself. Chris happened to glimpse Terapat enjoying the company of two saucy cabaret women. There he sat, inside the thatched gazebo with his legs ostentatiously crossed. He looked a right dandy, thought Chris, but he guessed Terapat made the young women feel at ease. Perhaps they felt safe with his effeminate nature.

As the clock neared midnight Chris's plans for an ideal end to the evening were, nonetheless, spoiled, when he whispered to Salinee, 'Can I kiss you?'

She shook her head and said, 'I cannot.'

'Why not?' Chris's lashes blinked angrily.
'The staff will talk,' she explained.
'God's teeth,' he protested and walked off in a huff.

Chris was determined to welcome 1987 in properly, so he approached one of the saucy cabaret women. Her big white teeth gleamed as she produced a slow, lingering grin and the silver light of the moon struck her two sparkling brown eyes. Midnight had now arrived and throughout the hotel lips joined other lips. Whilst half-concealed beside the arch of the footbridge, Chris thrust his lips towards the woman's cheek. Suddenly, an arm grabbed his shoulder and pulled him to one side. In frustration Chris turned to face the culprit. It was a waiter.

'Lady man,' the waiter replied to Chris's scornful glare and he gave Chris a pacific smile.

Chris's scalp froze and he swallowed at the thought of kissing the elegant lips of such a pretentious transsexual, indulging in a taste for elaborate costume. The transsexual hitched up his dress, produced a derisive grunt and, with a slightly nervous eye awaited Chris's response. Chris said nothing and calmly strolled back to the bar.

'Salinee,' Chris said softly, 'did you know the women in the show are all men?'

'Yes, all the hotel staff know.'

'I nearly kissed one of them,' he said shrilly, 'why didn't you tell me?'

Salinee hesitated, shrugged her shoulders and explained, 'You never asked me.'

'Oh!' Chris replied with resignation.

Then it occurred to him why Terapat had been in such animated conversation with the cabaret transsexuals. Terapat's man about town image should ensure that at least he had a good night.

The following morning Chris awoke with his customary New Year's Day hangover. The time was 8.50 and it suddenly occurred to him that the New Year celebrations had only just finished back in the UK. It was a sobering thought. Chris drank an effervescent cure and crept outside. Disgruntled waiters and waitresses tidied up the party decorations in a lackadaisical manner. This reminded Chris of the waitress Apinior. She was now married to a Thai man and had left the hotel a couple of months earlier.

During the next few days all of the hotel guests departed without any new arrivals checking in. The daily tour bus would come and go with all its passengers returning to Bangkok. Chris was mystified, but pleased. It was high season and there was no reason for it. One morning his curiosity got the better of him.

'Salinee,' Chris asked, 'why is the hotel nearly empty?'

'I don't know – ask Yuwadee,' she replied.

Chris wandered over to the reception desk. Yuwadee was leaning back at ease, reading a woman's magazine. 'Yuwadee,' Chris enquired, 'why aren't there any new guests?'

She placed her magazine down and opened the register. Then, leaning forward slightly, her face became serious.

'The hotel is fully booked,' she said and something in her tone warned Chris not to ask anymore.

'Oh!' Chris exclaimed, and changed the subject by saying, 'Salinee told me you have a French boyfriend.'

'Yes, I go to France this year,' she declared with shining eyes.

'Are you staying in France or coming back to Thailand?'

Yuwadee paused for a few seconds and began to nurse the flame of hope that flickered inside her.

'I don't know,' she replied, shrugging her shoulders.

'Look out,' Chris hollered, 'the bird is eating yer magazine.'

Yuwadee leapt from her chair and wrestled the magazine from the toucan's beak. Chris returned to the bar with a broad grin on his face.

By mid-afternoon, the quiescent hush and stifling heat had slowly lulled everybody into a drowsy torpor. With his elbows propped on the bar and chin between his hands, only the constant drone of the ceiling fans kept Chris awake. Gazing through the open window a green lizard caught his eye. Chris watched in amazement, as it hung precariously from the stem of a leaf whilst lapping up tree ants. Then the lizard leapt out of sight and was lost inside the dark green interior of the bush. Chris took another drink and listened.

Through the window he could hear a faint, distorted noise similar to an electronic crackle of a walkie-talkie. The churning of the ceiling fans seemed to intensify. It was one of those moments when Chris just knew something was about to happen. Salinee and Chris stared at the fans. They appeared to be working properly. Chris held up his hand for silence.

'What's that noise?' he whispered.

'It come from outside,' Salinee said mysteriously.

They both stood up and peered out of the window. They stood there awhile, motionless, hardly daring to breathe. Some of the hotel staff lounging in the shade of trees also stood up. They too were bewildered as to what was happening. The strange noise reverberated along the river, bouncing off the craggy rock formations like a pinball, only to fade away into a deathly hush as the forest muffled the drone like a wet sponge. The noise came back again. Louder and louder it grew. Now everybody recognised the noise and they all looked skywards in anticipation.

'There it is,' Chris yelled, as a helicopter flew over the hotel at low level.

It zoomed up the river and out of sight. More electronic crackling drifted towards them, this time much louder. Chris sipped his drink and glimpsed the black gleam of a firearm through the lush greenery. It was a soldier. Salinee froze and Chris stared at her for a moment, stunned. The soldier was no more than ten metres from their window. The soldier turned round slowly and glared straight into Chris's eyes. Chris took a deep breath and looked at him in a casual a manner as he could manage. The young soldier grinned unpleasantly. At that moment, two jeeps came hurtling down the 'clenched buttocks ride' with more soldiers on board. The soldier near the bar gestured towards the jeeps. In an instant the other soldiers were galvanised into action, flashing their machine guns as they took up strategic positions around the hotel. The helicopter returned and flew down the river. Soon, its noise faded away, merely to be replaced by the intricate sounds of Thai woodwind, and percussion instruments. Salinee and Chris walked into the restaurant and peered over the parapet. Below, the soft and mellow melodies drifted skywards like butterflies rising on the wind. In the distance, and half hidden through the feathery branches came a military gunboat that oozed two pleats of white water across the breadth of the river, and behind it, rocking in its wake came a luxurious wooden raft pulled upstream by two chains. A group of musicians sat on the bamboo floor, whilst the soldiers on board the gunboat watched the moss-green jungle with a steely gaze. As a whole, this bizarre scene would have dovetailed well with a Hollywood movie. The hotel's newest guests had arrived for the night.

'Salinee,' Chris enquired, 'who is on the raft?'

She shrugged her shoulders and strolled over to Yuwadee. Yuwadee approached one of the soldiers and spoke to him. A few minutes elapsed and Salinee returned to the bar with a severe frown on her face.

'It is an important general,' Salinee explained.

'Oh! I see.'

Up to that point, Chris had not really felt the presence of the military in Thailand. He knew that many Thai governments had been formed after several military *coups d'état* and nepotism was ripe throughout its military hierarchy. Not surprisingly, this general appeared to have his own personal safety high on his list of priorities. Yuwadee insisted that she knew nothing of the bizarre affair. Apparently, only the hotel manager knew they were coming.

Evening arrived and the relentless dark heat was stifling. Chris sat at the bar and through the window he could see God's tapestry spread out across the night sky. The appearance of the sweat-streaked headwaiter garbed in a moth-balled red uniform and black bow tie instantly brought a wry grin to Chris's face. The general ate dinner on his raft and the word got around that he was well oiled with drink. His soldiers soon found out and a few bottles of cognac and brandy were pilfered from his private bar. Outside, in the darkness, shards of yellow light would flare up through the veil of vegetation each time a careless soldier lit up a cigarette. Soon, the high security lapsed into a free and easy booze-up. Even Chris was allowed to wallow in the drinking of the general's pilfered cognac. This really was sampling the rose-strewn path of power and self-indulgence, thought Chris.

Early next morning when Chris turned up to eat breakfast, he was amazed to see half a dozen gorgeous women sitting together in the restaurant. Each had long black hair that flowed over their shoulders and their red lips gleamed in the morning sunshine. They still wore evening dresses that ranged from the elegant to the glamorous. It was a sight to awaken any man from a hangover and the waiters hovered round their table like flies on a jam sandwich. In spite of this, there was a tinge of self-denial about the women, like an unspoken competitiveness between them. Chris imagined that their modest appetites were a deliberate attempt to remain in the general's entourage. Certainly, they were glaring examples of the general's fringe benefits and, who knows? with their palms well greased it was difficult to judge who exactly was taking advantage of whom. Later that morning, the soldiers and the General's raft departed as quickly as they had arrived.

Ever since Salinee and Chris had returned back from Chiang Mai, the hotel had flowed with gossip and rumours. The waiters were the worst. On numerous occasions they would approach Chris and enquire if he had slept with Salinee. The implication was obvious. They were men and Chris was sure they too had had expectations in the past, not only for Salinee, but for most of the young women working at the hotel. So far, Salinee had eluded all of them. Nevertheless, if they now considered her to be sexually active, then perhaps they could move in after Chris had returned home. Chris trusted Salinee completely. They were now courting each other, and he was convinced she would never go with somebody behind his back. On these irritating occasions, Chris always explained that Salinee was a good girl, in words that were all the more forceful for being delivered in an off-the-cuff manner. In an attempt to still the rumours further, Salinee would purposely allow the elderly woman from the kitchen to chaperone her each evening. Chris would swiftly go back to his room, thus confirming his whereabouts to anybody who cared to know. However, these elaborate shenanigans were to soon back-fire. One morning, Chris approached the bar to find a melancholic Salinee.

'What's the matter?' Chris asked her.

'Chris,' she said, shaking her head sadly, 'the staff at this hotel are no good.' There was an uncomfortable silence, and then she produced her dictionary. To Chris's amazement, she pointed out the word 'masturbation'. Chris was taken aback for a moment.

'Why do you want to know about this word?' he asked with a puzzled brow.

Salinee hesitated and said, 'Some staff watch you in your room last night.'

'What!' Chris exclaimed, adding, 'How did they see me?'

'I think they have small hole in wall,' she replied.

'Who saw me?' Chris asked angrily.

Salinee shrugged her shoulders and said, 'I think some waiters.'

Chris was vexed to be without any means of finding who the culprits were, without raising a complaint. On the other hand, he feared for Salinee's job if he did complain to the management.

'Well, I hope they enjoyed it,' Chris huffed, in a nonchalant tone.

With all this in mind, Chris immediately changed his room and the incident was forgotten.

It had been a great holiday. Events had turned out far better than Chris had anticipated. He had been introduced to Salinee's mother and seemingly passed the test. So all in all, there was no reason to feel sad when it was time for him to return home. To the contrary, of course, he felt absolutely gutted when it was time to say goodbye. A growing crowd of staff came slowly out of the hotel. Nobody had eyes for anything except to witness the big goodbye. With still no kiss for them to gossip over, and with their eyes fixed on each other, Chris announced to Salinee that he would return in May. Chris boarded the tour bus and waited, hoping for a slim chance to talk to her again. The driver started the engine. Chris gave the driver's reflection a look between appeal and rebuke. Chris turned once more to Salinee and they waved to each other through the glass. Then she was out of sight. Salinee of course took it all philosophically, but once again Chris was angry at this tedious setback. So this was travelling for pleasure, he thought with pent-up anger. Chris felt that nobody should have to go through this. It was totally unfair that Salinee did not live around the corner from his house. They couldn't even talk to each other on a telephone. All he had to look forward to were four months of hard work and a load of letter writing. It seemed so long until he could see her again.

In Bangkok's airport Chris met up with a tanned Martin and his mother from the outbound flight. Martin and Chris were both depressed and said very little. There were no smiles, no theatrical masks. In the departure lounge they opened two bottles of duty-free red wine and glumly watched their bottles empty away. Martin's mother also remained quiet. Chris could sense there was something wrong. Martin nervously flicked his thumb and shot embarrassed glances at Chris. Finally the wine loosened their tongues.

Looking into his frank, ferret-face, Chris cautiously asked Martin, 'Well, did yer get the visa for yer girlfriend?'

'We didn't get one,' Martin replied mournfully.

'Wot wuz the problem?'

'We could have got one – but I changed my mind,' Martin said mysteriously.

'Why?' Chris objected.

'Because the embassy told me that...' His voice trailed away and then he continued with, 'They told me that my girlfriend had taken three other men to the embassy to try and get a visa.'

Chris turned to face Martin's mother. She shook her head in disgust. They drank some more.

In an attempt to make him feel better Chris said, 'I had trouble with a woman from Pattaya once.' Martin's mother threw Chris a glance. 'Her name was Wanna,' Chris added, 'and she threatened to cut her wrists in my hotel room.'

'Oh! They all do that,' Martin replied solemnly.

Chris was speechless and in shock.

Soon afterwards, it occurred to Chris to ask him, 'Have

yer ever had one of these women say that they want to have yer baby?'

'What!' Martin exclaimed, 'I've never heard that one before – it doesn't make sense for them to say that. After all, it would frighten their customers away.'

16

The Silent Strike of the Gavel

As Chris had promised, he returned to Thailand in the following May. This time Salinee had arranged a four-day holiday on the island of Phuket. Whilst Chris gazed through the hotel brochure, it appeared she had made a good choice. In spite of this, he was fairly disappointed that Salinee had not purchased aeroplane tickets for the 900 kilometre journey to the south of Bangkok. Like croci in early spring, Salinee's frugal nature was beginning to see daylight. In one way Chris was pleased, as he considered frugality to be a good character trait. But in reality, after many years of living on her meagre earnings, Chris imagined she had thought it too perilous to place a deposit on expensive aeroplane tickets. Of course, once he met up with her again he instantly paid for their air-conditioned bus and hotel accommodation.

The overnight journey down the thin elephant's trunk that borders Burma and Malaysia, was an uncomfortable one. During the night Salinee and Chris tossed and turned in their cramped seats. With the borders so close, they were now travelling through a politically sensitive area. They were unaware that, whilst they drifted in and out of their restless sleep, the bus made an unscheduled stop. With Chris's eyes still closed, he suddenly felt a sharp prod to his arm. Chris opened his eyelids, and was confronted by the beam of a flashlight and the unmistakable humming sound of a battery-driven motor. He rubbed his lashes and peered at the lens of a video camera. Chris was taken aback, as the lens was pointing straight towards his face. Chris sat up straight, his body tense as a rod. He could just make out the rigid profile of two resplendently uniformed figures. A policeman with a rapt expression on his face, watched as his colleague recorded every wrinkle, pore and bristle on Chris's face, as if mapping it like a spy satellite would. Chris protested by lowering his gaze to stare at the floor. The police cameraman panned to his left, and repeated the same light-grasping rape of Salinee's face. His colleague followed the lens with his flashlight. Chris looked at Salinee. She was awake now, her long-lashed eyes glaring back at the lens. All the passengers were recorded in the same manner. Even a mother breast-feeding a whimpering, hungry baby was imprinted onto the videotape. Chris was speechless and felt intimidated, but the Thai passengers seemed unconcerned. The uniformed officials returned to the bus driver and one of them checked the passenger manifest with his flashlight. His eyes became blazing orbs, as he pointed a finger towards a discrepancy. The bus driver shrugged his shoulders, whispered into his ear, and passed him something hidden in his fist. Rather furtively, the uniformed officer slipped it into his pocket and departed with his colleague. Chris peered through the window and under the star-filled sky he could see the two policemen join another sitting inside a car. Shards of red light flashed all around, tearing the official masks from their heads as it illuminated their corrupt, grinning faces. They talked with stooped shoulders and heads bowed and the gleam of their eyes cast oblique glances towards the driver of the bus. Chris's face grimaced with disgust, and he glanced at his watch. It was 3.00. Chris returned his gaze to the three policemen and was dismayed to see them flag down another bus. He turned to face Salinee and tapped her arm.

'Salinee,' he asked, 'why are they filming us?'

Salinee asked another passenger who explained in her own language.

'Chris,' Salinee explained, 'they are looking for Burmese thieves.'

Chris shook his head sadly.

'Take a good look at everybody,' he whispered, 'do any of us look like bandits?'

Salinee remained quiet and closed her eyes. Chris sat in deep thought, open-eyed and muttering for hours, churning the events over in his mind. He did not believe the policemen's explanation. He was sure the filming had taken place for some secret political agenda. Chris struggled to fall asleep. Eventually, he gave up and waited for the first glimmer of sunrise.

Dawn arrived and Chris was still gazing wistfully out of the window as Salinee woke up. As they travelled further south, it seemed as though they had entered a vast theme park, a geological paradise in fact. Aeons had past and what remained of a once generous landmass had now been weathered and sculptured into a surreal statement of grotesque art, art that nature had seen fit to embellish with lime-green mosses and plants, which hung from every cleft and fissure as skin fits the flesh of a beast.

The bus crossed a vast bridge that linked the mainland to the island and arrived at the bus station in Phuket town. Whilst sitting in their taxi, Salinee and Chris glimpsed their first view of the town. It was built on the rubber and tin boom of the last century and still retained its beautiful colonial-style houses that were once owned by rich rubber barons. Phuket Island turned out to be a romantic paradise. There, huge granite-like corks of rock project upward from the molten blue ocean as if about to reveal an underwater wine cellar and all the shapes in the shallows show up like bottle-green cultures, growing, as if seen under a microscope. Salinee and Chris shared a two bedroom, air-conditioned beach bungalow that seemed to say, 'Welcome to romance.' All in all, the sun, the sea and the palm trees all induced a sense of contentment and happiness. They held each other's hands and walked along talcum-powder beaches, kissing with only the surf to watch them.

One day they boarded a long-tailed motor boat and travelled to a neighbouring island, where a colourful village of Muslim sea gypsies lived on stilted houses. The gypsies are skilled fishermen and their cherub-faced children learn to dive at an early age in search of lobster, crab and prawns. That very same evening Salinee and Chris ate exquisite seafood in honour of their efforts. Inside a candle-lit beach restaurant, Salinee's face glowed and flickered with ardour. It was almost one year to the day that Chris had first laid eyes on her. Slowly and surely the auctioneer raised his gavel. She was falling in love with him. But Chris sensed that Salinee had to ask him one question, one question that needed confirmation in her mind. If she were to fall in love with him, would he continue to travel to Thailand and see her? After all, it was a lot of money. Whilst standing on the beach with the thundering surf rising and collapsing along the sand, Salinee pitched her question.

'Chris, ' she said, 'it is too far to travel for you to see a girlfriend.'

The air was suddenly prickly, charged with a high value of consequence that sent small shivers rippling down Chris's spine.

'No it isn't, ' was his quick and honest reply.

At that moment Salinee's lovely almond-shaped eyes widened, and a broad smile spread across her face. The gavel had struck without a sound. She had fallen in love with Chris and he knew it. Chris knew the exact moment Cupid's sting had struck her and it was now indelibly engraved in his memory forever.

'Okay,' she said cheerfully and they kissed.

Common sense dictated that the only remaining thing for her to do was to visit the UK. It was her chance to test the water so to speak. After all, Chris was sure there would be a culture and language shock. So far he had spoken to Salinee without a trace of his Black Country accent. Nevertheless, Chris was determined that this would not be the case in England. There was no point in glossing over the cracks. Chris needed to show her the reality of what she was letting herself in for.

In an attempt to give Salinee some flying experience they returned to Bangkok by aeroplane. Salinee sat in silence, her eyes frozen in fear as the air hostess demonstrated how to inflate the life jackets. Salinee could not swim and that single look at the air hostess's inflation technique spoke more adequately than any words could have done. Pretty soon, Salinee was a trembling mess.

Chris held her hand and said, 'It's all right, you won't need to do anything.'

He hoped the experience wouldn't put her off from coming to England and prayed for a smooth flight. They took off and, against Chris's advice, Salinee decided to tuck into the airline food. She knew it was included in the price of the air ticket and there was no way she would allow it to go to waste. Her cheeks paled before Chris's eyes as she peeled back the foil and sniffed the heady food. The aeroplane shook and the nauseating odour numbed her appetite. They landed in Bangkok, with Salinee's calling card left behind in the shape of a sick bag filled free of charge.

To Chris's surprise it hadn't put her off. Back at the River Kwai Village hotel, Salinee told Chris that if he sent her the money she would definitely come to England. Once again, Chris would have to rely on Harry, the daily tour guide to deliver his letters. Harry did not seem to mind, as the novelty had now worn off. It had almost become second nature for him to deliver a letter at least once a week. Chris thanked him for his efforts and he returned to England a few days later to prepare for Salinee's visit.

17

Blighty

With Chris's bank account almost depleted, it was now a case of returning to the overtime grindstone. It took 14 months before he was in a position to send Salinee a cheque for £1,200. By that time, Chris was looking much heavier. The lonely evenings had taken their toll and he had sought comfort in food and drink. Then to Chris's irritation, came the silence once more. Had she received the money? Was she coming? The men in his office pounced at the opportunity to use their sharp turn of phrase. They suggested that Salinee had taken his money and ran away. Chris could not dwell on such morbid comments and simply grinned, foolishly. Unknown to all of them, Salinee had originally asked for £3,750. Chris had refused and sent her the more realistic amount. After six weeks there was still no letter. Chris was ashamed even to mention it to his parents.

Then the day came when he arrived home to see a creased and tattered airmail envelope on the kitchen table. To Chris's dismay and horror it had no stamp. In the letter, Salinee wrote that she was due to arrive at Heathrow on the 21st of November 1988. Chris was furious. It was only a few days away. There he stood, holding a delayed letter that contained vital information, and Salinee had not bothered to put a fucking stamp on the envelope. The letter had travelled thousands of miles without being franked. Chris was aghast. Nonetheless, he believed his guardian angel had come good again and yet he was still angry. He wanted to give Salinee a piece of his mind for being so careless.

The 21st of November finally arrived. To a moderate extent, Chris readily displayed his inner feelings of excitement as he cheerily waved goodbye to his parents and caught the early morning coach to Heathrow. However, once again the whirligig of luck spun all of his preparations into chaos. In the faint light of a chilly dawn, Chris heard thumps and thuds from outside and, to his horror, a thick cloud of black smoke billowed past the window. The coach driver pulled onto the hard shoulder. Chris's coach had suffered a blow-out. Under normal circumstances the repair would have been routine. But not on this day, this day of all days the hot tyre had wrapped itself round the axle and solidified into a black crust. They could not budge it. Chris felt ill at ease sitting with idle hands, but there was nothing he could do. They still had approximately 35 miles to Heathrow and before long many of the passengers succumbed to panic. Chris could not have envisaged such a pandemonium. His fellow passengers had flights to catch and very soon the coach resembled the stock market City desk with frantic telephone calls on mobile phones. Chris scarcely listened to what the others were saying, eager for the time when he could escape to another coach. Thankfully, he was allowed to board the following service due to his absence of luggage.

Chris arrived at Heathrow two hours late, half-expecting to find Salinee carrying her suitcase and wearing a belligerent scowl on her face. He looked round in vain. Salinee was nowhere to be seen. Chris's heart began to pump at a furious rate. Where had she gone? Chris asked himself. Chris felt he had let her down by not arriving on time. In his panic he almost forgot to breathe. Had she gone away in search of him? Chris stood still and waited awhile, sweating profusely as if he was back in the tropics. Perhaps the men in the office were correct: she could have taken his money after all. Chris's mood changed. He now felt aggrieved and full of self-pity. He flounced about patting down his unruly strands of hair until, to Chris's astonishment, his name was announced over the p.a.

'God's teeth!' he gasped and wondered what had happened.

At this point he began to feel woozy. Chris proceeded to follow their instructions and was escorted by a uniformed official through 'staff only' doors and corridors. Then the magic moment came, as once again Chris cast an eye at his love. There she stood, waiting calmly in passport control. He pulled himself together and felt much better. Salinee had been stopped from proceeding any further until Chris had arrived to meet her. He tried to put on a sympathetic expression and gave Salinee an apologetic hug in front of the busy queues. They were in England now and the Thai social taboos could be forgotten awhile. Rather curiously, Chris also had to walk sedately through customs and he hadn't even been abroad. In one way he rather hoped that he would be stopped, as Chris was sure his response would have raised even the most diligent of customs officers' eyebrows. Chris knew he must have looked a little perturbed, but nothing happened. Salinee and Chris were allowed to walk straight through, with only the slightest of quizzical glances from the customs' officers.

When they stepped outside, Salinee experienced the reality of the British Isles. A strong, bone-chilling gale blew from the Arctic. She seemed suddenly overcome with a fit of the shivers, shaking and trembling as if possessed. Chris threw his arms round her thick, olive-green coat, a coat that no English woman would have worn in 1,000 years. In fact, it reminded Chris of children's wallpaper, with its patterned black puppies spread all over, puppies with glittering dog collars that attracted astonished glances from every direction.

'Salinee,' Chris asked, 'where did yer get this coat?'

Salinee wrinkled her brow and said, 'Can you talk slowly please.'

Chris repeated his question.

'I have problem with coat,' she replied vaguely, and explained, 'I think they only wear in north of Thailand.'

'It makes yer look big,' Chris moaned.

Salinee patted his enlarged stomach, smiled and said, 'You look fatter.'

'Wuz yer sick on the plane?' Chris asked, hoping to change the subject.

'Little bit.'

'Are yer nervous about meeting my parents?'

'Little bit.'

'Cum on, let's catch our coach. It'll take us about three and a half hours to get home,' he explained.

They boarded the coach and, to Chris's frustration, Salinee soon fell asleep. Through the window Chris looked fondly at the slush gutters, which hitherto as a motorcyclist he had hated so much. He wanted Salinee to gaze out of the window with him and see frozen church spires, snow-capped hills and slush valleys. The snow was rapidly melting and for the first time in her life she had an opportunity to see evidence of a snowfall.

Eventually they arrived home, after Salinee had snoozed through the entire journey. The lean figure of Chris's middle-aged mother stood waiting on the front doorstep, her face decorated with a broad smile. There she was, sporting a new hairdo as if welcoming royalty. Chris's parents' home was a two bedroom ex-council house, which his mother had encouraged his father to buy in the late sixties. Spotting a financial bargain, whether it is during shopping, or putting cash away for the future, was always his mother's forte. Inside the house, his mother and father welcomed Salinee with open arms. Here, Salinee was faced by a lushly furnished retreat from the outside elements and, elsewhere, such hitherto unknown items as gas fire, fitted carpets and airing cupboard. After Salinee had warmed her limbs beside the fire, the three of them showed Salinee her bedroom. Like a true gentleman, Chris had passed his own bedroom over to his girlfriend. Faced with sleeping in Chris's room, Salinee commented that the bedroom door would not shut properly. It had never bothered Chris in the past, so nothing was ever done about it.

Suddenly and rather tactlessly, his father shrugged his shoulders and blurted out, 'We're not a hotel.'

Chris cringed, and Salinee and his mother exchanged worried glances.

'Don't worry,' his mother said to Salinee, 'nobody will go in yer bedroom.'

That night Chris slept downstairs in the living room, but not before he had a glorious wrestle with his blanket, pillow and borrowed camp bed, all of which had become contortionists.

The next morning promised to be a better day, the gale had gone and a cool-lemon autumn sun shone weakly. Salinee and Chris strolled through his neighbourhood holding hands like teenagers. Chris was full of enthusiasm and dowager-like pride. They stopped at his old school playground and peered through the railings.

'Salinee,' Chris said, 'this is my old junior school.'

'What is junior school?' Salinee asked him.

'It's for children aged seven to eleven,' he explained, adding, 'my last year there wuz horrible. On the fust mornin' back from the school holidays, my headmaster decided that the playtime bell would fit me like a glove.'

'Chris,' Salinee interrupted, 'talk slowly please.'

'Sorry, during the rest of the school year I never had a

playtime. My job wuz to watch the clock and gallop round the playground like the goofy rabbit in *Alice in Wonderland*.'

'What's *Alice in Wonderland?*' Salinee asked.

'It's a children's book,' Chris said quickly, 'wintertime wuz the worst. I would keep falling over on the ice and all the children would laugh at me. Yer know, children love snow but I grew to hate it.'

Salinee stood in silence, totally bewildered as to what the hell he was saying. For the first time it became quite clear to Chris, that this was going to be more of a problem than he had first anticipated. The language and everyday knowledge one takes for granted was totally lost on Salinee.

They strolled through the park. In the far corner stood a tall clock twined in an ivy overcoat, its motionless hands hung forlorn and useless on a square face. There they stood awhile and Chris offered to take Salinee's photograph in front of the rusting timepiece.

'Chris,' Salinee grumbled, 'the clock is broken.'

'It's all right,' he insisted, 'nobody can tell from the photo.'

Chris took the photograph and their interest in the clock attracted a couple of teenage boys. As they left, Chris caught sight of them eyeing the clock, no doubt with the idea of vandalising it when Salinee and Chris had left.

'Salinee,' Chris urged, 'cum on, let's go to the supermarket. I promised my mom we would buy yer some rice, and some oriental food.'

'I'm all right, I can eat English food,' Salinee replied in a tone that suggested self-pity.

'Salinee, yer wuz struggling to eat yer dinner last night. It's easy to find some Chinese food for yer,' he explained.

'Okay,' she said quickly.

Whilst sauntering along the supermarket aisle, Chris was in seventh heaven and felt that no one else in the world had a girlfriend like his. Salinee's eyes tingled as she recognised some Thai ingredients. In spite of this, Chris watched with interest as she paced up and down the freezer picking up unfamiliar packages.

Finally she put aside her reticence, and asked, 'Chris, what are fish fingers? – Fish do not have fingers.'

Chris quickly turned round. To his relief nobody had heard her.

'They're fish meat in the shape of a long finger,' he whispered, and added, 'have yer got wot yer want?'

Salinee nodded and they went back home.

Later that evening Chris rummaged through his videotapes to find a suitable movie for Salinee to watch. Chris and his parents had noticed that she was struggling with the many contemporary television programs. A black and white movie classic, which spoke good plain English, was required. Eventually, after some deliberation Chris decided to show Alfred Hitchcock's version of *The Thirty-Nine Steps*. They all sat down and relaxed. A memorable scene went as follows:

Richard Hannay –	'Have you been in these parts long?'
Farmer's wife –	'No, I'm from Glesga. Did ye ever see it?'
Richard Hannay –	'No.'
Farmer's wife –	'Oh, ye should see Sauchiehall street. Whit all its fine shops, and Argyle Street on a Saturday nicht whit the trams and the lights.'

Chris glanced at Salinee. She was finding it increasingly difficult to understand, and now had a bemused sparkle in her eyes as she sipped her lemonade. The movie continued:

Farmer –	'Aye I might hev known. Making love behind my back. Get out.'

Richard Hannay – 'Now just a minute.'
Farmer – 'Get out of my hoos before I . . .'
Farmer's wife – 'Och aye, go . . .'

'Salinee,' Chris asked, 'do yer understand what they are saying?'

'No, are they speaking English?'

'Well, nearly. They're Scottish,' he explained.

The house erupted into laughter. So that was Salinee's first full day in England and it proved to be the benchmark for the rest of her visit.

In the days that followed, Salinee slowly adapted to her environment. She was a fine example of how *Homo sapiens* had spread around the earth. The human species is an assimilative social animal and has flourished strongly in most environments. Salinee was now throwing caution to the wind by tucking into English food on a regular basis. Chris's parents also decided to venture into the unknown by allowing Salinee to cook a full Thai meal for them. The news had leaked out around the family and they were agog to hear the final outcome. That evening Chris returned home from work and stood by the garden gate. The kitchen windows were open. He could smell the savoury food, hear the sizzling *wok*, and the clatter of dishes and cutlery. Joyous anticipation was whetted as he entered the house and saw that his mother had unearthed the best china, along with a new tablecloth and matching napkins. They sat down at the table. Salinee and Chris exchanged glances as his father sampled her zestful and aromatic soup. Chris's father sighed with satisfaction and his eyes sparkled in epicure's delight as he swilled it round his tongue.

'Salinee,' his father said, 'I think this is the best soup I've ever tasted.'

'Why don't yer try the other stuff as well,' Chris urged him, adding, 'but be careful of the red chillies.'

His parents' spoons wandered over the table, picking out unfamiliar items at random to place onto their crowded plates. They attacked the meal with a good appetite.

'I'd never have believed Chris would end up loving foreign food,' his mother said.

'When he wuz a child,' she added, 'he wuz very finicky about his food. If we went to eat at somebody's house and there wuz dirty crockery in the kitchen, he would hardly eat a thing.'

Chris's father blew his spoon and sipped the soup.

'Yer know, Thai food smells totally different from English grub,' his father put in.

At that moment Chris remembered an incident from his childhood.

'One day,' Chris said, 'when I cum home from school. I told my mom that I'd bin thinking of roast beef all day and hoped we'd got it for dinner.' Chris exchanged glances with Salinee to make sure she understood, and continued the tale without losing the thread. 'My mom said that we'd got lamb chops, 'cos we'd had roast beef on Sunday.' Chris's mother continued to eat, but she looked puzzled, and his father was none the wiser. 'When I took my socks off,' Chris added, 'they smelled of roast beef.'

Now his mother began to giggle as she too remembered the tale. But his father still looked bemused, even as he chewed an awkward noodle hanging precariously from his lip.

Chris continued with, 'So I took them to the kitchen and asked my mom to smell them.' Chris turned to face Salinee and pointed an accusing finger at his mother, saying, 'Do yer know wot she said?' Salinee shook her head politely. 'My mom said that it wuz raining after she'd done her washing and she'd hung my wet socks over the oven to dry.'

Chris's mother burst into laughter. It spread round the table like an infectious affliction and only stopped when they could get no more air into their lungs. All in all, the meal was a total success.

During another evening the telephone pealed and to Salinee's joy it was Yuwadee. She had now married her French boyfriend and was living in Paris. Whilst in Thailand, Salinee had written a letter to her friend explaining that she was to visit England. For that short moment in time, that telephone conversation almost transported the three of them back to the River Kwai Village hotel. Things were looking good, thought Chris. Salinee was able to see that with the aid of modern technology she could be in contact with a close friend in Europe. Even more so, her mother's café had recently acquired a telephone. So Salinee's right to maternal comfort was soon exercised a few days later, with a telephone call of sheer exuberance and joy.

In spite of this, the verbal contact with her mother soon unlocked darker emotions, mainly in the shape of homesickness. Apart from trying to comfort her, Chris asked himself, what else could he do? She had travelled all this way to be with him and yet he felt guilty at her predicament. When she felt homesick, Chris would wonder if it were his fault. Perhaps he was not showing enough affection towards her. Had he dodged reality by dreaming up a rosy future for both of them? These thoughts, confusing, and never quite understood, became soul-destroying at times. Chris was vexed to think that his dream might not be realised. Some days he could just tell by looking at Salinee's face that she was suffering inside. On those days she would be as quiet as a dormouse and her face would be noticeably paler than the cheery robust countenance that Chris had seen in Thailand. But he never saw her drop a tear. Luckily, her sad thoughts did not linger more than one day at a time and, as for the next day, she would transform back into her usual vivacious self. Chris's parents had also noticed her homesickness and his father advised him to make a special effort in showing his love towards her. It follows from all this that his father's advice on the subject was of some practical value. Chris had been a bachelor for so many years, so perhaps he had tended to stick to his own routine, especially when in his own environment. Because Salinee was now in England and staying in his parents' home, maybe Chris had simply assumed that every thing would fit together like a jigsaw puzzle. His quest for marital bliss seemed a long way off. So Chris took his father's advice and put in a special effort, by showering Salinee with love and tenderness. Each evening they cuddled and kissed inside her bedroom before she fell asleep. Chris would then settle down for the night on his sagging camp bed.

At work, several men vented their annoyance on Chris by criticising his handling of the whole affair. With all his travelling expenses in mind, they assured Chris that he was the only man who would be financially better off, after marriage, rather than *vice-versa*. In spite of this, their greatest concern was that he had neglected to expose Salinee to their heritage and culture. Their laconic mode of speech persuaded Chris to buy two expensive concert tickets to hear the BBC Philharmonic Orchestra. They were to perform at the town hall and the concert was to be recorded live and broadcast on Radio Three. Nothing was left to chance. Chris brought Salinee an elegant evening dress, handbag and smart coat, thus forcing her to discard the green coat on this special occasion.

The night of the concert had arrived. With feverish excitement they took their seats, and craned their necks to have a first peep at the musicians. Chris straightened his back and looked up. High above their heads, looking like a black widow spider dangling by a single thread, hung the ominous BBC microphone. The orchestra began to play a soft and mellow piece. The audience sat bolt upright, in a deathly hush, fully aware that every cough or scratch could be recorded for posterity. Chris heard a click next to him and saw that Salinee had opened her handbag. Feeling uneasy, he hastily placed a forefinger over his lips and urged she remain quiet. Salinee smiled and Chris turned to face the orchestra. The music continued. Then, Chris heard a rustling noise next to him. Chris seethed with impatience and turned to face Salinee. To his horror, she had opened a bag of potato crisps. Salinee seemed totally oblivious as to Chris's concern and offered him one. Chris shook his head vehemently. The best he could do was to smile bravely and utter not a word of complaint. It was during this period of limbo, that Chris's ears attuned to every crunch, no matter the distraction of the other sounds coming from the orchestra. The people in front turned round. They did not pass any remarks about the noise, but their tell-tale look of derision written across their faces said it all. Chris had to assume a stern expression and say nothing. He found himself ignoring the concert and concentrating entirely on the microphone above their heads. What would the recording sound like when it was broadcast? Chris thought. Chris visualised thousands of listeners from around the country complaining of sunspot interference. Eventually, Salinee finished her crisps and crushed the bag into a small ball. Chris sighed with relief. However, at this point, she produced a can of lemonade from her bottomless handbag. In a flash, Chris wondered what else she had got in there. Perhaps she had brought the whole corner shop with her. Now his patience was exhausted and in desperation he threw his hand over the ring pull. Salinee looked startled for a moment, until Chris silently pleaded with her not to open it. She obliged and Chris could relax until the intermission. Presently, the music trailed off and rapturous applause echoed around the hall. The intermission had arrived and it was his chance to interrogate Salinee.

'Salinee,' Chris whispered, 'wot are yer doing, why did yer bring all of this food and drink?'

'I don't really want them, but your mother gave them to me,' Salinee explained.

'Oh! I see.'

Chris exhaled slowly in resignation that it was not Salinee's fault after all. However, the fact that Salinee had chosen to eat during the performance only helped to confirm his growing suspicion that the Thai's relaxed approach to life was something he would have to tolerate. As for the rest of the concert, well, his girlfriend slept peacefully through it all, thus squandering the opportunity to sample Britain's so-called culture.

For a woman whose parents would have protected her from worries and conflict during early childhood, Salinee must have led a sheltered life in comparison to western children. In those childhood days, there would have been no television in her home town and her only view of the outside world would have come from a performance of shadow-puppetry or a costume drama by a visiting theatre company. Her absolute courage in flying around the world should not have been underestimated, Chris thought.

Nevertheless, her courage was to be seriously dented when a newsflash came onto the television screen. It was the evening of the Lockerbie flight disaster. As the news reports filtered through of burning debris falling onto the small Scottish town, Chris could see the fear on Salinee's face. The next day was even worse, with photographs of the disaster bringing the tragedy into everybody's home. Anybody who was due to fly at that time would almost certainly have flown with deep anxiety, especially as it soon became clear that it had been a terrorist bomb. It was also a clear example of where the United Kingdom and the United States stood in the hierarchy of world news. If something serious happens here, Chris reflected, it is immediately flashed across the world quicker than the trade wind. Whereas, if a similar thing had happened to Thai citizens then after the first few days the news would have been put on the back burner, eventually vanishing into oblivion.

It was sometime during the previous months that the salmonella egg scare had reared its ugly head. The news programmes were still running the story. The excessive news coverage puzzled Salinee.

'Chris,' Salinee asked one evening, 'why do they keep talking about eggs?'

'Cos they've got bacteria inside,' he replied and pointed out the word 'bacteria' in her dictionary.

'All eggs have this,' she blurted, adding, 'you should cook them well before you eat.'

'I know!' Chris had to admit, fully knowing that he loved runny boiled eggs.

She was right of course, Chris had always noticed that the Thai people cooked their eggs solid in a high temperature wok. Salinee was a farmer's daughter and was fully aware of such obvious risks.

One Sunday as the rain fell on the sodden garden and dripped down the window, Chris decided that he would take Salinee to London and York. When they stayed in London she considered it just another city, no better or worse than Bangkok. However, she was shocked to see that England also has it fair share of homeless street beggars. Salinee admired York for its lack of bustling streets and her photographic film soon came to an end in her attempt to secure lasting pictures of the ancient wall, cobbled streets and quaint houses, though it was not long before she took sour to the idea and wanted to return to Chris's parents' house. Chris considered that this was a good sign. Perhaps she felt safe with his parents.

The rest of his family treated Salinee as if she were a celebrity. Little by little each of them invited them into their homes. Chris guessed they were all curious as to who this woman was. To be honest with himself, apart from his parents, Chris did not give a toss what anybody else thought of her. He already knew how his parents felt, as he had overheard his mother talking to a sister on the telephone. She had said, 'I don't think I could find an English girl better than Salinee.' Chris's mother was right: neither could he. That was why he had resorted to travelling afar in search of love, hoping to find someone somewhere. From what Chris had seen in Thailand, most men had not succeeded. There was the haunting memory of Youst, the Dutchman who had stayed at Salinee's hotel. Then, of course, there was Martin, the ferret-faced man who had taken his mother to Thailand in hope that she might help with his girlfriend's visa. The last time Chris had seen Martin he was totally gutted, his mother too. His so-called girlfriend had opened her legs to all and sundry in an attempt to migrate to England.

Chris felt lucky to have found Salinee. However, he still felt puzzled about the meaning of life and love in general and he assumed that his guardian angel had taken good care of him. It all seemed as though they were two pieces of earthenware that had been glazed and fired on separate continents. Salinee and Chris was not a matching pair, but they had found each other by fate. They had, Chris supposed, reached that moment when the only remaining thing to do was to get engaged. They both knew it and there was no need for Chris to propose marriage.

Salinee's visit had carried them into January 1989 and it was time for her to return home. Her main concern was that she now had to try and get her old job back. If she were successful she would write and let Chris know. If she failed she would have to inform him as to which hotel she was working. It could have been anywhere. But wherever it was Chris promised her that he would meet her.

Chris kissed Salinee at the airport and said, 'When I cum and see yer again I'd better see yer father.'

This was the closest he had come to popping the question.

'When will you come?' Salinee asked.

'In a few months. What does he think of me?' Chris asked, wondering.

Salinee hesitated a few seconds and replied, 'He does not know about you.'

'What!' Chris cried feeling unreasonably cheated.

'My mother would not tell him I have come to England.'

'Why?'

'Because he might say no,' Salinee's eyes filled and she started to sniffle.

Chris hugged her. Oblivious to the gloomy sadness all around them, the information board clicked over and urged Salinee into the departure lounge. It was time to say goodbye. Chris watched with trembling hands as she left him and strolled down the corridor. She reached a corner, turned round and waved goodbye. Then she was out of sight.

The next thing on Chris's agenda was to return to Thailand and set up a meeting with her Chinese father. Under normal circumstances this was something to look forward to. However, Salinee and her mother had certainly put him in an awkward situation. In fact, it was an awesome challenge. How would her father react when Chris turned up on his doorstep to ask for his daughter's hand in marriage? The Chinese people had many old and traditional customs, thought Chris. Would he allow one of his daughters to marry a foreigner? Chinese elders were always respected and if he refused what the hell would they do?

The whirligig of luck was spinning again, and Chris felt as if he was caught up in some half-real, crazy *maelstrom*.

18

Dowry

Chris lost weight and returned to Thailand four months later. It had been three and a half years since his first visit and Bangkok had changed. Taller, commercial skyscrapers now dominated the small and seedier hotels, evidence perhaps of economic growth. Like giant mirrors, they would reflect the afternoon sunlight from their glass and metal facades, so that the streets below shone with an almost diamond brilliance.

The River Kwai Village hotel had also changed. Salinee now worked as the restaurant cashier and there were more rooms located on the river. Advertised as Raftels, they were a slightly cheaper option than the land-borne rooms. Although not Chris's cup of tea, they provided an opportunity to get closer to nature with the river rushing only inches below the floorboards.

However, during this holiday, he too was expected to embrace nature. This time Chris was to stay in Salinee's home, a genuine Thai country house next to a farm. Salinee had warned Chris that her home had no luxuries such as running water, or air-conditioned rooms. But that was not Chris's main concern. Meeting Salinee's Chinese father for the first time had now taken top spot in the anxiety charts and this of course was the main reason why Chris had returned so quickly. Chris approached the idea with trepidation and, far too soon, he found himself sitting on a bus bound for Kanchanaburi province.

Whilst Salinee had stayed in England, her father had found out about his daughter's escapade. He had not taken it well. This, fuelled with malicious gossip, had caused him to seek an urgent *tête-à-tête* with Chris. Chris wanted to marry one of his seven daughters, four of whom had already married Thai or Chinese men. Chris wondered, whether her father would react with vehement repugnance at pooling the family genes. His gut feeling was that Chinese males had one priority in life, which was to keep the family name and bloodline pure from external, so-called weaker families. The Chinese people might even have considered that being born Chinese was winning first prize in the lottery of life.

Chris's stomach churned when Salinee uttered the dreaded words, 'Nearly home now.'

The bus began to slow down as it entered a small village. It pulled up beside a row of houses and shops with rudimentary, crude frontages that ran along the edge of the main highway. Salinee and Chris stepped onto a dusty forecourt in front of a roadside café and the bus left, leaving a trail of salmon-orange dust in its wake. They were nearly smothered in it and Chris watched with a rueful grin as the dust slowly dispersed to leave a fresh, more rural essence. An ageing, arthritic dog wandered towards Chris and rubbed its nose against his travel bag.

The café was a white, two-storey street block, with the ground floor and forecourt used for the business. The upper floors appeared to be the bedrooms. Inside the café, Chris could see an elderly woman sitting at one of the four wooden tables. Chris looked closely at the woman and recognised her. She was Salinee's mother. Her mother had seen their arrival, but continued methodically to pound away with a large pestle and mortar, whilst chewing her much-loved betel leaf and nut paste.

The left-hand corner of the shop was obviously used for cooking. A huge sooty *wok* sat idle on the gas stove and on the floor, swarming with loathsome flies, stood a large tin from which came a strong stench of vegetable waste. Chris followed Salinee towards her mother. The zestful tang of crushed chillies hung all around her.

'*Sawasdee krap*,' Chris said smiling affably.

Her mother nodded, straightened her back and spoke to Salinee in her own language. Chris sat down to a table. The arthritic dog rubbed its nose against Chris's leg and sat under his chair. Chris ran his fingertips along the wooden tabletop and rattled a glass condiment set containing chilli oil, fish sauce and toothpicks. Over the years, drops of chilli oil had nourished and tainted the dark brown tabletop and now its grainy surface had a sheen that resembled fading lacquer. Chris raised his eyes. Pinned to the walls were dusty and tattered posters of Hollywood movie stars. Tom Cruise in *The Color of Money*, and Richard Gere in *An Officer and a Gentleman*.

A grim-faced middle-aged woman with ruffled, sable hair emerged from a room at the rear of the café. Looking rather gaunt, and clad in a fading cotton dress, she looked at Chris with a long, disillusioned stare.

'Chris,' Salinee said, 'this is my older sister.'

'*Sawasdee krap*,' he said gladly.

'*Sawasdee ka*,' the sister replied solemnly.

Chris turned to face Salinee and wondered why the two sisters he had met so far bore little resemblance whatsoever to her.

A cherry red Toyota pick-up truck pulled onto the forecourt causing a cloud of dust to fly into the air. The driver entered the café and ordered some food. The man sat down at a table, lit up a cigarette and opened a newspaper. He lingered on this awhile and then casually turned to face Chris. Suddenly, the stranger's face was one of dismay. Chris was a foreigner, whom hitherto the stranger had only seen outside the village. Embarrassed, the stranger quickly turned to face his newspaper. The arthritic dog abandoned Chris in favour of the more promising customer.

Salinee's sister turned on a bottle of gas that stood under the stove and lit the hob with a match. A blue flame roared with ferocity and she began to chop up meat with her baleful meat cleaver. Flies danced above the meat and swooped onto the bloody flesh in between swipes. Salinee threw a handful of red chillies and garlic into the sizzling wok, whilst her sister added the meat. Chris sniffed the spicy fumes and his eyes watered. It was all too much for him, so he stood up and walked onto the forecourt rubbing his eyes with his hand. Salinee followed and tried to comfort him. Chris, now feeling slightly embarrassed, refused her help.

He waited a few minutes until his eyes cleared. The sky was a kingfisher blue with a slight breeze to temper the heat, so Chris decided to take a look around. Behind the café, about 300 yards from the main highway, lay a dry riverbed with green hills beyond. Chris peered down, as if looking into a precipitous gorge. There was a strange grimness to that riverbed, Chris thought. It now swarmed with loathsome vegetation, insects and reptile life, all of them rioting on the remains of fish and river creatures. That land belonged to the river and they had no right to live there. All this made it possible to imagine how it would have been before the river had been dammed. Perhaps buffalo carts used to trundle along the very dirt track were he now stood. Salinee had once told him that as a child she often saw water buffalo go down the steep bank to put out from the shore. Even her father used to fish the river with a net, though his talents were a lot broader. In World War Two he had cheekily sold black market ice cream to the Japanese soldiers.

Chris was wilting a little when he returned to the café. The cooking had finished and the man was eating his meal.

Chris returned to his seat. Salinee opened the glass doors of a huge refrigerator and handed Chris a Singha beer.

'Salinee,' he asked, 'how much for the beer?'

'It's okay,' she replied and explained, 'you are our guest.'

'Oh!' replied Chris, feeling quite pleased. He took a large gulp of beer and asked, 'do I sleep here?'

Salinee smiled and explained, 'No, you stay in my father's house. Finish your beer and I will take you to see him.'

Chris could not share her optimism at meeting her father, so seeking a little Dutch courage he drank his beer in one large gulp. This instantly brought a look of dismay to her mother's face and her cavernous, crimson mouth was agape for several seconds.

Chris followed Salinee down the main highway. After a few hundred yards they crossed the road and joined a dirt track. Trees and bushes grew on each side and a bungalow gleaming brightly with white masonry paint loomed out of the dark shrubbery. Two fierce sounding dogs began to bark.

'Chris,' Salnee said, 'be careful of the dogs. They bite you if you get too close.'

Chris hesitated, and drew in a deep breath of foul-smelling air. They continued on, strolling past the decapitated top half of a car. Sad and skinny-looking hens clucked and ran out from under the rusting roof. A few black feathers flew through the broken windscreen and the dogs barked even more. Here, there were plants in pots, but they had all died through lack of water. To Chris's left, and almost in harmony with the chickens, began the sounds of grunting pigs. They approached the decaying pigpens, which now leaned over to one side. There, the air was laden with unsupportable odours and piglets played in vile conditions. Amongst all of this, almost odious by its proximity was a brightly-coloured butterfly flexing its wings like an elaborate brooch. Chris gazed at the bungalow. Each dog had been tied to a concrete pillar to the left and right of a patio frontage. Salinee shouted in Thai. An old man lay prostrate on a wooden table. He coughed, rubbed his rheumy eyes and sat up. Then, with a slow stroke of his meaty hand, wiped several beads of sweat from his brow. He gave Chris an indignant glance. Chris shuddered. Leaning against a walking stick, the old man forced himself to his feet and hobbled towards the dogs. The bones of his old frame barely contended with the ravages of time and he looked as though he had a migraine. The ingenious old man used the hook of his walking stick to gather in a frayed rope and he stood on it with his bare feet. For the meantime, both dogs were out of harm's way. It was now Salinee and Chris's chance to enter the house and rather hesitantly they strolled through the small gap in between the snarling canines.

By Thai standards, thought Chris, the bungalow was certainly not impoverished. Perhaps middle class, but by western standards Salinee's father lived frugally. The floor had the same coarse look as the walls and paint had been splashed on the concrete at some time. Salinee's father returned to his polished tabletop and sat on it.

'*Sawasdee krap*,' Chris muttered nervously and gave him a box of duty-free cigarettes.

In an instant the old man's eyes lit up at the sight of the cigarettes and he grinned. Chris had broken the ice.

Salinee showed Chris to his room. The bedroom was small, with a single bed that had one sheet and a large sausage-shaped pillow. No duvet or blankets would be required here. Covering each window frame were fixed wire-mesh nets, that distorted the view outside into iridescent hues. The glass windows would need to remain open day and night and these wire nets were Chris's only defence against the dreaded mosquitoes. Chris glanced around in search of the most important and yet simplest of household items.

'Salinee,' he asked, 'can I have an electric fan?'

'Yes, of course. I'll get you one.'

A few seconds later she returned with a small nine-inch diameter fan.

'Haven't yer got a bigger one?'

'Yes, but my father uses it. I'm sorry but this is all I can give you.'

'All right, can yer show me the shower and toilet.'

Salinee escorted Chris to a room at the rear of the house. Through a window he could see a sparse yellow-leafed sugarcane plantation that was not doing very well and in the distance were hills, dreamlike in the haze. Salinee opened the door, and the damp smell of wet dog turned Chris's head. He looked at it gloomily. The shower consisted of a large water tank and plastic bowl.

'Chris,' Salinee explained, 'you fill the bowl up and when you stand over the drain pour the water over your body.'

Chris hung around unwillingly, nodding his head in approval. He gazed at the toilet with concern. It resembled an upturned gutted crab shell and a brown residue hung around its sides. From that moment on Chris just knew that his next four days were going to be an uncomfortable experience. His heart sank, but he had to do it, just as Salinee had trusted him by staying in his home. Chris soon came to the conclusion that her father seemed intent on being self-sufficient and pursuing his old-fashioned lifestyle regardless of modern influences that now surrounded him.

'Salinee,' Chris asked, 'where are yer sleeping?'

'In the café with my sister. Shall we go back now?'

'Okay,' Chris replied, worrying about the dogs once more.

Dinner was fried rice with pork. It was quite good; after all it was a café and there were more customers now that evening had arrived. In spite of this, having observed the preparation of the food with deep reservation, Chris found himself searching for human hairs and cooked flies. There weren't any, of course, but he still had to look.

Now it was his turn to be introduced to friends and family. Salinee's nephews and nieces considered him a strange curio. The children satisfied their fascination by staring at Chris's grey-blue eyes and stroking his fair-skinned arms. Later, Salinee's cockeyed sister made an unexpected visit from the Tamarind farm. Chris was also introduced to two plump brothers and another sister who turned out to be a nurse. The nurse closely resembled Salinee and she used the opportunity to try and improve her English, which after a few beers Chris was willing to participate in.

That night Chris lay naked on his bed, feeling light headed with alcohol. He listened to the stirring of a wind chime and the whine of an intruding mosquito. The faintly bitter smell of wood smoke drifted through the meshed window as evening fires were lit on distant farms. The bedroom light was switched off, but that which came in through the window illuminated a lizard scurrying along the bedroom wall. Outside, the noisy insect world buzzed with excitement and a cockerel, fooled by the silver moon, greeted the next day.

The following morning Chris lay on the bed, awake, as the sun's rays angled down from a gorgeous blue sky. He cast an eye over his naked body and, to his horror, his legs, chest and arms were covered with mosquito bites. Chris instantly wondered about his 'meat and two veg' and gave his penis and testicles a good examination with a worried gaze. Luckily, they were clear, and he swore that from that moment on he would sleep in his underpants.

Salinee's father had wanted Chris to visit his favourite Chinese temple so, later that afternoon, Salinee, Chris, and her cockeyed sister travelled north-west in the tamarind scented pick-up truck. After leaving the main highway, they made their way along a single dirt track that cut its way through cultivated farmland. In the distance, a range of hills partly covered with cotton wool clouds grew nearer. The gorgeous grandeur of a turquoise-coloured temple stood high on a smaller, much closer hill and gleams of gold light rebounded from six of its orange tiers. A duller, cone-shaped construction stood next to it with its apex missing. At first sight, Chris thought it to be a ramshackle ruin, of sorts.

'Is that the temple?' he asked Salinee, wondering.

'Yes, the gold temple.'

'Wot's the broken temple on the right?'

'It's a new Thai temple. They want to build it taller than the Chinese temple,' Salinee answered with a wry smile.

'God's teeth! I don't believe it. Can't they get on with each other?'

'Oh no,' Salinee assented, shaking her head slowly, 'the monks used to fight with *kung fu.*'

'Wot, like Bruce Lee?' Chris said quickly.

The two sisters laughed.

'Thai people like Bruce Lee,' Salinee's sister shyly put in.

They pulled up near a shop and café. Here there were no tourists. An ornamented tiled courtyard paved their way to the entrance of the temple. Created through a marriage of art and engineering, Chris could not have wished for a nicer place to visit. A gardener pottered about his terracotta pots and white gardenias dripped water from a good hosing. Encased in a large glass case embellished with golden fretwork along the edges, sat the porcelain figure of a laughing Buddha. This jolly face, shaven head, and squinting eyes reminded Chris of the laughing policeman found in some of Britain's seaside towns.

Rather cheekily, he pretended to search for the money slot and said, 'Where do yer put the money in?' Salinee projected a scornful glare in Chris's direction, so he suggested, 'Shall I take a photograph?'

Chris aligned the two sisters beside the Buddha and, to his annoyance, a mange-ridden black dog walked in front of the lens. The dog turned to face the camera. Chris recoiled in horror as the dog now resembled a hound from hell. Its hideous head was twisted out of shape by years of cancerous growths and flies circled and crawled over a weeping, sticky eye.

'Salinee,' Chris said sadly, 'it's terrible to let it suffer. Why don't they put it to sleep?'

'The dog lives in the temple,' Salinee said vaguely, adding, 'the monks believe it is somebody born again.'

'Yer mean reincarnation?'

Salinee nodded and Chris hastily snapped the photograph as soon as the dog had moved on.

The six-tier temple had hundreds of stone steps that spiralled round the main structure. To the north they were briefly plunged into the luxurious shade. Here, Chris would insist on stopping for a breather. However, it was a futile act, as all too soon he would climb some more and return into the stabbing sunlight. Chris was in a state of exhaustion when they finally reached the top. However, up there, the panoramic view was worth all the effort. Through the arches, Chris could see the cloud shadows race across the countryside and, to his delight, a cool breeze blew in between the gaps of several bronze bells hung from the eaves. On the tiled floor lay an abandoned pillow and blanket. It intrigued Chris.

'Wot's that for?' he asked Salinee.

'Some monk sleeps here,' she explained.

'Natural air-conditioning,' he remarked with a wry grin.

Chris peered across the short distance to the Thai temple, and heard stonemasons chipping away. All round the construction lay a labyrinth of bamboo scaffolding, bending and flexing in the breeze, from which several workmen sat rather precariously on swaying planks. Chris was aghast, wondering if they had any health and safety guidelines to follow.

The three of them lingered awhile until it was time to return. As Chris was the only male of the party, he decided to take up the lead position and strode down the steps with his mouth half-open in a happy dream. Suddenly, a hand grabbed his shoulder and jerked his body backwards. Chris turned round. It was Salinee's sister and she pointed to the step below his feet. Chris was horrified, not to say panic-stricken. He stood quite still, with hunched shoulders and pigeon-toed feet. A green snake, no longer than 18 inches hugged the shadows. Salinee's sister took a sharp look at the situation and spoke to Salinee in her own language. There was a tone of panic to her voice. The situation was grave. They were trapped for sure. The long, scaly, limbless viper slithered down onto the next step. It was in the sunlight now and, below, in the full blaze of the sun, a shadowy forked tongue licked the stone. A cold shudder ran down Chris's spine. The shadow of the forked tongue had induced it, the very symbol of evil. The reptile repeated its actions, wending its way down the stone steps. The three of them followed a step at a time, trying to anticipate the reptile's every move. Would the snake change its mind and decide to turn round? Chris asked himself. If it did, then there was nothing for them to do but to climb up those damn steps again. The whole scene represented man's struggle with nature. There was no other expression for it. The viper was in control. It had taken everybody half an hour to reach the top of the temple. In spite of this, they were now forced to make an unhurried descent that lasted more than an hour. To everybody's alarm, the snake would linger for minutes on end, as if to mock everyone with its piercing, glass marble-like eyes. It seemed an eternity, but they did reached the bottom unscathed and the snake went on its merry way into the dark bushes.

'Salinee,' Chris asked, 'wot would yer do if it bit me?'

'We go to doctor,' she replied mysteriously.

Chris gazed around, looking for signs of a first-aid centre.

'Where's the doctor?' Chris asked, wondering.

'In Kanchanaburi,' she calmly told him.

'God's teeth!' he exclaimed. 'That's one and a half hours away.'

Salinee and her sister said nothing.

Chris turned to face her sister and said, 'Thanks, I think yer may have saved my life.'

She smiled and he saw she had quite a gleam in her cockeyed organs of vision. But in reality, Chris knew that his guardian angel had secretly intervened.

Later that evening, as Chris sat enthroned under a ceiling fan in the café, he wondered why Salinee was taking so long to return from her father's bungalow. He looked at his watch. She had been more than one hour now. Presently, a sad and sullen Salinee returned.

'Wot's the matter?' Chris asked her.

Salinee sat at his table and there was a slight twitch of her nose. She appeared to have been crying.

'Chris,' Salinee said tremulously, 'I have to talk to you about...' her voice trailed away. She paused for a few seconds in deep thought and continued with, 'I forget the word.' Salinee stood up and went to a room at the back. She returned with her English/Thai dictionary and pointed to the word 'dowry'. Of course, Chris's understanding of this word was 'property a wife brings to husband at time of marriage'.

'Salinee,' Chris said firmly, 'I don't want any money from yer family.'

Salinee looked puzzled, and explained, 'In Thailand the man pays the money.'

'Oh!' Chris exclaimed, 'how much will I have to pay?'

'My father not love me,' Salinee said sadly, 'he say he want 600,000 baht.'

Chris did a quick calculation in his head. The answer was approximately £15,000. His heart sank. Chris could not believe it. He stood up and walked outside. Salinee followed. There was no way Chris could afford such an amount of money. He was convinced that her father had inflated the dowry in an attempt to destroy their relationship. An air of palpable gloom hung over them.

'It's too much for me to afford,' Chris protested.

Salinee nodded in agreement.

'My father does not like you,' she said, with trembling lips.

'Salinee,' Chris said, 'I want to marry you.'

Tears fell from her eyes.

'You can only marry me,' she sobbed, 'if you pay the money.' Salinee held his hand. 'Chris, I love you, but I cannot marry you if my father does not like you. If I walk out the door, I will never see my family again.'

Chris looked into her tearful eyes and realised that whilst her father was alive, Salinee would obey his wishes.

'Chris,' Salinee said, 'I want you to find someone else. I love you but it's not fair for you to wait.'

Chris sighed and his face grimaced. In a strange and metaphorical vision, Chris felt as if he had been struck by lightning, killed on the spot. From that moment on his life would be turned upside-down. Earlier that day, his guardian angel had saved his precious soul, but at the expense of losing the woman he loved. But even a guardian angel could only perform one miracle per day. In one way he wished he had been bitten by the viper and had died in Salinee's arms. Then he would never have known the tragic circumstances that were to follow a short time later. With his life now in tatters, Chris was dead, as sure enough as if the venom had ran around his veins like embalming fluid. He would have to start all over again, reborn as a sad and bitter man, just like that hideous hound in the temple. There was no justice at all in this shitty world, he thought.

19

Bamboo, String, Bronze, Silver and Gold

Chris drew back the curtains and rubbed his tired eyes. He struggled to gain his bearings and then he remembered where he was. Chris exhaled slowly. He never did like Nakhon Sawan. It was now more than six years since he had first met Wanna in Pattaya. This day was the culmination of 17 months' hard work, which in reality was a pure face-saving exercise. Chris blinked and sucked in his breath many times, knowing that he would never forget this dawn. This was the beginning of the rest of his life. This was his wedding day. Suddenly, he felt a nervous rumble inside his stomach and fearing diarrhoea rushed straight to the toilet.

A little later, Chris hung shyly around the hotel lobby waiting to meet his parents and wedding guests. Being an only child, his mother and father would never have missed this day. But other family members had also come to Thailand: an uncle, auntie and cousin. However, what puzzled Chris the most was that a married couple who were friends of his parents had also decided to tag along. It intrigued Chris, as he was not related to them and the cost of the holiday was certainly not cheap. Nonetheless, whatever their reasons were, they seemed to enjoy being drawn into the euphoric pre-wedding and travel preparations. All in all, Chris's guests formed a stew-pot of personalities that would enrich any ceremony.

In one respect alone, though, his wedding would be

unlike anything they would have experienced before. His wedding was to be a Thai-Buddhist ceremony and this could well have been Chris's downfall, but for his insistence to Wanna that she kept him in the dark as to what would happen. This way, thought Chris, his innocence would keep him well clear of any ridicule if anything went wrong. In spite of this, and rather mysteriously, the only advice given by Wanna was to fill his pockets with plenty of money.

The ceremony was to begin at 9.00 in the morning. At 7.00 Wanna's chubby brother met Chris in the hotel lobby. Chris and his guests boarded the mini-bus and the brother proceeded to ferry them to Wanna's home village. Her brother had the disconcerting habit of driving near the side of the road and his use of the horn resembled an ambulance on an emergency call, which would render startled motorcyclists to shake in his baleful shadow.

It was 8.00 when they arrived at the village and Chris thanked Wanna's brother for his less than sobering lift. Because the village ice shop was shut all day for the wedding, a neighbour had agreed to let Chris stay with them until the start of the ceremony. Their house was clean and well furnished, with fine teak furniture from the north of Thailand. This was Chris's last chance to go to the toilet. He became agitated and found he used their facilities more and more as the clock moved towards kick-off time.

Soon, it was 9.00 and Chris glanced at his watch like an impatient rail traveller. Presently, he saw the mysterious outline of two young men come bouncing towards the house, each held a six-foot high jade-green sugarcane branch with blade-like leaves. The woman of the house handed Chris a bouquet of yellow orchids and he cradled the flowers like a newborn baby. Chris stepped outside and under the cloudless, sapphire sky took several deep breaths. Chris's parents and guests joined him and a few other villagers gathered behind. It soon became clear that he was to lead a procession towards Wanna's home. The two men with the sugarcane branches now wore jolly faces and each stood to the left and right of Chris. They thrust their sugarcane branches aloft and Chris set off, parading down the dusty highway like a village carnival. The procession grew in length each time they passed a villager's home. Perhaps the whole village had been invited, thought Chris. Chris turned round and saw a crocodile of 30 or more people following, many of whom were carrying dishes of food and fruit covered with cling film. What Chris liked most of all was the cheerful high spirits that went with it all. Everybody wore smart clothes and this filled him with pride. He continued a little further and, to his astonishment, two strapping teenage boys ran out from behind a bush carrying a long piece of bamboo. They stood in front of Chris, forming a barrier with the bamboo. With a bemused expression on his face, Chris queried their actions, protesting that he was about to get married. Their pacific smiles soon told him that their actions were part of the pageant. Chris would have to pay out some money if he was to proceed any further. This was why Wanna had advised him to fill his pockets. Chris now felt rather foolish and handed the boys 20 baht. The two boys removed their barrier and joined the procession.

Chris left the main highway and joined a dirt track that led towards Wanna's house. Built of wood in the style of a single-storey Swiss chalet, the simple house bore witness to the poverty that Wanna's family lived in. Without warning, two small boys appeared from behind a tree and with stern expressions on their faces made a pretence of being child bandits by demanding money from Chris. They also held up the procession, by stretching a long piece of brown string across the dirt track. Chris joined in their fun and paid them. Rather cheekily, they asked for more. Chris obliged and continued towards the house.

Here, more people stood waiting. It was almost like entering a hall of mirrors. Altogether, more than 100 people had turned out to see this foreigner marry one of their own. Chris noticed that the yard had now been cleaned up. There was no rubbish or clucking hens and the water buffalo had been moved from its tethered position under the house. In the yard lay a dozen or so tables, on which soup dishes steamed on food warmers. Caterers, garbed in white aprons cooked Thai food in the shade of a tree. There was no breeze and the air was sweetened with cabbage, garlic, chilli and the aromatic smell of roasting pork and chicken. Then Chris realised why there were no hens pecking around the yard. He grinned and said nothing to his guests.

Two of Wanna's nieces, aged approximately ten and twelve, appeared from inside the house. They held a chained, bronze belt across his path and demanded money with giggling voices. Chris could hear several clicks. He turned round. Some of the guests had begun to take photographs. Once again, he dug deep into his pockets. The girls stepped aside. The two men with jolly faces now lay down their sugarcane branches and allowed Chris to enter alone. He walked up the steps and felt glad to enter the shade. By now, almost half an hour had elapsed and his Thai adventure had followed a familiar pattern. Chris was sweating profusely, due to the heat and his stifling wedding suit. Inside the house there was still no sign of Wanna, so he proceeded towards the bedrooms.

Two of Wanna's three sisters now blocked his path with a silver bracelet. Chris greased their palms and rather sheepishly crept towards Wanna's mother who stood outside her daughter's bedroom. Wanna's mother was a meaty, middle-aged divorcee who looked in poor health, but her spirits were high and she too held a barrier across the bedroom door. Chris hoped that this was the final barrier, as it was a small, solid gold chain. Once past it Chris could enter Wanna's bedroom. But what would happen next? Chris asked himself. He had no idea and felt uneasy. His mind went wild with pagan theories. The fact that Wanna was inside the bedroom was rather significant, he thought. Would her mother close the door and allow him his hymeneal rites? Chris hoped not, he could not have had sex with 100 people waiting outside. They would be timing him with their watches, perhaps marking him out of ten. He was not one of Pat Pong's sex performers, although he had recently read that Pat Pong was soon to change into a bloody street market. Was there nothing sacred? Anyway, instinct told him to back off a little and calm down. Chris felt easy once again and emptied his pockets with a large donation to the family coffers.

The door was flung open. Inside, Chris could see Wanna sitting bolt upright on the bed, surrounded by the sweet odours of blossom. Wanna looked a picture and was ripe for marriage. He gave Wanna the bouquet of flowers. Her powdered cheekbones came alive with a fine sprinkling of glitter and her cherry red lipstick shone with chambering and wantonness. Wanna wore a carnation pink blouse and a scarlet red dress embellished with golden braid. In keeping with the traditional Thai wedding costume, a decorative silk sash ran over her shoulder and across her chest.

'Wanna,' Chris said softly, 'yer look beautiful.'

'Thank you, Kiss,' she replied in a voice that quivered, 'I am shaking,' she added tremulously.

Chris leaned over and kissed her on the cheek.

Whilst gripping her trembling hands, he said, 'Calm down, everything will be okay.'

Outside, Chris could hear the tinny reverberations produced by the whispering gaiety of dozens of tongues.

'What happens now?' Chris asked Wanna.

'We go outside and make blessing to the spirit-house,' she explained.

Wanna stood up and her sisters entered the bedroom to make final adjustments to her hair and dress. The sisters hung a garland of white jasmine and red roses round Wanna's and Chris's necks.

Then, rather hesitantly, Wanna and Chris strolled outside to the waiting crowd. Somebody gave each of them a plate of food and a burning incense stick. Wanna held a whole, cooked chicken, whilst Chris juggled with a fresh leg of pork. The scented smoke from the incense sticks clung to the happy couple like an early morning mist. The crowd all watched keenly as they carried the cooked chicken and leg of pork towards the northern end of the yard. Here, stood the small *papier mâché* shrine of a spirit-house. Resembling a lavish bird table, the shrine sat high on a post just above eye level. Chris had seen these spirit-houses almost everywhere in Thailand, with their miniature human figures peering through the open front portals. The rapt attention on the faces of their guests encouraged Chris to observe Wanna very carefully. He copied every move she made, pausing timidly whenever she made the slightest of movements. A wooden table stood beside the spirit-house and an exotic rug with a tasselled rim lay in front. Chris looked carefully at the rug. Its durable flat weave created a colourful carved effect against the dry, dusty yard. Wanna placed her sad-eyed, boiled chicken onto the table and Chris followed suit with his leg of pork. A guest gave Wanna an eggshell-blue china teapot and she carefully poured out the cold tea into matching cups. The cups were then placed onto the table. The bride and groom knelt on the carpet and each stubbed their polished shoes into the soil. With their incense sticks now held tightly between the palms of their hands, Wanna and Chris prayed to the miniature clay figures. There was an uncomfortable silence all around.

Even the flies seemed to hush up awhile. Chris almost expected the painted figurines to wink at him. Such was the importance placed by the crowd on this religious offering. Wanna and Chris kept perfectly motionless, whilst more shutters from the mass of cameras clicked away. Suddenly, Chris felt extravagantly clumsy and absent-minded. He worried about his performance. Chris did not relish the prospect of appearing to perform the ceremony incorrectly. He took a deep breath to calm himself down. The happy couple stood up and perambulated around the yard to yet another spirit-house. They repeated the performance with growing confidence. By this time, Chris had forgotten his stifling suit and was simply enjoying the ceremony. He felt glad that he knew nothing of what was to happen next.

Presently, they returned to the house and sat on a leather sofa. Chris had not seen the sofa before, so he assumed it had been borrowed from a family friend especially for the wedding. Chris's parents and Wanna's mother joined them, and they all sat in admiration as the guests gave the bride and groom their wedding gifts. Not the usual toasters, towels or crockery, but slaughtered chickens, vegetables and baskets of fruit. Then, a group of guests gave the happy couple a dismembered pig, with its butchered legs and hindquarters spread out on a table. Chris waited with anticipation for the head to arrive. It did so and they placed it directly in front of him. For several minutes it appeared to stare at Chris with inebriated, lazy eyes. Chris felt guilty, as if it were his entire fault that it had been decapitated. By this time the table in front of the sofa resembled a butcher's shop. Then, Wanna's close relatives brought out their gifts, all of which were sealed inside white envelopes. Wanna and Chris declined to open them in front of the others, as they suspected money to be inside.

Now it was time for Wanna's mother to display her dowry of £2,000 to the guests and, like a jolly Father Christmas with a sack of gifts, she swung the polythene bag over her shoulder and pranced around the yard with a broad grin on her face. This brought jubilant laughter to all and sundry. Chris also smiled, but there was in his bemused face, something quizzical, as though feeling cheated.

The table was eventually cleared and a sticky Thai desert was pushed towards Wanna and Chris. This was to be their final enactment of the day. The significance of the sticky balls meant that they would stick together until they died.

'Kiss,' Wanna urged, 'swallow a ball quickly.'

From the tone of her voice Chris could guess what was coming. He picked up the spoon and hesitated. Several guests jostled for better positions. Chris probed the plate with his spoon and quickly chose the smallest ball he could see. Chris swallowed it. Now the cameras were let loose, capturing his reaction to the pungent aftertaste. Chris defied all of them by displaying no emotion whatsoever and then, rather slyly, he sipped a glass of water after the moment had been forgotten.

Now the happy couple were free to join the other guests at their dinner tables. The feasting began, with bottles of beer and Thai whisky, all of which were freely available. But as Chris had expected, they were never allowed to relax. Everybody wanted their photograph taken with the bride and groom. Chris had never stood in front of so many lenses in such a short time. There was, for him, no control over the photographs, no artistic input, no exposure or framing decisions to make: nothing but hope and a quick prayer that at least someone knew what they were doing. Chris soon found out that it was far more practical to remain quiet and let the other people chat to Wanna about their family affairs. All in all, the day was so serene and fascinating, in a timeless, oriental way, which Buddhism so often projects to the outside world.

To cap it all, later that evening when they had all

returned to their hotel, to Chris's surprise, the hotel staff were holding their annual party. The newly-weds and guests sat outside watching the fun around the swimming pool. Soon, the word spread that there were honeymooners staying at the hotel. Wanna and Chris were the guests of honour and they all enjoyed another free party. That day was their moment of fame. Chris had succeeded against all the odds. He had returned to Pattaya and married Wanna within 17 months. Chris knew what to do. His experiences with Salinee had been a dry run, so to speak. Wanna's visa had not been a problem. Although she was a prostitute, she was registered as a member of the staff working at the Nipper Lodge. Thus, nobody at the British embassy knew of her real job. Even Chris's parents were none the wiser, and although they were still reeling in a state of confusion after Salinee's unexpected absence from the proceedings, they had greeted Wanna with open arms. Chris had turned his own emotional turmoil into a success. Once again, his guardian angel had come good.

Chris's wife's car headlights shine through the front door windows as she turns into the driveway. Chris looks at the clock. She has arrived home on time. Once again, Chris confronts the same agitation of mind. At what stage should he tell her that there is a Thai message on their answer machine? He goes over the question again and again in his head. Her family only telephone from Thailand to inform her of a family crisis. The message had disturbed Chris, as he suspected they wanted more money.

'Hello darling,' Chris says and kisses her.

She smells the cider on his breath, but that is no surprise to her.

'How is Jintana?' Wanna enquires.

'All right, she enjoyed the nice weather in the park.'

Chris hesitates for a moment, and adds, 'By the way, yer have a Thai message on the telephone.'

A look of anxiety contorts his wife's face and the colour drains from her cheeks to resemble scattered ashes. Wanna drops her shopping bags and quickly walks to the telephone. She listens to the message.

'It's my mother,' Wanna says, 'she sounds drunk. I cannot understand what she is saying.'

'Why does she sound upset?'

'I don't know why.'

Wanna looks at the clock and shrugs that it's okay.

'I will telephone her tomorrow and find out.'

Wanna sits down and pulls her socks off.

'Kiss,' she says, 'today an English customer in the Chinese supermarket where I work could not understand what I was saying, is my English still that bad?'

'Yer English is fine now,' Chris says pensively, 'it should be – yer've lived here for yonks.'

Chris continues to drink his cider and they both watch the television.

'Kiss, when will you get a job?'

'I don't know, I . . .' Chris pauses a few seconds and adds, 'I don't understand wot the problem is. After all, everything is paid off – isn't it.'

'Yes I know that,' Wanna says, 'but people at work keep asking me.'

'Are yer embarrassed 'cos I ain't got a job?'

'Yes.'

'Well I ain't,' Chris's lashes blink angrily. 'Look, if I had a low-paid job and I wuz still werking, would yer be happy?'

'Yes.'

Chris get frustrated and retorts, 'Well just imagine I'm still werking.'

'What do you mean?' asks Wanna.

'Wot I mean is, when I wuz werking I wuz earning the

equivalent of three years' salary in one year.' Wanna nods. 'Not only that, I saved all the extra money and put it in the bank. So if I don't get a job for two more years, it won't make any difference whatsoever – will it?'

'You have already been out of work for one year,' Wanna says quickly.

Chris takes a large gulp of cider and refills his glass. Inside his head Chris considers the pros and cons of telling his wife the real reason for his unemployment. Chris decides to say nothing.

Later, they both go up the stairs and on entering their bedroom Chris says, 'I've just taken Jintana's pyjama top off, she wuz sweating like a pig.'

Wanna gets out of the bed and goes into Jintana's bedroom. Chris gets frustrated.

Wanna returns and says, 'Jintana is all right now.'

'I've just told yer she's all right,' Chris says, 'I wuz the one who checked her out fust – why did yer have to get up and take a look?'

'Can't I look at my own daughter if I want to?' Wanna says angrily.

'Yes, I wuz only joking.'

Still upset, Wanna protests, 'I know sometimes you think I am hopeless.'

'No I don't,' Chris says humbly, 'but I do have to watch yer sometimes. I'll never forget the time when I cum home to an empty house and found the kitchen window wide open. The only thing yer could say in yer defence wuz that yer'd turned the alarm on.'

Wanna says nothing and they kiss goodnight. With his eyes open, Chris stares into the darkness. 15 minutes elapse and he breaks the silence with, 'Did yer lock the back door when yer cum in?'

Wanna bursts into laughter and Chris joins her as he realises what he has said.

'See,' Wanna says, 'you do think I am hopeless – don't you?'

Chris leans over and kisses her cheek. Soon, they fall asleep.

20

Split Wedding Ring

The following day, Jintana enters their bedroom. Chris peers at the alarm clock. An awful sight greets his tired eyes. The clock reads 6.00.

'Oh no!' he groans and quickly seals his eyes shut.

His daughter walks round the bedroom and Chris tries to detect which way her short steps are taking her. Whom will she approach? Chris wonders. He hopes she will approach his wife first.

'*Jintana gin nom,*' Jintana says.

Chris's request has been answered. His daughter has selected her mother to make a milk drink, which means Chris can stay in bed a little longer. Chris drops off, into a light slumber. An hour later, he is woken up again by his daughter's angelic voice.

'*Por,*' Jintana says, '*derm cha mai?*'

'Yes please,' Chris replies, 'tell yer mom I want a cup of tea.'

With intense excitement, Jintana runs down the stairs and Chris rather hurriedly gets up. Presently, they all eat bacon and eggs for Sunday breakfast. It takes longer than anticipated and Chris watches the clock with deep anxiety.

'Darling,' Chris urges, 'let's get a move on, it's nine thirty.'

His comment is wasted on Wanna. Most married men, reflects Chris, will testify that a woman has a different timescale from their own gender. However, over the years he has now come to the conclusion that Thai people never stick to a rigid daily routine. Thais quite often leave Chris with the impression that they can afford to deride and evade the petty restrictions of the rat race. This can be frustrating for Chris, as on certain occasions Wanna appears to be as unhurried as a Galapagos island giant tortoise. Today is one of those occasions.

'Hurry up please,' Chris pleads to Wanna, 'we have to pick up mom and dad at ten-fifteen if we are to make the christening service on time.'

'Kiss,' Wanna retorts, 'you were the one who got up late.'

'Maybe so, but did yer have to mess about arranging the flowers on the table? Yer haven't even found time to telephone yer mother.'

Wanna just ignores his comments, as wives usually do on these occasions.

'Jintana,' Wanna says, '*Gow pom mai.*' Jintana keeps still whilst her mother ties a ponytail in her daughter's hair. Meanwhile, Chris continues to run round the kitchen like a March hare. Jintana grabs the opportunity to join in the mayhem by insisting someone pick her up.

'Jintana,' Chris shouts, 'put yer coat on now!'

Their daughter jumps and rolls round the kitchen floor in protest.

'*Jay yen yen,*' Wanna says and accidentally steps on her daughter's hand.

Jintana yells out and cries.

'*Mai pen lai ka,*' Wanna says in an apologetic tone and promptly picks her daughter up.

But even then, despite the pain, their daughter flashes Chris an insolent smirk of satisfaction. Quite often, depending on the circumstances, his cherub-faced daughter can convey a melting persuasive charm and on other occasions, like now, she can make Chris's blood boil. Chris shakes his head. Jintana has won again, he thinks.

Finally, they all arrive at the church late. It is a modern church, with no spire or gargoyles. They walk inside and see that handbags now occupy all spare seats. The regular parishioners have known in advance that strangers are about to invade their place of worship. Today is a Christening Sunday, thinks Chris, and on these special occasions the habitual parishioners will show the new people how proper Christians behave every Sabbath. Chris and his family stand alone at the back. A middle-aged woman clad in a rather smart black suit approaches them.

'Hello,' she boasts to Chris, 'we seem to be busy today.'

Chris soon sees that her proud expression transforms to a vindictive smirk. There is an embarrassing silence.

'Would your family like a seat?' the woman eventually asks.

'Yes please,' Chris replies.

In a well-orchestrated ritual, they are escorted towards two shining black handbags.

'Excuse me, Ethel and Rose,' the woman says, 'would you mind if these new people could sit next to you please?' Her words had derided the word 'new'. In a show of reluctant solidarity, the two gaunt, elderly women remove their handbags and place them between their heels. Chris and his family sit down and Wanna follows the ceremony.

'This is a new experience for yer, isn't it,' he comments.

'No it isn't,' Wanna assures him, 'I went to Alex's christening. You remember, the one you would not come to.'

In a few words, Wanna quotes the salient points of a conversation they had had three years earlier. Once again, Chris has been skilfully reminded that he had let his wife down. Chris remains quiet.

Six babies, parents, and godparents are invited onto the

stage. Chris's godson, Adam, is there as well. He too is to become a godparent.

'Wanna,' Chris asks, 'does this mean I'm a *grand-godfather* to baby Lewis?'

He looks at his wife's puzzled gaze. She does not understand his jest. In a strange and macabre way the congregation listens in silent anticipation. You can hear a pin drop, thinks Chris, as they wait to hear screams of sheer terror. Finally, physical contact is made between holy water and a startled skull. Laughter echoes round the church, thus proving Chris's theory correct. Perhaps next time they may want to watch the children during inoculations, or even tooth extractions, he thinks.

The christening ceremony continues and Chris glances up at the stained-glass windows. Shafts of sunlight transform into blues and greens as they cut through the glass. There is dust in the air and the tiny particles are caught in the beams. He follows the inclining rays across the room. Splashes of kingfisher blue and peacock green fall gently onto a security sensor and control panel. It is a sign of the times, thinks Chris, that a church of all places needs such a hi-tech security system.

An elderly man with a pious look on his face stands up at the end of their row. Chris turns round and sees a few others standing in the congregation. They are all wearing similar suits and appear to have been strategically placed throughout the building, as if to protect a head of state or VIP.

'Wanna,' Chris observes, 'this is wot I've bin waiting to see.' Earlier at home, Chris had deliberately collected three 50 pence pieces, one for each member of his family. Chris did not want to suffer the embarrassment of searching for change whilst in church. After all, he thought, the regulars would have frowned upon him as if he had belched explosively during a prayer.

What follows is a pure dramatisation akin to a Hollywood movie. A ceremonial-looking velvet pouch hung from a carved wooden handle is passed to each row of the seated congregation. The people standing up watch with an owl-like gaze, as if a retired Mafioso is collecting their protection money. Chris grasps the varnished handle from Wanna and slides his hand inside the soft velvet pouch. Three coins are dropped inside and he slowly removes his hand to show that it is empty.

'Wanna,' Chris whispers, 'I feel like a bloody thief. They certainly don't trust us newcomers.'

Jintana's leg starts to perform her dance.

'*Bai yow nai hongnam,*' Wanna says and escorts her daughter to the toilet, forcing everybody to stand up as she passes along the row. Whilst Jintana is in the toilet, the female vicar invites all the children to leave and attend children's church. Chris sits and watches as, one by one, a parent or guardian accompanies a child down the aisle. Now the vicar's forehead creases with torment. Her sermon turns more adult in content, with racism, money and adultery all put under the spotlight. After a short period of time Jintana and Wanna return, raising eyebrows in their immediate vicinity. Wanna has done it again, Chris mutters to himself.

'Wanna,' he whispers, 'all the children have gone to children's church.'

Chris points towards the rear and Wanna looks behind her. She stands up and once again escorts Jintana along the row, thus disturbing everybody for the third time. The sermon continues and Chris drifts into a torpid state.

Half an hour elapses and the vicar's sermon ends. Everybody files out of the church and Chris waits in the foyer to meet the rest of his family.

'Where's Wanna and Gintonic?' Chris's mother asks, surprised.

'Mom,' Chris says, 'yer granddaughter's name is Jintana, – they're both in the children's church.'

He points a finger to a back room.

'Tut . . . I'm sorry,' his mother says apologetically.

A female relative shows her face and says, 'Hello, Chris, I didn't see yer in the church – wuz yer sitting at the back?'

'Yes,' he replies, 'we wuz late.'

She pauses and sympathetically enquires, 'Have yer still got no job?'

Chris shakes his head and says, 'No – still nothing yet.'

Her chubby face shows little concern.

Chris hastily turns round and looks for Wanna, whilst mumbling to himself, 'If only she knew why. But I can't tell her. I can't tell any of them, not even my wife.'

In the distance he sees Wanna and Jintana's smiling faces. They walk towards him.

'Wot wuz it like inside the children's church?' he asks Wanna.

'It was good,' Wanna explains, 'just like a playgroup – Jintana enjoyed it.'

'Did they know Jintana is Buddhist?' Chris asks, with a sardonic grin.

Wanna looks around the room and tells him, 'Shush . . . it doesn't matter.'

Chris sees his mother and father, and suggests, 'Cum on, let's go to the pub – they've got a buffet on.'

They all get into Wanna's car and Chris takes up his usual role of directing his wife through the back streets of the town.

'Did that Thai woman telephone yer?' his father asks Wanna, mysteriously.

'Which Thai woman, dad? There are lots of Thai women over here now,' Wanna remarks.

His father rephrases his question.

'The one who has just married an English man from Stafford. Yer know, they met on the intercom.'

'Yer mean Internet,' Chris remarks.

'Oh! Yes,' says Wanna, 'she telephoned a few weeks ago. She is a little bit homesick though.'

'Give way and turn left here,' Chris interrupts.

Wanna compresses her lips impatiently.

'Gintonic,' Chris's mother says, 'did yer enjoy the . . . tut! I'm sorry, I can't think of the words.'

'Christening,' Chris say rapidly, 'and it's Jintana, not gin and tonic.'

His mother looks round at him sadly and shakes her head.

'Tut . . . I'm sorry . . .' she says and pauses in deep concentration, 'my words are slow today. Jintonic, did yer enjoy the Christmas?'

They all laugh, with his mother producing that wonderful silent snigger that shakes her body like a jelly.

Chris's mother was still suffering the effects of a severe stroke she had had eight years earlier. Chris will never forget that terrible dark, dank December day. To listen to his uncle's plaintive voice over the telephone sent shivers down his spine. Then came the shock and horror as he saw his mother's unfamiliar, twisted mouth resting on that hospital pillow. No longer would she be light on her feet, her walk, close to a dance step, gone forever. Chris instantly blamed her benevolent and mild disposition, those numerous, restless nights worrying about other people's problems. Nevertheless, to blame her character would have been wrong. She was what she was and having found herself in a sanatorium at the age of 18 with tuberculosis proved she was a survivor. With resolute determination and a new antibiotic called streptomycin, she had been cured within six months whilst numerous others had fallen by the wayside.

Wanna continues to drive and asks, '*Jintana, bai yow nai hongnam?*'

Her daughter shakes her head.

'Wot did yer ask her?' Chris enquires.

'I asked her if she wants to go to the toilet,' explains Wanna.

She drives into the pub car park and they all get out. Above their heads, an aeroplane cuts a silent path across the blue sky, squeezing snow-white vapour like toothpaste from a tube. The other guests arrive and they all split up like clans from a Scottish glen. For several minutes the virgin buffet remains untouched by human hands. Nobody wants to be seen as the first to deflower its ornate presentation. Finally a child is urged to take a sausage roll and the feasting begins.

'*Jay gin alay?*' Wanna asks Jintana.

'Ham sandwich,' Jintana replies.

Wanna fetches her daughter's food.

'Has summat happened to yer wedding ring?' Chris's father asks, as his eyes rest for a moment on Wanna's bare finger.

'Yes dad,' Wanna replies, 'it split open last Saturday when I was at work.'

'Well when yer get it mended I'll pay for it, 'cos Chris still ain't got a job.' Chris gives his father a derisive glance and goes to the toilet. As Chris re-enters the smoke-filled room, he glimpses his auntie Dawn. Eleven years older than Chris, she still retains those quintessential elements of swinging sixties' gloss. Even now, this middle-aged woman cringes if Chris calls her auntie. Rather furtively, Dawn blindly juggles with a bottle of Bailey's Irish Cream under the table. Liqueur glasses are quickly emptied and filled, whilst a lookout watches the licensee behind the bar. Then, like a magician pulling a rabbit out of a hat, she pulls out a bottle of Scotch whisky from her bulging handbag. Chris too empties his glass and passes it under the table. As time elapses, more alcohol is consumed and the revellers drop their guard. Half-pint glasses are now clumsily filled with the coffee-coloured liqueur. This brings a derisive glare from the licensee as she empties the ashtrays. The party goes on as such parties do, with frequent drinking and spasmodic outbreaks of laughter.

Eventually, the celebration is over and everybody goes home. Chris crawls onto the settee and plunges into a deep, black sleep. He wakes up two hours later, heavy-eyed and with his tongue feeling like the bottom of a parrot's cage.

'Have yer telephoned yer mom?' Chris croaks to Wanna.

She looks at the clock. In Thailand it is 10.00 in the evening.

'I'll do it now,' she replies.

Wanna picks up the handset and dials her mother's telephone number. Chris listens closely to the conversation. Wanna speaks Thai, but Chris can tell by her tone that things are not well.

'Wot's the matter?' he whispers into Wanna's ear.

'Shush,' she says, 'my mother is crying.'

Chris listens quietly and then Wanna sheds a tear. Chris goes into the kitchen and pours himself a glass of cider. He drinks it and pours out another. As he returns to the drama he sees that Wanna is weeping some more. Chris sits down and waits. Forty-five minutes elapse before Wanna puts the handset down.

She stares at Chris and speaks softly, 'I can't get her to listen to me. It looks like they need some more money.'

'Fust of all,' Chris declares, 'I'm still out of werk.'

Wanna looks unconcerned.

'My brother is in trouble with the police,' she whispers, 'they need some money to bribe them.'

'Wot! I don't believe this, hasn't he got a lawyer?'

'He's signed a confession for stealing cars.'

'Flipping heck!' Chris exclaims. 'Hasn't yer mom any money left. She's already borrowed a load from us.'

Wanna shrugs her shoulders philosophically.

'When did all this happen?' Chris asks.

'Last Saturday.'

'Wow!' Chris exclaims, 'that explains why your wedding ring split.'

Wanna seems unconvinced.

Chris drinks some more and says, 'This is unbelievable. Wot about yer mom's bank account?'

'The money is all gone,' Wanna says with raised eyebrows.

'Has she bin boozing again?'

'I told you it's for my brother,' Wanna corrects Chris.

'I bet,' Chris says haughtily.

Wanna frowns and gives him a malevolent glance. Wanna gets angrier, as Chris continues to spout off the obvious.

He resumes with, 'I feel like I've bin werking for yer family for years.' He drinks some more and adds, 'why did yer brother steal some cars?' His voice emphasised the word *steal.*

'Kiss,' Wanna says, 'I'm tired now – give it a rest please.'

'Yes, all right.' He drinks some more and adds, 'He's bin stealing stuff for years. Probably from yer mom as well. Telephone her again and tell her to get a lawyer fust thing tomorrow morning for yer brother.'

'Oh, not now, Kiss,' Wanna says with intense annoyance.

Chris pours himself another drink and says, 'I bet yer glad yer married me. Look how good my family has bin.'

Wanna already upset, sees the red mist and says crossly, 'Oh! I want to be sick, you haven't had a job for ages. Look at you, I think you're having a mid-life crisis.'

'Don't be bloody daft, mid-life crisis my arse,' Chris yells sternly.

'Well why can't you get a job then?' Wanna asks bitterly.

Chris also gets angry and shouts, 'Look we've bin through

this before. I've paid the damn house off and all yer give me is a load of grief – anybody would think the wolf wuz knocking at the door.'

Chris sits down and waits for Wanna to put Jintana to bed, his temper raging and building up inside like a dormant volcano. Nobody knows what he has had to endure, every day suffering the ridicule of people who assume he cannot get a job and all along he has had his own secret project: a simple project, just to teach their daughter the English language. All he wanted to do was to be able to talk to his own daughter.

Chris's heartbeat strums an eerie two-tone chant that fills the room with heathen vibes. Chris looks round, and beneath the ordered beauty of his surroundings he finds elements totally alien to his understanding. The vulgar chill of the chant and a distant drumbeat draw him towards a Thai painted canvas. Warm and tropical, the painting hints of a steaming malarial jungle with an overgrown temple and, silhouetted against a paler sulphurous smoke are shrines of red-throated demons, reclining Buddhas that drip green and brimstone-snorting tigers that sit and smile haughtily. Clouds of steam drift across the shadowy jungle, amber steam lit from candles flickering within the ancient stones. Evil enters the room and Chris feels a surge of rage sweep up his body. The alcohol fuses lying brain cells with truth cells. It is time he told Wanna the truth.

Chris's wife comes down the stairs and he yells, 'Yer just don't understand do yer? Yer never will. Wot we've got in the shape of Jintana now, isn't wot we'd have if I wuz at werk all fucking day.'

Wanna's face flushes with anger. Chris walks into the kitchen, grabs a long thin blade and cuts himself a slice of cheddar cheese. He returns, shouting and waving his arms.

'I gave up a high paying job just to be able to talk to my own fucking daughter. She couldn't even fucking speak to me at weekends. It was bollocks.' Chris paces round the room, elbows the door and shouts, 'Talking Thai with Jintana is so fucking quaint, but it's no fucking good when her teacher pencils her down as wanting special educational needs, is it?' Chris stands there, taking deep breaths and continues to wave his arms. Wanna reels back as a disembodied, alien light repeatedly flashes across her face. Wanna says nothing, but Chris can see hatred and derision in her eyes. The ambience is redolent of brimstone. Two evil embryos, Siamese twins bearing the names 'Separation' and 'Divorce' are conceived. They grow rapidly. Their umbilical cord begins to suck the very life out of their marriage. Chris looks down at his empty glass. In the guise of a halo, a circle of white light runs round its rim. Chris must terminate those evil twins and this drunken argument now.

His guardian angel intervenes and Chris utters the winged words, 'Goodnight Wanna, I'm going to bed.'

Chris goes into the kitchen and returns empty-handed. He staggers up the stairs.

Later, Chris wakes up at 3.00 in the morning. Wanna is not in their bed, and then he remembers his drunken rage. Chris gets up and goes down the stairs. He sees a chink of light shining under the kitchen door. Chris opens it. Wanna is sitting at the table with slumped shoulders. Her red-rimmed eyes stare at the cruet set. She has been crying.

'Are yer all right?' Chris asks softly.

Wanna says nothing to her *bête noire*.

'Cum to bed. I'm sorry about last night, but I had to tell yer the truth. I had to do it.'

'I can't sleep,' Wanna replies quickly.

'Okay, cum to bed later if yer want to, it's up to you.'

Chris goes back to bed worrying if this is the end of his marriage.

The following morning Wanna is quiet. Chris decides to go for a walk and returns two hours later. 'Kiss,' Wanna says in a serious tone, 'I want to talk, can you sit and listen to me, please.'

'Wot is it?' Chris asks, whilst still standing.

'Last night I felt that you didn't love me anymore. For the first time I thought about leaving you.'

'I do love yer and I love Jintana. I want us all to be happy. After all, look wot I had to do to marry yer.'

'I thought you was going to kill me with the knife,' she says bitterly.

Chris's eyes turn on her in disbelief.

'Wot knife?' he asks.

'You kept waving a knife in the air.'

Chris frowns and says, 'I don't remember holding a knife.'

Wanna looks into his eyes. It is a piercing stare that only a wife can deliver. She sees that Chris is sincere. He has no knowledge whatsoever of a knife. There is a long silence and they both sit down.

Finally, Wanna says, 'Kiss, I need a friend I can talk to, I want you to listen to me like a friend. I need to talk to someone who I can trust.'

'Are you sure you want to talk to me? What about all the Thai friends yer know?'

'They gossip too much,' she says flatly.

Chris nods in agreement.

'I wish we lived in Thailand and not in England.'

'No,' Chris protests, adding 'I married yer so yer could find a better life in England.'

'Yes, I know,' says Wanna.

'We have to stay in England for Jintana's education,' Chris insists.

Wanna sighs.

'Look, I'll sell my windfall shares and give yer sum money to send to yer mom.'

Wanna nods. Chris gazes at their daughter. Jintana is

playing with her toys. She is the only reason, thinks Chris, why he is still married to her mother. In spite of this, there is not a single day that passes by in which Chris does not think of his true love, Salinee. Chris kisses Wanna and their daughter sees their embrace. Jintana walks over and hugs her parents.

'By the way,' Chris says, 'when I went for a walk this morning, I popped into the library and looked at a psychology book.' Wanna's eyes tingle. He continues with, 'There's a name for a certain condition when a person loses all interest in material things. The person can often give up their job or business and go back to college or even take up a project more dear to their heart.'

Wanna looks at Chris with a wry grin, and says, 'Go on, tell me what it's called.'

'It's called the classic mid-life crisis,' Chris says, humbly.

'See, I told you so,' Wanna says, haughtily.